The Little Coffee Shop of Horrors

Anthology 3

Tether Falls Press

Contents

Introduction

Time for endings and new beginnings. This will not be a normal introduction; this is the behind-the-scenes version. For those who have already read volumes one and two, welcome back. For those who are reading this one first, welcome aboard. There are several things to discuss about this volume, how it differs from the others and what the future holds. If none of that interests you, please jump to the first story.

A quick history: Joseph Carro is an author and editor. He is a graduate from the Stone Coast MFA program in Maine which has graduated many impressive authors. Joseph is one such author.

He is also my nephew. And my stepbrother. Confused? Thought so. Joseph and I have often proclaimed ourselves to be the only uncle/nephew horror co-authors in the business since we have found no others. However, even if they exist, we are damn sure the only ones who are uncle/nephew/stepbrother coauthors.

We grew up in poverty. Eventually I went away to college through scholarships and working three jobs. Unknown to me during that time, Joseph ended up in a foster home. To rescue him from that situation, my mother adopted him. That is how we became stepbrothers.

It was at my mom's funeral in 2019 that this anthology series was born. (I will avoid the sorrow of her passing.) There, Joseph and I reconnected and this idea I had floating around. It was something that we could work on from a distance. We had tried a movie project together years earlier, but our writing styles were too different and the distance too far.

The idea was for authors to visit 12 different coffee shops around the country and allow the setting to determine a story. No preconceived notions, no pulling from a slush pile. We decided to kick it off with just the two of us to start. We quickly realized we were on to something. We both created stories we likely never would have otherwise written. It was then and still is exciting.

However, like I mentioned above, life happens. To edit an annual horror anthology has always been my dream since I was young. That doesn't mean it was always Joseph's dream. (His interests are far more eclectic than mine.) Volume two was when things got more difficult. Life issues were affecting Joseph more than they were me, so it was harder for him to produce as many stories.

It takes a lot to write six complete stories while also doing other work and writing other projects. That is why I authored more stories than him for volume two. We got it out a bit late, but it contained some great new stories, and we added drink recommendations.

The plan was to eventually publish this anthology with the traditional one author per story structure, but it felt right to close out the first three volumes as a trilogy from me and Joseph. It has been a treat to work with such talent from my own family and to do something together. The trilogy felt right. By book four we could transition to other authors.

Except life continued to happen. We missed releasing volume three last year. I was not going to even think about doing it without Jospeh, so a year off it was. This year was a make-or-break year. We could not delay any further, or it would stray too far from my dream of editing an annual anthology. Joseph came to the plate with some awesome stories as usual but fewer than before. That left me with more than normal to write (I don't mind, like I said, this was my lifelong dream). That was when an idea hit.

Why not add someone to the family? I follow Ellen Datlow online because I treasure her work (and because I dig her travel pics). At some point she mentioned that two authors make a collection while three or more make an anthology. But our book has always had 'anthology' in the title. We planned to become a traditional anthology by volume four. Why not make it official with volume three?

It is with great excitement and joy that I introduce a name you have already seen on the cover: S. Alessandro Martinez! He is the Stoker nominated author of ***Helminth*** which you should absolutely check out. I am a fan of his and have gotten to know him through HWA. If I trusted anyone to leap into this passion project, it would be him. And Alessandro delivered a banger!

That makes volume three a true anthology. Volume four in the future will be straight up a fresh lineup of authors. Will Jospeh and I still author a story each in future volumes? Not sure yet, but the two of us are in this together so we will edit the future volumes together at least.

I am also happy to say that life has gotten better for Joseph as of the time of this publishing. Had things been this way then, we might have had more stories from him. But it is more important that he used the past year to live outside the page.

If you wonder why Joseph has never written an introduction to any of these, it is because I would rather have him drafting his killer stories. There are plans for a special project in the future, and for that we will finally give Joseph the reins on the introduction.

Since I have the microphone, I just want to say how lucky I am to have worked with Joseph through these three volumes.

He is a top-notch talent, and I am lucky to have such a great writing partner. I will always treasure the books we put out. If you ever get the chance to meet him at an author event, please do. He is a great guy besides being just a great author.

So, from me, Joseph, and our newest author Alessandro, I hope you enjoy this caffeinated concoction of stories that could only come from visiting twelve different coffee shops around the country. Raise your cups of coffee and give a toast to the last of The Little Coffeeshop of Horrors Anthology as it was, and toast to what it will become in the future. Thank you all for coming on this journey with us.

A toast to the readers as well. You all are the cream in our coffee. We couldn't do this without you.

Now let's all turn the page...

Books A Million Café

SOUTH PORTLAND, MAINE

This story is one of two written during the week of my mom's funeral. (As mentioned in the introduction.) I was at a hotel by myself during the ten days I was home. The days were spent with family but at night I was alone at the hotel.

A Books a Million store with a café was within walking distance of my hotel. It was perfect for distracting me from my sorrows. I spent many evening hours typing away on my laptop. This was 2019 and places were still open late. The café was located just inside the entrance to the right. Straight ahead a world of books, and to the right caffeine and sugar.

This coffee shop had banners everywhere advertising their blended drinks. I am generally a black coffee kind of guy, but I needed to drown my sorrow in something, so I ordered one of the crazy blended drinks on the menu. It was delicious and hit the spot.

The place is cozy, with lots of seating. Something about being near the entrance and watching people from my home state come and go made me feel better. I left home at eighteen, but I will still die a Mainer. Being there felt like home.

What inspired the story was that this bookstore is near the Maine Mall. The mall is the only one I know of in Maine and covers a square mile of real estate. It was where my friends' parents would drop us teens off for a day at the arcade.

I did not have much money like my friends and video games were going up in price, so I had to play older, cheaper games and settle for watching them play the newer ones. That was where Skee ball comes in. I do enjoy it and used to win tickets, but never enough for any good prizes.

They still have an arcade there, but it is bigger now, and more like Dave and Busters (a Californian adult arcade/bar). I visited that new Maine Mall arcade (upper floor versus first floor when I was younger) but I Did not play anything because I was too sad. But I was happy to see an arcade still existed.

As for the story? It involves teens and an arcade of course.

DRINK RECOMMENDATION: I call this one the **Go For It**. Find the densest calorie blended drink you can find at your local coffee shop. Get all the calories in one cup like any good teenager would do. Then kick back and read Skee. I think you will have a blast.

Skee

PAUL CARRO

Nicky fed the ten-dollar bill into the change machine in the mall arcade while Charlie stood by, waiting for his cut. Their mom had two rules: split the money and don't become MC kids. She was always worried about them becoming milk carton kids. Charlie and Nicky sometimes wondered if they would someday spot their own fathers on milk cartons. Charlie was seven, his brother thirteen, and they shared the same mom, but different dads. The fathers had one thing in common: both split when the boys were young. Charlie did not even know who his dad was. The man left when he was three.

"Hey, halfsies," Charlie said when Nicky handed off too few quarters.

"Same number of games, Mom said, not the same amount of money. Dragon's Lair is fifty cents. Can I help it if you still play the baby quarter games?"

Before Charlie could protest being called a baby, Nicky went off looking for girls, friends, and Dragon's Lair. Charlie wandered further into the arcade while deciding how best to spend his quarters. His first stop was the prize booth. There, high on a shelf above the rock band mirrors, snake whistles, Bazooka Gum, and finger traps, sat the grandest of all prizes. An Atari. Not the newest model, but close enough.

Charlie wanted desperately to win it so he could fight Space Invaders all day long without getting ripped off by his snot-nosed brother. The price of the game system was three-thousand tickets. Charlie had saved only two hundred tickets so far. Many games paid out tickets, but the one Charlie always earned the most on was skee ball.

To get there, he passed by the basketball hoops where high-school aged kids jeered each other on. Next was the punching bag, where three older bullies from around the neighborhood scored high numbers with every punch. Jimmy, Roy, and Bo. Rumor was that their own parents were afraid of them. Charlie steered clear. The terrorizing trio made mincemeat of kids no matter their age. They were equal opportunity bullies. (That they were not ageists was about the only good thing anyone could say about them.)

Unable to control himself, Charlie stopped briefly by the Flip-It machine. The machine comprised enormous masses of quarters that hovered near the edge of a spill tray. Players dropped a quarter in a slot, aimed it, and hoped to push the existing change into the payout catcher.

Charlie could not resist and tried two times. Each time, his coins only added to the existing pile. *Stupid, so stupid,* he thought. He knew it was a scam, just like the hoop rims being too tight on the basketball toss, and the claws too loose on the claw machines. But had Charlie scored more quarters from the Flip-it, then he could have played more skee ball.

No longer a "cool" game, arcade management relegated the six skee ball machines to a dark, isolated corner of the arcade out of view of other arcade patrons. It was as if the owner was ashamed to own them. The six machines sat between a fire exit door and a supply closet that smelled heavily of puke and cleaning supplies. How both odors could be present at once mystified Charlie.

The area, lit by black lights, appeared as night even in day, which was creepy, but it made his teeth and hair look cool. Skee ball was how Charlie collected his initial two hundred tickets. Three thousand felt so far away. As creepy as the space felt (the runway on which players hurled balls was blood red), Charlie enjoyed the game.

Each unit was like its own little bowling alley if the bowling lanes curved toward the sky at the end. Rather than knocking down pins, the player aimed the ball toward a series of PVC tubes with points painted on them. The tubes in the center ranged from ten to fifty. Two pipes in the upper corners were worth a hundred points each. Charlie thought those corner PVC pipes looked narrower than the pipes with lower scores.

The worst was the ten-point marker because it served as the default ball catcher. If one missed all the tubes (a possibility even with nine balls per game) the ball settled at the base of the machine where it dropped into the unprotected ten-point hole. Shooting for the elusive hundred-point tubes (the biggest ticket payouts) usually ended in a miss that rolled into in a ten. Solid fifties were the best strategy but boy how those hundred pointers beckoned.

What made the game scary beyond its remote location was its motif. Covering the top of the machines was a series of backlit images. Combined, they formed a panoramic view of a circus with dancing clowns and whirling machinery. But hanging dead center of the whole thing was a clown's face.

The clown's face was not part of the image, rather a three-dimensional animatronic made of something as shiny as porcelain. Its white face glowed menacingly under the black lights and wore a jester's style hat. The hat split in two above the rim, each half a different color with one yellow, the other black. A jingle bell topped off each half of the hat. The clown's face remained mostly in repose, looking down, but occasionally it raised its head to speak.

Charlie hated it whenever the face came to life. It was creepy enough when stationary, but once animated, it displayed a creepy smile, a bulbous nose, and glowing purple eyes set far back in its sockets. The glowing eyes were bright enough to cut through the black lights above the machines. Despite Charlie's disdain for the animatronic, he normally used the machine one over from the face. It was his lucky lane that always produced more tickets. (He tried them all and would have used the one furthest from the face if all things were equal.)

Ready to get his game on, Charlie inserted a quarter. The balls rolled to the front of the machine with a satisfying rumble. It was then that the clown raised its head. The purple eyes reminded him of his friend's Light-Bright game.

"You're a baller. A skee baller!" the clown said.

Its mouth moved when it talked, further unnerving Charlie. After it spoke, it fell into a strange laugh that drooped into slurred speech at the end before the eyes extinguished and the head tilted back down into stillness. God, Charlie hated the thing.

Charlie played two quick rounds and came up short on tickets. He eyed the quarters in his hands. It was not fair how his brother always shorted him. Sometimes he thought his brother was as big a bully as the three gathered around the punching machine. If Charlie won the Atari, then he would not need to worry about coins anymore. But he only earned ten more tickets after two failed rounds. He would be old enough to work at McDonald's by the time he won enough tickets.

The hundred tubes in the corners were the answer. He needed to try for them. Charlie was good at lining up shots and hurling the ball. Once in a groove, he could repeat the throws with some accuracy. It was time for a full-on push. He lined up the shot, launched the ball down the side. It hit the ramp, arced high, hit the hundred tube's edge, and bounced away. The ball danced around but settled into the dreaded ten-point slot.

"Eat my shorts!" Charlie screamed in frustration.

Charlie rocketed the next ball which flew into the net, chugged around the space like a rubber ball and finally dropped into a roll, scoring a whopping ten. That was it. Aggravated, Charlie grabbed ball after ball and launched them into nothingness, just whipping them. Tens became his friend. Finally, he was down to his last ball.

"Come on, figure this out."

He lined up the shot, aimed carefully for the hundred and launched it much softer than normal. The ball rolled, arced into the air at the ramp and headed right for the hundred! Charlie raised his hands in victory before it even landed. Thunk.

"What?" Charlie lowered his premature victory hands.

The ball sat wedged behind the hundred-point tube. It never made it into the hole. Not even the ten. It was simply stuck. The game remained in play, waiting for a ball that would never arrive.

He had to get it moving. If the ball did not drop in a hole, he would not get his tickets (as few as they might be). Charlie yelled toward the arcade for a worker, but the music blared too loud. No one could hear him. The arcade itself was deafening with all the games playing at once.

"Ball is stuck," the clown said with a laugh.

"No shoot, Sherlock," Charlie replied.

"Get the ball," the clown said.

"You get the ball," Charlie said, frustrated.

"No. You get the ball."

What? Charlie eyed the animatronic. Did it just answer him back? Impossible. He had to get a worker. He turned to leave when the clown spoke again.

"Pussy."

"What did you say?" Charlie turned, shocked.

"Get the ball, get a prize," the clown said before falling into the low energy laugh.

A prize? What was the prize? For freeing a stuck ball? Then it hit Charlie. What was to keep him from walking up the runway of the game and dropping the balls in manually? He was small, he would fit under the net. If anyone saw him, he could say he was freeing the ball. If it worked, he could do it with every game.

After checking the coast was clear, Charlie stepped onto the ramp. His stomach knotted up over the feeling that he was doing something wrong. But someone had to loosen the ball. He arrived at the top of the machine, reached for the stuck ball, and screamed.

A hand shot out of the hundred-point hole and grabbed his arm! Its grip was vice-like, so powerful the grip hurt, and he could not pull free. He cried out for help, but no one could hear him over The Tubes singing *She's a Beauty* over the speakers. Charlie pulled harder, but the hand gripping him matched him pound for pound and then some.

Wherever Charlie's arm was, it felt colder than any New England winter he ever experienced. There was no fighting it. He could not free himself, but then, just like that, it let go. Like part of a team faked out in tug-o-war, Charlie flew back on his ass. Lifting his now freed arm, he observed it change corpse blue back to its normal pink.

Charlie scrambled back to the front of the machine. He wanted to run, needed to, but suddenly tickets spat out from the machine. Bing, bing, bing. They kept coming. By the time it stopped, he had two hundred! Suddenly, he did not feel like running. The clown's face came back to life.

"Bring me someone, win a bigger prize!"

It laughed itself into silence and sat there, just an animatronic mascot for skee ball machines. Charlie flexed his hand.

There was nothing wrong. He had to have imagined it. He had an overactive imagination because he loved the *Twilight Zone*. Sometimes he wondered if Rod Serling was his father.

"Imagine, if you will, that I am your father," Charlie sometimes said in the man's voice while watching the show. He nailed the voice, so maybe the man was his father. But then Charlie could do Donald Duck as well, and that math simply did not work out.

There was only one way to find out. Charlie inserted a quarter. He threw the first ball, yipped at scoring a fifty, but then froze, waiting to hear the oomph of someone in the machine getting hit by a ball. Nothing. He shot the rest of the balls and scored well. It was his lucky machine, but nothing else happened. Strange. The tickets came out normally. A decent round, but nowhere close to two hundred.

"Bring me someone and win a thousand," the clown said.

The animatronic head went still but remained in the operating position. Its grin and purple gaze remained fixated on Charlie.

"A thousand tickets?" Charlie asked.

The clown nodded, never powering down. And did its grin grow wider? Then a voice behind him startled Charlie more than the clown.

"Well, well, well, it's my lucky day. I am trying to get the *Dio* mirror and I'm twenty tickets short. That's almost as short as you are, runt," Jimmy Jasper said.

Jimmy was one of the three amigos at the punching machine. His buddies were not with him, not that it mattered. Jimmy shoved Charlie to the ground and ripped the tickets from his grip. Charlie panicked.

"No, I need those," Charlie said, verging on tears.

"Two hundred? On skee ball? How did you get so many tickets? Never mind, doesn't matter, I just scored." Jimmy swaggered back toward the arcade.

"I cheated!" Charlie cried out.

That intrigued the teen who turned around. He crossed his arms (dang, those were some muscles). Jimmy shrugged to suggest he was waiting.

"You can walk the balls straight to the holes and dump them in. Problem is, I do not have a lookout and I'm scrawny, so can only carry one ball at a time, but you..."

"Great idea kid. Glad I thought of that. And I can carry nine balls. Put a quarter in," Jimmy said.

Charlie nearly argued over who should supply the quarter, but he wanted to get his tickets back, so he kept quiet. Either the bully would score using the new system and they would share the loot, or Charlie could grab the tickets back when the teen's hands were full. Neither plan seemed ideal, but it was all Charlie could come up with.

They loaded Jimmy's arms with all nine balls. Jimmy mentioned he planned to do the same routine with his crew in the future, but until he found his friends, he expected Charlie to act as a lookout. Charlie was looking out—for an arcade employee. Once a worker arrived, Charlie would ask the adult to get his tickets back. He used adult loosely; some workers were the same age as Jimmy.

A net hung near the game's top. Designed to catch stray balls, it acted as a spider web to Jimmy, who fought his way through. Once past the obstruction, the bully dropped a ball into the hundred-point pipe. The teen grinned when the digital score advanced on a nearby display. Jimmy dropped another, then another.

"Wax on, wax off kid, this might just work," Jimmy said, finally down to his last ball.

As Jimmy dipped the last one in, a hand shot out of the tube and grabbed the bully's arm. Charlie got a good look at the arm rising from the tube. The hand was deathly pale, and the arm had a polka dot sleeve with a ruffled cuff.

Jimmy did not cry out, simply grunted in surprise. Accustomed to brute force solving everything, the teen yanked his arm as if it would be no big thing to free himself. It proved to be a big thing when the bully met firm resistance. He could not pull free. It was then the teen realized his plight.

"Hey, help me, kid," Jimmy yelped before being yanked into the hole up to his elbow. "It's cold down there. Why is it so cold? Whoever this is, I will kick your ass... ungh!"

The clown's arm pulled Jimmy all the way to his shoulder. Then the impossible began. Charlie never had proper furniture growing up. Their home was a mishmash of lawn sale finds, like the two director's chairs his mom purchased for the boys. The chairs collapsed easily, and the heavy, hinged-wood pinched Charlie's fingers to blood multiple times. But it was the chairs' loud disassembly that bothered Charlie the most. The clip-clap-clop of the wood when folded down to store in the closet was deafening and violent.

Once Jimmy went into the hole past his shoulder blade, his body disassembling sounded like the chairs doing the same. Clip-clap-clop! Down the hole went the bully. Jimmy's screams turned girly as his body twisted, broke, and toothpaste tubed itself down the hundred-point hole.

That such a big guy could fit made little sense, but in the blink of an eye, all that remained was a single foot stuck out of the hole. It wriggled about but did not appear under the control of someone. It shook more like that of a limb that realized it no longer had a driver. The Chuck Taylor knockoff sneaker slipped off the foot and fell onto the skee ball game ramp.

There was blood (though less than what Charlie would have expected from such an ordeal). The blood poured over the machine before settling into rivulets which fed into each of the point holes. Jimmy's blood flow scored everything from ten to a hundred. But the blood did not remain visible for long. It soaked into the machine like someone with a straw was slurping up spilled soda. The red runway helped camouflage the whole thing, anyway.

Jimmy vanished along with Charlie's two hundred tickets. At least momentarily. Bing, bing, bing. The chime sounded while the machine spit out tickets at the game's front. They appeared endless, more than Charlie ever saw come from any machine. His eyes grew wide as he tore the tickets away and counted them. A thousand! As promised. The clown came back to life.

"Bring me someone for a thousand more," it said and went silent.

Before Charlie could consider such an offer, hands landed on each of his shoulders. The two people responsible each tried to spin Charlie around, but in opposite directions. The bullies gave up and stepped in front of him. Roy and Bo stood there, scoping out the area. Charlie pocketed his tickets quickly, hoping the teens would not notice the bulge. They seemed annoyed, but then again, it was hard to tell where they were concerned.

"Hey kid, you see Jimmy anywhere?" Roy asked.

Charlie grew angry that he had to worry about losing his tickets again. It bothered Charlie how bullies harassed so many people but could never bother to learn the victims' names. Angered, Charlie considered sharing how their buddy screamed in a puberty voice moments earlier. Eventually, the teen sounded like Freddie Mercury at his best. *Jimmy really hit those notes,* Charlie thought. Unable to come up with an answer, Charlie shrugged.

"Said he was trying to score with a girl," Bo said. "He must have scored."

"A hundred points," Charlie said.

The duo squinted in confusion, then raised fists into fake punches. But they were out of juice from the punching machine earlier, so they simply wandered off. Out of quarters and in a daze, Charlie sought his brother out and went home.

Charlie barely slept that night, and when he did, he dreamt of the clown prancing through the mall. Everywhere Charlie went, the clown was there, popping up as an employee at

Dairy Queen, Chess King, Spencer's, and Burger King. Was the previous day a dream as well? There was only one way to find out. Charlie needed to go back, but it was not up to him.

His mother wanted the boys out of the house all summer. Charlie wanted to be out but not by himself, and Nicky had many friends, so he hung out with them instead of his younger brother. Only when Nicky went to the mall, or the beach, did their mom force Nicky to bring Charlie along. If Nicky was simply seeing friends, he went on his own. That morning, Charlie begged Nicky to go to the arcade again, but Nicky had other plans. Or did until Charlie promised to take only a single dollar out of the ten their mom usually coughed up. That was enough for Nicky to agree to haul his brother back to the arcade.

Armed with only a single dollar, Charlie approached the skee ball machines, surprised to find a family of four playing and having a blast. The clown seemed well behaved, only talking scripted stuff about everyone having a ball. The youngest girl seemed frightened of the clown as much as Charlie was, but the other family members simply laughed at the animatronic antics. Charlie met the girl's gaze, pointed at the porcelain face, and shivered. The girl laughed, feeling a little better with a sympathizer in her midst.

Charlie left and went to stare at the Atari while waiting for the family to finish. Charlie's hand kept returning to his pocket, where the thousand tickets begged to be redeemed. Was he really going to get three thousand?

He considered cashing out for other prizes and calling it a summer. But then he saw a kid yelling at his sister. She cried while he called her a brat. Other people fought in public, always bigger against smaller. That was the world. Beat down the already downtrodden. The world had plenty of jerks and Charlie was open to seeing where the day took him.

Charlie returned to the skee ball machine and inserted a quarter. The clown appeared normal. Charlie had to wonder whether he was hallucinating the previous day. But how to explain the tickets?

"You're a baller. A skee baller!" the clown said.

"And you're a real psychopath," Charlie said.

"That's not very nice. Step closer and say that. I do not bite. Well, not exactly," the clown said.

Its face grinned so wide, Charlie thought he might pee himself. The clown broke out into laughter, its animatronic face coming along for the ride. It stopped laughing so suddenly that it startled Charlie.

"I'm just kidding. Bring me someone and earn a thousand tickets," it said.

"I can't. I'm all out of bullies," Charlie said.

And he was. Charlie could not do that again. He felt guilty even though Jimmy was a jerk. No, faced with the clown,

Charlie could not find it in himself to deliver someone else to the clown. Except the Atari was within reach.

A teenager appeared nearby in a work uniform. His nametag read Han. No way was that his real name. It had to be a cool employee thing to do. The kid was scrawny like Charlie and had a lot of acne. The worker seemed upset.

"Why do kids puke so much?" Han said.

The worker opened the supply closet and reached for the mop and bucket. He filled the bucket with water from a hose attached to a sink inside the closet. The clown winked at Charlie. Charlie shook his head. He did not know Han; it was not fair. Except Han seemed miserable. But how to get him to the holes? Charlie remembered Jimmy's plight the day before. Charlie took off one of his shoes and tossed it to the end of the skee ball machine. It landed near thirty.

"Hey mister," Charlie said. It took the kid a moment to realize he was a mister. "I lost my shoe."

"Weird. I found one there yesterday. How did it happen?"

Charlie shrugged, and the guy shook his head. Han stepped onto the machine and made his way along the runway. He ducked under the net, reached for the shoe, and the hand reached for him! From the forty-point hole this time. The kid never cried out. His face went white, and he seemed scared, but he never even said a word. Not even when his body totally flipped upside down like he was in a handstand, his feet licking high against the net.

Unlike Jimmy, Han appeared more flexible. Fewer bones popped as the arm pulled him down into sludge size to fit into the tube. How the teen's head fit, Charlie could not fathom, but it worked somehow. There was more blood this time. It exploded all at once, like a popped sack. It sprayed the net, the wall, every inch of the game, but like before, the game seemed thirsty and slurped it all up.

Once it finished its meal, the game spit out another thousand tickets. Charlie took them and held them to his chest. He was so close. The clown seemed intent on sharing in Charlie's joy. Its face lit up, its eyes glowed brighter than before, as if happy about the meal.

"Bring me another, and get a thousand more," the clown said, gargling, as if it was choking on blood.

Suddenly, everything was real. As bad as Charlie felt for what he had done, he was so close. The Atari called. But then, so did his brother.

"Hey Sasquat," Nicky said. "I'm out of quarters. Time to go. Wow, how many tickets did you get? I want to get a Japanese headscarf to tie around my leg like *The Karate Kid*. The chicks will love it."

Sasquat was one of the many nicknames Nicky used on his brother. Charlie had to go number two when they were in the forest once. He had no choice; it was coming out. His brother made fun of him, saying rather than spotting a Sasquatch, he had encountered the more elusive Sasquat. That was on top of buttmunch, turdhead, and a laundry list of other names. In a perfect world, Charlie could have told his brother about everything. But he could not tell his brother a thing, and if he did not share the tickets, his brother would beat them out of him.

He had no choice.

"Hey Nicky, thanks for letting me have the cereal surprise. I know you usually take them. Very cool of you for once," Charlie said.

Charlie poured more milk on his cereal and ate a big spoonful. Normally, they went through cereal too fast in the house, so their mother bought the cheap stuff. But in recent weeks she started buying better brands with better toy prizes inside the box. Charlie assumed after recent events that his mother felt bad for him. She probably also wanted more reasons for him to stay home. No need to worry about that, he thought.

"So, Nicky, Nickster, buddy, brother of mine. I scored a high score on Space Invaders again. Thanks for trying to retrieve my shoe that day. I was worried mom might be upset if I came home without it. You at least tossed it to me before, well, you know. Han had left it right there when he got slurped up. Mom still cries about you a lot."

Nicky stared back from the back of a milk carton. Charlie poured the last of the milk to freshen up his bowl, then he tossed Nicky into the trash. He left his dishes in the sink and went off to play with his Atari. He had gotten good at it over the past month, though occasionally he wished he still had a brother to play it with.

Chaumont Bakery and Café

SANTA MONICA, CALIFORNIA

This coffee shop is relatively new to Santa Monica. Mixed used residences have sprouted up all over Los Angeles in recent years. Apartments on top, gyms, businesses, and restaurants at the bottom. In this case, the coffee shop and bakery combination occupy the ground level front corner of a massive apartment complex.

While its coffee offerings are relatively modest, the food is excellent, especially their pastries. The shop is all windows so sunshine floods the space creating a warm, welcoming environment. The seating is fantastic because it is a mix of communal table seating, single tables, and comfortable table-free seating off to one side. If you are there to work, you have plenty of space. If you're there to read, you have comfortable seating in which to do so. If you are there to eat, well your stomach will thank you.

The clientele and staff are friendly and nice. Almost too nice. That is where the idea for this story came in. I imagine half the customers probably live above the coffee shop. But all the customers seem so nice. Anyone who has lived in a large building knows not everyone is nice. There is always one neighbor or questionable character.

That is where the idea for this story struck. What really goes on in those mixed housing units? Time to meet Paisley.

DRINK RECOMMENDATION: I recommend hot tea. Something with lemon or peppermint. I feel that is what Paisley would drink.

Tenants

PAUL CARRO

Let me tell you about Paisley.

She is a pen chewer for one. I only mention it for two reasons. One, it is what she is currently doing on the couch in the living room. Second, there is no reason for her to chew on one because who uses pens anymore? She keeps them on hand to tap an indecipherable Morse Code and to snack on, that is all. I cannot get her to stop, nor would I wish her to. It is one of the little quirks that makes my girlfriend unique.

Our apartment is a steal. Two bedrooms and two baths, though we do not use the second bedroom, only for occasional guests. We do not get many guests, though. Despite the apartment being sizeable, it sits in a questionable part of town. Rather than bring guests home, paisley visits her friends often. Sometimes she spends the entire night or even a weekend, often on a whim, without notice.

Does that make me jealous? No, it is a relief. I find great joy when Paisley vacates for a few days. Does that make me a bad boyfriend? No. It is the reality of our situation. See, once upon a time Paisley worked full time for a tech company at an office with her friends. Then the world happened, and it forced her to work from home.

Don't get me wrong. Paisley is beautiful with long, flowing red hair. Many people lean into blondes or Brunettes, but I have always been a sucker for redheads. Paisley is a stunner, with green eyes and freckles for miles. When she stands naked, the freckles on her body seem to form arrows pointing to her promised lands.

'Right this way. Follow the twin trail of freckles here and here for boobs (quite symmetrical, I might add, with outies for nipples that are oh, so enticing). Need a little more than that in your life? Follow the next freckle path to the promised land of the pussy.'

Okay, I should stop there. Do not want to get anyone too excited, especially myself. You know us guys, poor decision makers when we get horny. That will come into play soon. I am getting there.

I am a few years older than Paisley and was already living in the apartment when she moved in. I graduated from college a few years prior, while she had just graduated when she moved in. There were issues early on when she moved in because she brought home so many college friends. One by one, each of her friends moved away from the college town and she eventually switched to bringing home her work friends.

That worked out much better because the work friends were more responsible and never trashed the place. Even better still, the work friends preferred to meet elsewhere. Not saying her tech friends were stuck up, but many visited our humble apartment once and refused to return because of the neighborhood as I mentioned. Her friends preferred more upscale neighborhoods or venues.

Then there was Justin. Justin was a "friend" from work who she brought home occasionally. I sensed there was something between the two and it bore fruit when one day she slipped into the bedroom with him. She thought they were alone, but no, I was there. Before I could decide how best to respond, the guy was already done. He finished too quickly. I could tell it frustrated her. Paisley was probably thinking what I was: *Cheat just for that? Sixty seconds?*

I waited for the putz to leave before following through on my anger. I do not know what would have happened had I confronted him in the apartment live time. Things would have gotten ugly. Instead, I got his number from Paisley's cellphone (then deleted it from her phone) and called him. To say my call surprised the douche canoe is an understatement. My threats were a success. The man never returned to the apartment.

There was no reason to let Paisley know I witnessed her indiscretion. But the whole thing caused a rift. She was on edge, likely dealing with the fallout at work over the exposed relationship. I never heard what Justin said to Paisley after my call to him. Hopefully he simply ignored her as I instructed. She most likely suspected I knew something because back home, she walked on eggshells for some time. We would not survive another affair.

To be clear, I would never cheat on Paisley. She was my number one gal. I am no saint, though. Several of her female friends who visited were hot and I may have checked some of their socials out after their visits. Many posted very risqué photos on their socials. I made it a point to never follow her friends, but I sometimes used Paisley's phone to scroll through their pages.

Did I ever see any of them naked in person? Heck yeah. They would spend the night getting drunk, getting stupid, and developing an allergic reaction to clothing. We primarily used the guest room for those too fucked up to even Uber home. If any ever puked in the guest bedroom, the cleanup was on Paisley. I refused to clean up after her friends. They were hers, not mine. I had no interest in dancing in her world outside the apartment. She came home to me (most nights) and that was good enough for me.

Not as sociable as her, I had my own routines which were interrupted when she began working from home. I was so excited when she first moved in, I could not get enough of her. Every smile, every laugh, her floral scent that lingered in every room. But she spent much of her time out of the apartment at the start of our relationship. That was ideal. While she was at the office, I had TV time, couch time, and nap time. The apartment was my castle until my queen came home.

And because she was gone hours at a time, her return was always exciting, even if I had enjoyed a wonderful day goofing off rather than working. I was like a dog, happy to see its owner return.

Paisley coming home every day after work was the highlight of what was normally already a pretty good day for me. Once she began working from home and was there, like me, from morning until night, the excitement faded. The whole thing was an adjustment for both of us. I can roll with most things, so took it mostly in stride, but I could tell she struggled to adapt.

She developed the pen chewing habit after sitting at her desk for too long. She sometimes took the laptop out to the balcony, but the internet was not as good out there. Something seemed to keep her internet from working as well as it should. For that reason, I made sure not to use any devices myself when she took her many Zoom calls.

Her being home all day was not ideal, but like I said, we adjusted. Okay, I adjusted. Something about being in lockdown had Paisley on edge. I always preferred her without makeup and with simple (or no) clothes on. Now that she needed to appear on camera at a moment's notice, she wore clothes all the time. Sometimes (the rebel that she was) she wore nothing below the waist and a dressy top to take her calls. It took everything in me not to crawl on all fours below the desk and give her a good time while she took the call.

Seeing her prance around the place in only a top with her ass and pussy hanging out drove me crazy, but she was technically at work. On days when she did the half-dressed thing, I had to control myself, otherwise I might get caught walking around naked myself on her work camera.

There was one person, though, who increasingly could not control himself, and he showed up much more often once Paisley started working from home. Wilhelm Johnson, "Big Willy," as he called himself, was the property manager. When male tenants asked about the nickname (I asked at one early in my time at the apartment) he shrugged and said it was a goof. But when women tenants asked, he smiled and danced his eyes down to his groin. Subtle enough to keep out of trouble, but suggestive all the same.

Probably playing a numbers game, hoping to get any woman desperate enough for him to pay a visit. He was tall, but not big. The man was lanky with an Adam's apple that always rose over the top button of his chambray shirts. Chambray shirts and navy Dickies. That was his eternal outfit. He never mixed it up. The food stains on his clothing were sometimes different, so there was that.

I considered moving out even prior to Paisley moving in because of Wilhelm. When I first moved in, we received frequent notices on the door requesting entry into the apartment. The notes never came with the legally required amount of time for notice. I would let him in, though, and he always scoured the place for anything illegal, as if I was doing something wrong. I was struggling to pay rent and was sometimes late, so having him around made me nervous.

Eventually, he would get around to what he really came for, inspecting fire alarms, or whatever else his excuse was. But by the end, he always left while eyeing me as if he would catch me next time. After Paisley moved in, things got worse. He found so many more reasons to enter the apartment. When he did, I noticed the way he looked at her. I could also tell Paisley was uncomfortable, but like me, she understood she had to keep the landlords at bay. The price for the unit was too good to walk away from.

After Paisley worked from home, the man showed up more frequently with increasingly flimsier excuses. He some-how seemed to know which days she went bare down there. I closed the curtains to the balcony whenever I could, but Paisley was quick to open them. I assume that was how Willhelm knew Paisley was half-dressed. His new excuse related to the bathroom. That was where our lives would change drastically.

One day when paisley went out for a weekend. (Finally!) Big Willy entered our unit. I assumed he thought the place was empty because the car was not in the parking lot. It had been some time since either of us ventured out. Grocery delivery meant one never needed to leave their apartment (ah, life in a college town).

Paisley was on edge recently, hearing things, thinking someone was behind every corner. She told friends some of her panties were going missing. I had no such fears. The washer dryer combo in the house was in such a cramped space that it was amazing we did not lose garments to the washing machine gods more frequently. There was even a gap in the wall where items could fall through.

But on the day that Big Willy let himself into our apartment, everything made sense. The man entered the restroom and tinkered around. I hid in the kitchen as the man called out repeatedly, doing his best to make certain he was alone. It would have been easy enough to show myself, but I wanted to know what he was doing, so I followed his path through the house undetected. The man stopped occasionally and listened. I was not a ghost, so he probably heard my breathing or rustling of my clothes despite my attempts to be quiet.

If he was not up to something nefarious, I don't think he would have been so paranoid about sounds in the apartment. He should have been okay encountering a tenant if he was on the up and up. He was not. I knew for certain after glimpsing something small in his hand as he entered the bathroom. When he returned from the bathroom, the object was gone. He placed a camera in the bathroom! Disgusting. What a violation of privacy.

It took everything I had not to confront the man, but I had a feeling he was not done. Sure enough, the man went into the bedroom and dug through drawers, sniffing panties. Unbelievable. He pulled them from her panty drawer, which meant they would all smell like fabric softener. As pervs go, he did not seem to know enough to grab from the hamper.

I needed time to figure out what to do, so I discreetly made my way to the kitchen and made a noise. Big Willy yelled, asking who was there, nerves in his voice. He at least had the sense to worry about being caught. Willy followed the sound to the kitchen and found a spatula on the floor. It innocently could have fallen from the counter, but it was enough to frighten him off. (Yes, I had dropped it to startle the man.)

Once he was gone, I moved to the balcony and closed the curtains. I hoped he noticed they were open when he entered and might freak out at seeing them suddenly closed. But if the man rushed to the parking garage and saw the car still gone, he might doubt if they were ever open at all. I hoped the whole thing made him worry.

Meanwhile, I needed to stay out of the bathroom while enacting a plan. While I wanted the man to wonder if anyone had been home, my entering the bathroom would confirm it because of the perv's camera. If he saw me so soon after installing the camera, there would be a confrontation that could end on in eviction, even though the slimeball would hopefully finally get fired. The man likely did this to other tenants over the years and still had his job. No, the situation required something more permanent.

Using the kitchen sink as a urinal was gross, but I needed to stay out of the restroom until dark so he would not catch me on camera and know I was home. The bathroom had a small window so the room remained bright even with the lights off during the day. But even if there were no window, the camera might have night vision and motion sensors. I would assume it had both while I fashioned a plan.

Once it was dark out, I put my plan in motion. Using the man's perviness against him, I slipped into one of Paisley's robes and wrapped my head in a towel (I do not know how women do that; it took me five tries.) Then I took Paisley's laptop and headed into the bathroom, leaving the lights off. I glimpsed a tiny red light from the small camera, which was set at an up-skirt angle on the toilet. Easy to miss if one did not know where to look. I remained as far from the lens as I could, giving only flashes of a robe about to be removed. Then I gently turned on the shower, running light water.

Once that was done, I placed the laptop on the floor and played a video of a woman satisfying herself. The woman was vocal. It was the type of over-the-top carnality that would draw the predator into the open. I snuck out of the bathroom and waited.

I never used the door chain when Paisley was gone because her jaunts were too erratic. I never knew whether she was coming or going and could not chance falling asleep while she tried to get back into the apartment. That was part of the reason Big Willy likely assumed no one was home when he entered earlier. *If the chain is not locking, then come knocking*, was probably what the guy thought.

Except now an unlocked chain would mean an invitation since he believed "Paisley" was home and in a shower enjoying herself. (I did not realize how graphic the video was until it started playing, but it was too late to change it.) I chose a thirty-minute video to give him time to respond, but the perv was in the apartment in five.

I left a single candle burning in the living room so he could see, but otherwise left the whole place dark to make it easier for me to hide. Big Willy smiled at the dim lighting, probably taking it as a sign of romance. Still, he used the flashlight app on his phone to better navigate the place. Willy approached the bathroom where "Paisley" was having a grand old time.

With his free hand, Willy rubbed his groin. Gross. Total perv. The man stepped into the bathroom, and I followed. Once inside, the man grabbed the tiny camera, which meant he wanted no evidence of what was to follow. (He failed to notice the laptop, which was dark on screensaver even though the audio continued.)

Big Willy dropped his pants and underwear down around his knees. He started stroking something that did not live up to his nickname, then yanked the curtain open. The pants around the knees served me well.

Without fear of a camera catching me in the act, I charged with the utility knife in hand. Willy spun and locked eyes with me, his phone lighting my face. The empty shower had surprised him, but he was more surprised to see me.

"You!" he yelled.

Then he was gurgling. One swipe of the utility blade was all it took. Ear to ear at his throat. He was immediately choking on blood and grabbing his throat with one hand while the other grabbed the curtain. Like a reverse scene from Psycho, he fell into the shower, pulling the curtain off its rings. I left the water on so most of the mess would go down the drain.

Big Willy watched me go to work, grabbing his phone where I opened the notes app to write out his suicide note.

It described how being a perv weighed heavily on his soul, and how stalking Paisley was too much. She did not deserve someone like him watching. It was disrespectful. I made sure within the note to have him offer his sincere apologies to her while also admitting to watching other tenants in the nude.

Then I checked his media files. Sure enough, the camera had sent video to his phone. I deleted the video of me in the bathrobe, but verified that yes, he had filmed other tenants. Many. I forwarded a few to Paisley with a specific apology to her, saying he was the sick one. He had a problem, and she never deserved such treatment. I forwarded them so Paisley might feel some closure but also because I was worried the evidence would remain locked in his phone once it reset to screensaver.

That way, the police would have evidence if the phone was encrypted. The cops floated around the property for weeks. Paisley continued staying with the friend she had been visiting when the whole thing went down. She did not wish to be on the premises while investigators worked the scene. I made my own arrangements, remaining close enough to monitor the action. A new property manager came by, this one a woman. She lived on one of the landlord's other properties, so would not be on site as often. That alone was a relief to me.

The new property manager seemed nice from a distance, but I never spoke to her. She was too busy with contractors who replaced the shower curtain with a sliding glass door. (Upgrade. Score!) They also cleaned the place, threw up some fresh paint, and the apartment was like new. But the contractors seemed on edge during the work, complained of hearing unexpected noises. Sadly, I sensed where all that was going.

When Paisley returned, she could not get comfortable. She too heard noises and appeared on edge, uncomfortable if not in her own skin, at least in her living space. The jerk property manager had haunted the place while he was alive, but it was as if the workers and Paisley felt he haunted it after death.

Less than a month after returning to the freshened-up apartment, Paisley visited her family in Minnesota. She was done with life in the college town, which meant she was done with me. Though heartbroken, there was no way I was going to move. No way I could financially. No, the apartment was under new management, and everyone bought the suicide, so I was in the clear. It was time to live my best life there even though without Paisley I grew lonely.

Eventually, a new tenant moved in. I thought I was partial to redheads until I met this blonde. This one did not work from home. She was a teacher. I would have to deal with the jealousy because she brought guys home frequently. She was a looker, this one, so men braved the terrible neighborhood to hook up with her.

I was just happy Big Willy was gone. He evicted me five years earlier. I had nowhere to go then, so I moved into the walls of my old apartment (I discovered an opening to the spaces between apartments near the washer/dryer combo while an actual tenant there.) I built myself a life there in those walls where I would watch Paisley until she left for the day, then I would roam freely around my old place. Paisley had better furniture than I ever did, so that was nice.

But the new tenant has already proved to be an upgrade. She has sex often, and I get to watch from the discreet holes I long ago drilled through the bedroom walls. I have many discreet holes. It was through those holes that I got to know the new tenant by watching her shower, fuck, gab on the phone with friends, and watch TV. (I had a suitable spot where I could watch her shows from high in a corner behind her.)

Yes, life with the new property manager and tenant had revitalized what had become a stale relationship. Paisley was great, but when she started working from home, my legs would cramp from being inside the walls all day. I was ready for change and welcomed my beautiful new girlfriend into my apartment.

Let me tell you about Stacey...

Starbucks

Niagara Falls, Ontario, Canada

Driving into the Canadian side of Niagara Falls, across the Rainbow Bridge, you're greeted with many chains familiar to those of us from the United States. IHOPs line the horizon, seemingly endless all over the landscape. Then you have your Hard Rock Café, and a massive Hershey store, and of course Starbucks.

Located within the Sheraton Fallsview Hotel, this Starbucks greets you as soon as you're in Canada, right before you hit the insane spectacle that is the Canadian midway. I began dating a girl from Canada and we met up in Niagara Falls. This was one of the first stops I made to get coffee to fuel my adventures.

As I sipped my coffee and stared out at the falls over on the American side, a story started forming in my head about a couple (naturally) vacationing to Niagara Falls until things go awry in a big way. It's hard not to be inspired by the majesty of the falls, but I wonder maybe if I had other help? Maybe the ghosts of Niagara were calling out to me, bidding me to take my place among them. After all, what is more haunting than the undying love between a man and a woman?

DRINK RECOMMENDATION: Since this is a tale about the haunting and powerful Niagara Falls, I suggest a slight variation in the traditional London Fog Latte – which I'll just call the Niagara Fog Latte just for fun. So, take your traditional Earl Grey Tea, get your steamed milk and hot water (equal parts) but instead of just the vanilla you'd normally use – how about some maple syrup for some old-timey sweetness and a nod to Canada's Maple Syrup empire. Enjoy!

Ballad of the Lost Bride

Joseph Carro

Some on social media love to ask what people's happiest moments in life were. When I see such posts, very few happy memories come to mind. It shocks me that some have so many, while others have so few. I would hope life balanced that stuff out better. I'm in the few good memories camp. But there were some.

The earliest I remember was my uncle Dustin gifting me a Nintendo Entertainment System complete with a bevy of games like *Final Fantasy*, *Super Mario Bros.*, and *Rygar*. Back then, my three siblings and I only had a dinky black-and-white TV, but we played the *hell* out of that NES. It was the first time in my life that I felt like the other kids. We'd always been poor, so my mom never had money for things like video games. Having the NES made me feel...*normal*.

The second time I recall being extremely happy was meeting one of my heroes from *Star Wars*—the mighty Chewbacca, aka actor Peter Mayhew. I ran into him while attending Super Megafest convention as a cosplayer. I took a photo with him, though my camera malfunctioned several times. Mayhew's assistant struggled to take the photo because my camera's battery door repeatedly slid open. Each time he tried to snap a pic, the battery dropped to the floor. I explained that the latch was broken but it took him forever to get it to work. The whole thing caused Mr. Mayhew to laugh out loud.

The camera malfunction gave me extra time to talk with *'Chewie,'* who was more pleasant and generous with his time than I ever could have imagined. I still have the autographed photo and smile whenever I look at it.

The third memory, and the happiest of my entire life, was the day I accidentally asked my wife Candace to marry me. Candace and I were in a deep conversation about something I cannot remember. We conversed while on our backs in bed, staring up at the ceiling, hands clasped. One thing led to another, and the subject of marriage came up (as it had more than once before) but this time it felt *different*.

I heard an inflection in her voice I'd never noticed before, which made me wonder if she was considering spending the rest of her life with me. We joked around constantly, so it was hard to tell when she was serious. When we first started dating, she mentioned she never wanted to get married. But that day in bed there was something in her voice. I floated something out there.

"Well, I mean, you *probably* wouldn't ever want to marry me anyway, right?" After asking, my cheeks grew hot. Evaluating what I'd just said in my thoughts, I decided I sounded dumb and childish.

"Yes, I would," she replied after a moment's hesitation.

My heart pounded and the world went silent. What seemed like an eternity passed as we lay in the growing darkness under a blanket of silence.

"Babe?" she said, hesitation tinged in her voice. "Are you okay?"

"Candy?" Most called her Candy for short, and I was no exception.

She didn't reply. I think she knew what was coming. I felt her hand squeeze around mine.

A decision fortified within my soul at that moment. "Candy, will you... marry me?"

"Yes," was all she said, before I pulled her close and we had the most passionate lovemaking session of our young adult lives.

Each kiss felt like our souls were entwining together, fusing us in spirit for eternity. The idea that she wanted to stay with me for the rest of our lives fueled my soul in a way that I've never felt before or since. In that moment, I knew that if it came to it, I would die for my wife.

The wedding was a first for both of us. We kept the proposal secret, and I went about getting the blessing from her father even though she'd already said yes. His name was Gordon, and I liked him, although he was a man's man, and I was a nerd who barely knew how to change a flat tire. Still, I tried to keep up with the man as much as possible when he helped work on our house (we replaced the plumbing twice before Candy and I were even married).

Sometimes I chatted with Gordon while he worked on his cars in the garage whenever we visited Candy's parents' house. I never had a father in my life, so it was a sort of neat experience to hand "dad" the wrench when asked or hold the flashlight while he screamed obscenities at the aging car parts he was tearing loose with his mangled and callused hands. He seemed to like me well enough, even though I was nothing like him, because we at least connected over fantasy novels and video games. He loved *Dragonlance* books almost as much as I did, and we once had an all-night gaming session playing co-op on his old X-Box during the holidays. If Candy was happy, he was happy, and I made Candy happy as possible, as often as possible. In the meantime, the man could deal with a little dorkiness.

Candy's mom, Anne, was a peach, always smiling and a proponent of Reiki—a sort of spiritualistic healing and meditation. She was genuinely interested in what I had to say, or at least never let on that she wasn't. Anne laughed frequently, which was infectious. She laughed hardest whenever Gordon did. I could watch the two of them conspire in levity forever and never tire of it. For both me and Candy, her parents were what we hoped to be when we reached their age.

For the wedding, Candy and I rented a small chapel in Portland, Maine. The gothic looking chapel was in a large cemetery. We wed in October and the trees were absolutely popping with color. We had flowers delivered to the chapel, but they were late. This caused a lot of initial mayhem behind the scenes as I frantically called the flower shop with the help of my groomsmen. They were my best friend from high school, my uncle who'd gifted me the NES, and my brother.

My memories about the ceremony are vague, but Candace showed up with her bridesmaids in a stretch-hummer outside while I waited in the chapel, increasingly lightheaded from the heat of bodies and my own nervous heart pounding blood through my shaking frame. All I remember clearly is that when my wife walked in through the chapel doors, time slowed to a standstill. In her I saw my future displayed before me in a series of cliché bullet points:

- Honeymoon.

- Buying a house.

- Have a kid.

- Watch the kid grow up.

- Be surrounded by grandchildren.

As she walked down the aisle, I grew lightheaded. My brother-in-law captured me on video, letting out a cry before fainting. I remember nothing about that, and I've never watched the video myself.

After the wedding, a line of loved ones waited for us outside the chapel. We did the hugs and kisses slow-walk mamba until we finally escaped to the car. From there we drove to our honeymoon destination of Niagara Falls. Not the American side, but the Canadian side.

The Canadian side was bright, colorful, with plentiful museums and shops, and even a midway area replete with carnival side shows and attractions. Candy and I had both been big fans of *The Office*. When Jim and Pam got married in Niagara Falls, we mentioned how cool that would be. That fantasy spawned by a TV show became reality when we chose the destination for our honeymoon.

The drive to Niagara Falls in Canada took about nine hours. Eventually, with Candy sleeping in the passenger side, we rolled through the gate at the Canadian border. Multicolored lights somewhere down below signaled the Falls. The checkpoint guard asked me what we were doing in Canada and how long we'd be there. Candy woke. While I handed the guard our passports and informed him that we just got married and were honeymooning in Niagara Falls.

He asked if I could roll down the back window so he could see inside. Upon spotting the "Just Married" slogan scrawled on the glass, he handed the passports back. His facial features softened, and he said softly, "Congratulations."

Candace beamed, despite her sleepiness, and I thanked the guard before we drove through and into the Canadian side of Niagara Falls. Immediately, the scenery changed to a carnivalesque atmosphere. Neon signs lit up the streets as we made our way to a boutique hotel overlooking the falls where we checked in. The room was honeymoon-worthy.

"I'm going to jump in the shower, babe," Candy said, giving me a wry smile. I could tell she was still very sleepy.

"Want company?" I asked.

"Only if it's my husband," she said, beginning to disrobe.

"Well, whoever your husband is, he's one lucky bastard."

She disappeared into the bathroom as I finished my sentence, a twinkle in her eye as she left a trail of clothing behind in her wake.

"We've got a lot to do today," Candy said, dressing herself as I rubbed the sleep out of my eyes.

"And whose idea was this?" I asked sarcastically. "I don't remember signing any sort of waiver or anything."

"Our first day of marriage and I'm already thinking about a divorce," she said, playfully throwing a flannel shirt my way that she'd picked out for our eventual photos. The shirt landed on my face, and I made snoring noises.

"C'mon, I'm serious babe," Candy said. I could feel her yank the blankets from my lower half and begin tugging one of my legs to get me moving. I laughed and pulled her to me. She giggled and let out a short, surprised shriek, and we kissed. The memory of the previous night flashed through my mind. By the way she blushed, I could tell she remembered as well.

"Alright, alright, don't divorce me. I surrender," I said. "I love you."

"I love you, too." She said, booping my nose with one of her long, slender fingers before sifting through our luggage once more, looking for items she thought we might need later. We were supposed to hike around the falls, grab a light lunch, and then explore the Canadian Midway.

I dressed with renewed vigor. The splendor of Niagara Falls was visible through our window, and the scenery took my breath away. The water cascaded in unbelievable sheets from the cliffs, sending spray into the air around the base of the falls where dozens of people had gathered. They looked like yellow-clad ants from our room several stories up.

Boats passed slowly, navigating close to the falls. The boats held dozens of tourists in rain gear taking cellphone photos or videos. I checked the time on my phone before throwing on pants and the flannel shirt. It was almost ten AM. We slept longer than we planned.

I was ready in just a few minutes. While waiting for Candy I Googled poutine places. I loved the Canadian dish comprising fries smothered in gravy and cheese curds. My belly grumbled in anticipation.

"How are we coming along, babe?" I asked, sitting on the edge of the bed. I could see her in the bathroom, flustering with several bags. To me, it seemed like chaos, but over the years together I grew accustomed to her process. It was just a very long one.

"I'm almost ready," she said, changing her shirt for the third time.

"Anything I can help you with?"

"Did you look up places to grab lunch? I am freakin' starving!"

"Already on it. Unless you're one of those monsters who hates poutine."

She turned and glared at me. "Oh my god, I love it. How does this shirt look? It doesn't look weird?"

"If by weird you mean sexy, elegant, and snackable, then yes, you look very weird."

She smiled and shook off any thoughts of an intimate detour. "Nice try, bud." She took the shirt off again and replaced it with another one she'd already tried on earlier.

I chuckled and stood up. After more trial and error, we were out the door and walking toward the falls while keeping an eye out for a café. We spotted a massive Hershey chocolate store, complete with a giant mock candy bar decoration three times the sizes of our bodies sitting against the front of the store like a sugary obelisk. Next to that was a Starbucks. There, we grabbed coffee and pastries before rushing to the falls area to make up for lost time.

"Oh my gosh," Candy said, taking in a deep breath when we arrived where both the American falls and the Horseshoe Falls were in full view.

The Maid of the Mist coasted through the waters below, its passengers looking like specks from our vantage point. Behind us, the Niagara Falls skyline stretched out like a panorama. The cityscape (if one could call it a city) was a mix of unique buildings fitting of such a grand backdrop. I took photo after photo, trying to get as many of the buildings in as possible before I turned my attention to the falls themselves.

"It's so crazy to see this in person," I said, snapping a few pics of the Maid of the Mist, the Falls, and the Horseshoe Falls in the distance. Soon I noticed an old building that seemed to call out to me.

"Actually, I want to know why nobody told me that all the buildings here in Canada look like they're from Star Wars."

"Everything reminds you of Star Wars," Candy said, rolling her eyes. "You and Star Wars. Why didn't you just marry Star Wars?"

"No, I mean it. Check out that tower." I pointed to a dome that looked like the Space Needle in Seattle. "That looks like something straight out of Coruscant."

The only weird thing about the building looking like something out of Star Wars was that Star Wars never gave me the creeps while the distant tower did. Not willing to talk more sci-fi, Candy gave me a kiss, grabbed my hand, and pulled me toward a nearby gift shop.

"Time's a wastin'," she said, laughing softly as we careened toward the overpriced mugs, tee-shirts, and memorabilia.

We'd had a hell of a morning playing tourists. Soon it was poutine time. We'd already walked along the Canadian side of the Falls, including Horseshoe Falls, where we took a few selfies. Further down, where the crowds had dispersed, we encountered an old power station. It was the building that unnerved me earlier in the morning. Something about its architecture and proximity to the raging waters intrigued me. An overturned steel wreck of a ship sat nearby in the waters.

The building comprised dark stone and cement. I guessed the architecture to be an early 1900s design. Elaborate decorations caressed the building's recesses, like intricate lacework delicately draped over a grand façade. Modern architecture leaned toward bleak shoeboxes which depressed me. I suppose that's why I found myself drawn to historic buildings. I liked to photograph such buildings, framing the images to bring their character to the forefront. The love that the workmen and women put into those buildings was something to be in awe of.

When I'd had my fill of photographing the old building from every angle (Candy waited patiently, sitting on the grass and enjoying the raging waters of the Niagara River, looking out over the shipwreck), we headed out for poutine. We gorged on the gooey, cheesy, gravy covered fries. After that, we agreed it was time to walk it off.

"How are we doing with the itinerary?" I asked, as we walked by a giant Frankenstein's Monster who stood three stories higher than the nearby Burger King.

The iconic Hollywood horror figure held a massive burger in his ginormous green hand. The sight of food (even artificial) caused me to rub my belly, which was full to the gills with poutine.

"I planned today as a simple walking around day. I wasn't sure how tired we'd be, and I wanted to make sure we got to see some of the city before doing falls stuff. Maid of the Mist is tomorrow, and then the day after that we walk across the Rainbow Bridge and visit the American Falls. Mom wants a pic. Did you know it's where she and Dad went when they got married, too?"

"Yeah, your dad mentioned it. I got a brief glimpse of the falls lit up last night through the hotel window. It was gorgeous."

"Ooh," she said, pointing.

I followed her finger to a cool-looking Victorian building. Sandwich boards on the sidewalk advertised tarot readings and fortune telling. The building was a funky lavender and teal combo. Black lace curtains hung inside the large bay windows.

A beautifully crafted wooden sign above the door read: '*Falls of Fortune Psychic Shop.*'

Before I could protest, Candy was already rushing for the front door. With a sigh, I followed. She always liked psychics and mediums. She had dragged me to one in Portland where the finger quotes psychic said the two of us had already been together in three other lifetimes. I didn't believe in the stuff, but Candy did.

Except occasionally, I wondered if Candy was a medium. Sometimes Candy had dreams that would come true. Though mundane, the dreams contained enough details that made me wonder if she was omniscient. Other times, she'd call when I was in trouble, like the time I got a flat. She called immediately. Once verified, she rang her dad to come change the tire. (That was embarrassing). She had a strange and mysterious way about her.

When we entered the shop, wind chimes tinkled. Incense filled the room. There was no medium in sight, so we busied ourselves with looking at various books and artifacts along some nearby shelves. Crystals, incense burners, and candles depicting David Bowie as a saint were all for sale. I flipped through a book on spirituality as Candy, finally too excited to keep waiting, rang the bell at the desk.

"Ah, you're one of those," I said, giving her the stink face.

"Hush," she said.

A voice emerged from behind the counter. "Hello, hello, my dearies," the woman behind the counter said.

The woman reminded me of Candy's mother, beaming, and dressed in flowy purple and blue floral clothing. Long, silver and gray hair flowed down her shoulders. I thought a psychic shouldn't need a bell, but she answered that question. Maybe she was psychic.

"I'm so sorry to have kept you waiting," she said. "I sensed your approach through the mists. My name is Marge, and I welcome you to my humble shop. Please, tell me what you were seeking from me today?"

"Well," Candy said, looking sheepish. "I was kind of hoping you might have time for a walk-in tarot reading."

"Oh, I am so sorry, dearie," she said, giving a big, exaggerated frown. "I am booked solid for the next couple of days."

"Oh, that's a bummer," Candy said. "It's okay. Figured I'd ask. Do you have a business card, though? Maybe we'll be back. We're on our honeymoon."

"Your honeymoon? Oh, drat." She handed Candy a business card and a fresh smile. "I am so sorry that I haven't time for a tarot reading. Because it's your honeymoon I can offer you a general reading. I have twenty minutes. I can fit both of you in."

"No thanks. You can give her the entire twenty," I said, motioning toward Candy.

"Aw, I see you definitely found yourself a keeper," Marge beamed, grasping Candy's hands and leading her to the back. "You can come, too, Mr. Keeper. You can call me Marge"

I wondered why she didn't guess my name if she was a true psychic. We followed Marge to a table in the back. The lighting was very dim, intimate, and the lighting shrouded the room like certain bars back in Portland.

"Sit, sit," Marge said, ruffling her skirts behind her to better sit on the chair with them as we took our own seats. Candy sat opposite her, and I sat in a smaller chair by the wall to give them their space.

"Okay, first off, just give me your name and age," Marge said, closing her eyes and grasping Candy's outstretched hands anew.

"Candace Linford," Candy said, before pulling one of her hands away from Marge's grasp, scrunching up her face, covering her mouth with her withdrawn hand, and then laughing. "Oops," she said, looking at me. "I guess it's Candace Buckley now." Candy returned her hand to the expectant grasp of Marge, who was still beaming.

"Aha, so married recently then. How old?"

"Twenty-seven," Candy replied.

"People call you Candy for short."

Candy glanced at me. I gave a smirk. Of course, it would be easy to assume people called her Candy for short, but I said nothing. I wondered how much this "quick reading" was going to cost. I guessed if Candy got some enjoyment out of it, it didn't matter.

"Yes," Candy responded, not betraying her surprise.

"I see that you've got some very loving family surrounding you. Your parents, they've been thinking about you a lot recently."

Again, Marge could have inferred that we just got married, so in that case, Candy's parents would have been involved in the wedding shenanigans over the past month or two. Of course, they would think about her.

"I hope so," Candy said.

"It seems they've been here as well?"

This one sent a chill up my spine, but I stifled the feeling. *Lucky guess.*

"Yes," Candy said. "They were married here back in the eighties."

"Aha," she said, smiling more broadly. "I knew it. They've been to see me before. I felt their aura on you."

Candy looked at me with wide eyes. I knew she'd immediately ask her parents if they'd ever been to see the psychic as soon as we left Marge's shop.

"The eighties were a very fun time. In fact..."

Marge stopped mid-sentence and leaned back. Her smile vanished and her face became grim. "You have the gift, Candy."

"Well," Candy began, "I sometimes wondered. I have dreams and things that are sort of weird and sometimes I think they come true."

"Candy, listen," Marge said, withdrawing her hands from Candy's grasp, causing Candy to smile nervously. "You've got to be careful, child. This area can be overwhelming for those with gifts like yours. It certainly has been for me."

"What do you mean?" Candy asked, looking very concerned. I sat up, unsure where this conversation was going.

"You must protect yourself. You possess a rare gift, a light that draws spirits seeking solace or resolution. But with this gift comes a vulnerability that acts as a beacon that some spirits, lost or restless, may be drawn to. To them, you may as well be the Rainbow Bridge you crossed to get here from America. They will try to use you to cross that bridge. Do you understand?"

"I...I think so," Candy said.

I wanted to leave but Candy was engrossed in the reading. Marge grasped Candy's hands again and leaned forward.

"You must understand, dear one, not all spirits are benevolent. Some may seek to use your connection for their own purposes, and by doing that, it could confuse or even hurt you. Has any of that ever happened to you before?"

"No, not really," Candy said. "I mean, I've felt like a weird energy before, but nothing that ever hurt or anything. Can that happen?"

"It's crucial that you shield yourself. You need to set boundaries between the world of the living and the realms of the departed. Come, we're running out of time. I will not charge you if you promise to heed my advice and follow my instructions."

I tried to figure out the angle. I was expecting a high price for the twenty-minute detour. It was weird that the woman was suddenly offering advice for free. Marge explained what to say if Candy felt a spirit trying to merge with her. She told Candy to imagine a protective shield around herself and say aloud that she only welcomed benevolent spirits and rejected all others.

Marge handed Candy a black tourmaline pendant, for grounding and protection, and told her to wear it while near the falls. The whole thing creeped me out enough that I leaped when a tall, lanky woman with dark hair in a bob entered and greeted Marge. The woman was the booked appointment, so it was time for Candy and I to leave. As we headed out the door, Marge grabbed my wrist, catching me off guard.

"Listen, Ethan, I know you're not a believer," Marge said, looking deep into my eyes with her own piercing blue orbs. "Please watch out for her. I didn't want to alarm her, but there's a spirit tailing her since the falls. The spirit is consumed with so much sadness and grief that it almost brought me to tears. Stay with her. Don't let her wander."

"I won't," I said. "Thank you." I walked out the door to an expectant and nervous-looking Candy, who embraced me in a hug.

"Well, that was something," Candy said.

"Yeah, well, I wouldn't put too much stock into it. I know you believe in them, but sometimes these mediums want to scare you and make you come back to their shop to buy more stuff. She probably has a bunch of those amulets she gives out every day."

"You think?"

"Yeah, I mean, did she even tell you anything that she couldn't have made up?"

"Oh yeah, that reminds me," she said. "I'm going to call mom and ask if they saw the psychic." She pulled out her phone and dialed, turning toward the falls while she put the pendant around her neck.

At first, I grew annoyed, then angry. This Marge woman had made my wife upset, and for what? Then, the chill I'd felt up and down my spine earlier returned as I realized Marge had called me Ethan. Neither I nor Candy had ever mentioned my name.

Things got weirder after Candy called her mom. Apparently, back in 1981, when her parents were in Niagara Falls, the newlywed couple had visited the psychic shop. Marge was younger and studied under her mother who ran the shop back then. Candy's parents received a reading from Marge, just as Candy had, but without any mention of spirits using people as bridges. Marge connecting Candy to her parents made Candy believe the woman was the real deal. The ominous warning sent Candy into a spiral.

We returned to our hotel room, where I tried to talk her down, but Marge's words had rung true. Candy spent some time practicing the mantra Marge shared. We decided to cancel our dinner reservations and order in some Indian food. Food delivery was not as fast in Canada, so it was going to take a while.

"I'm going to take a bath," Candy said.

"Okay, babe," I replied. "After you're done, do you want to walk down to the Falls to catch the light displays on the water?"

"Maybe. I'll see how I feel after the bath. I kind of just want to sleep and try to wake up tomorrow all fresh."

"Are you okay?" I asked, hugging her close and kissing her forehead. She crumpled into my arms. I hugged her tight, breathing in the scent from the top of her head. "You know I'm right here with you, right?"

"I know," she said. "I'm sorry. It kind of spooked me, is all. I didn't want to say anything, but the first night we stayed here, I had vivid dreams about a woman."

"You did? Aw, I'm sorry, baby." I stroked her hair and tried to comfort her. "I'm sure it was just anxiety. I mean, we just got married and everyone is already asking questions, like when are we having kids, when are we buying a house, yada, yada, yada. It'll pass."

Candy stiffened in my embrace. "This... This was different, E." E is what Candy called me for short. She broke our embrace and looked up at me with fear in her eyes. "The woman screamed. It was terrible. Angry and sad at the same time. When I think about her shriek, it makes the hair stand up on my arm. Look."

She raised her arm and displayed the pinpricks of gooseflesh. I tried to think of something to say, but she was not done.

"In the dream, the scream started in the distance but grew closer and closer. Then I heard wet footsteps. When I turned around, a woman in an antiquated wedding dress walked toward me. Her white dress was sopping wet, torn, and stained red with blood. The woman's skin was sloughing off, and she dragged one of her legs behind her. It was horrific. She spoke a name and then I woke up crying."

"And you didn't wake me? Babe!"

"You were asleep, and I didn't want to worry you."

I pulled her closer and tightened my embrace. "Please, next time, wake me up. I want to be there for you. I love you."

"I love you, too," she replied.

We stood that way for a long time. It took some time before I thought to ask the name spoken in the nightmare. Thomas. A name that meant nothing to me.

Candy finally took a bath. Meanwhile, I scrolled through television channels while waiting for the food. The driver soon texted me and stated he was circling the block because there was no parking available. He asked if I could come down instead. I poked my head into the bathroom to inform Candy.

"I'll be right back," I said. "Channel flipping earlier. Back to the Future starts soon. That gives us something cool to watch while we eat if you're up for it."

"Sounds good," she said. "Love you, babe. Thank you for being you."

"No, thank you. I'm so lucky."

I exited the hotel. Fireworks were going off over the falls. Had I missed a memo, and it was July 4th? The sky burst into brilliance with multicolored explosions. I watched the display for so long that I almost forgot about the food.

When I checked my phone, I found two missed messages from the driver. He was on his way back to the hotel. Traffic was horrible because of the fireworks. The fireworks could have been a nightly tourist thing or Canada had its own holidays that I was unaware of. I hoped the fireworks might be enough to get Candy out of her funk and out of the room.

I navigated through throngs of people gathered on the sidewalks watching the show. I positioned myself to see oncoming traffic, but the cars moved at a snail's pace. Despite wanting to watch the fireworks, I focused on faces behind the windshields, looking for the person who matched the profile picture on the app. Finally, I spotted him and flagged him down. With the car still running, he opened his driver's side door and handed off a large brown paper bag.

"I'm sorry, my friend," he said. "No need for a tip, I understand."

"Nah, it's okay, man. You're going to need a drink after tonight, from the looks of it." I handed him a $10 bill and waved, clutching my food as I made my way back to the hotel.

"Thank you, brother," the man said.

People were already honking at him to move forward the available three inches, and by the time I reached the hotel again, the smell of the butter chicken was practically making my mouth water.

To my surprise, when I entered our hotel room the bathroom door was open, but Candy was nowhere to be seen. I texted her and her phone rang from the other side of the room. She'd not taken it with her wherever she'd gone. While strange it was not one hundred percent out of character. She hadn't been feeling well, so she likely stepped out to get some air or went down to the front counter for Tylenol or something.

Nothing to stress about just yet, so I went about separating our food items onto the table. The restaurant supplied plates and utensils. I piled jasmine rice onto my plate and topped it with the savory, spiced butter chicken, the reddish-gold sauce seeped deep into the starchy mound. Taking a chunk of garlic naan, I sopped up the food greedily. After about fifteen or twenty minutes, I'd finished my plate. Candy still hadn't shown up yet. Weird.

It was time to look for her. In case she came back before I did, I left a note explaining that I was just going to go looking for her as she'd forgotten her phone and to text me if she came back before I did. I signed the note, '*Love you.*'

I took the elevator down to the front desk. The night-shift employee was busy tapping away on a computer. His nametag read Monte, and he looked up when I coughed.

"How can I help you, sir?" he asked, looking up briefly from the computer just long enough to flash me a cursory smile.

"Hey, yeah, we're staying up in room 207 and I was just wondering if you'd seen my wife at all? Do you remember her?"

"Ah, yes. You're the newlyweds, correct?"

"Yeah," I said, trying to flash a smile without betraying my anxiousness. "Have you seen her within maybe the last hour? I ordered us dinner, and she left the room but didn't take her phone."

"Yes, I saw her. She exited the hotel. You left not long before, so I assumed she planned to meet you. She wasn't wearing shoes, which I considered odd, but you are Americans."

Initially, my fears waned upon hearing that Candy left right after me. She probably forgot to tell me something. Maybe she missed which way I went and decided to watch the fireworks. Still, why follow me, I wondered? Why not text me? Why leave her phone behind and why walk barefoot?"

"Are you sure she was barefoot?"

"Yes. Her feet were wet. She tracked wet footprints through the lobby. We had to mop them up so nobody would slip."

I turned and saw the mop trail. The mop bucket was in a recessed area of the lobby and a hotel worker was placing down a wet floor sign.

"Is everything okay?"

"Yeah, yeah, It's just odd she left right after me. I'm going to go look for her. Maybe she got lost."

"The beauty of the falls can overwhelm people. My guess is that she just went out to watch the fireworks."

"Thanks," I said, barely registering what he said. I moved outside and looked up and down the street. Hundreds of people still wandered about, and traffic remained at a standstill. I walked around the block but saw no sign of her. Checking my phone came up empty. She hadn't returned to the room.

After one more trip to the lobby to make sure she had not returned, I set out on foot, deciding I needed to look further than just the block. I walked for a long time and grew more and more worried. The American Falls glowed red, white, and blue courtesy of light projectors on the Canadian side. The Horseshoe Falls changed back and forth from red to white. Had I not been so stressed out I would have appreciated the beauty of the falls and how the colors seemed to give texture to the water as it fell. The Horseshoe Falls, when they changed to white, gave the water a heavenly appearance.

It was the type of beautiful scenery that would have enticed Candy though, so I thought it worth checking out. By the time I reached Horseshoe Falls, there was still no sign of my wife. Then I noticed the interesting building we'd seen earlier, the old power station, and decided I'd check there just to be sure. If she wasn't there, I would call the police. It had been a couple of hours, and it wasn't like Candy to be gone so long without telling me.

With the static roar of the rushing falls in my ears, I walked until I saw the dark shadow of the power station against the backdrop of the city-light-polluted sky. There was strange energy in the air and the odd feeling the building evoked in me returned. It unnerved me enough to turn away and leave.

Then I heard soft singing coming from the shore next to the power plant. Whoever the crooner was, they remained hidden behind a copse of trees. The cadence of the voice was strange as was the song, but the voice was instantly recognizable. She continued to sing as I rushed toward the trees.

"Let me call you sweetheart. I'm in love with you! Let me hear you whisper that you love me too!"

I rushed to the tree line and saw her, barefoot, standing at the very edge of the raging waters, singing a song I'd never heard before.

"Candy!" I shouted over the sound of the rushing waters. "Where have you been? I've been looking all over for you. Are you okay? What's wrong?"

Candy stopped singing and turned slowly to face me. Her eyes looked dark. I snapped a few pictures though I don't know why. Part of me feared I might never see her again, that something was so incredibly wrong that there was no coming back from it.

"Thomas?" she asked, tilting her head. "Have you come to take me home?" Her voice and cadence sounded different from the way Candy normally spoke. The name Thomas sent chills down my spine. It was the name from her dream. Was Candy sleepwalking?

"Candy, get away from the water. You're too close. You've also forgotten your shoes."

I motioned for her to come closer. When she refused, I stepped forward. She moved backward. I stopped immediately, trying to keep her from moving closer to the water.

"Whoa, whoa, whoa," I said. "Babe, be careful! Please come this way."

"Heavens to Betsy, Thomas," she said in her new cadence. "This view is simply ducky, isn't it? Even at night. But it's brighter than I remember. It's been dark for so long, Thomas. It makes a girl's eyes tear up to see the falls after all this time."

Not knowing what to do or say, I stood still. I was at a loss about what she was getting at. I didn't relish the thought of having to dive in after if she fell in, but I absolutely would.

"Do you remember proposing to me here? Do you remember when we were married? I do. It's all I think about, really."

"What are you talking about?" I asked. "I'm not Thomas, I'm Ethan—your husband. Are you sleepwalking? Please, come away from that edge."

"My husband. Yes, I remember. In the year of our Lord, 1915, we stood upon this very spot. So much hope and love, Thomas. But something's wrong, my love. I remember you holding my hand, and then I remember the ground...falling away at our feet. Then dark water, then...nothing. What say you, Thomas? Why do such ungodly memories haunt me so?"

If she was sleepwalking, I needed to draw her away from the ledge but not startle her. (I don't know where I read not to startle sleepwalkers.) She withdrew from my attempts to reach out. Maybe, just maybe, if she thought I was the other person, she might come closer. At least close enough for me to grab her and pull her to safety.

"Yes, I'm Thomas," I said unconvincingly, but I noticed Candy react in the half-light. "Please, my...dear. Come away from that ledge and stand with me under the moonlight."

"Oh, Thomas, it really is you," she said. "How wonderful."

"Please, come away from the edge, darling," I said, extending my hand for Candy to take and trying to match her weirdly formal speech and tone. "I want to see you better here in the moonlight." My heart pounded.

"My love," she said, twirling in the grass. "You don't know what you do to me." Candy waltzed forward, extending her own hand to grab mine. Her hand was ice cold to the touch, and I tried not to withdraw mine in shock. Candy then said, "Dance with me, Thomas."

She rested her head on my shoulder. Fog clouded her breath. Her whole body was ice cold, and the surrounding temperature dropped twenty or thirty degrees. We twirled slowly round and round as Candy sang, and then looked up at me. Her eyes were black orbs. She saw the fear on my face and took a step back, grabbing the sides of her head in frustration.

"No," she said. "You are not he. I miss him so. Thomas, my love."

"I am Thomas," I said. But she was no longer listening.

That's when Candy ran for the water. I cried out, launching myself toward my wife. Everything seemed to move in slow motion. Candy leaped toward the raging waters. Just as it looked as if she would throw herself off the ledge, her right arm grabbed hold of a nearby tourist info sign. It was the strangest sight. One moment my wife was leaping for the water, the next she saved herself. But she appeared to struggle with something (or someone I could not see.

Candy cried out in her own voice. "No, please! Eleanor, you're gone. Thomas is gone! Look for yourself!"

I reached for Candy and tried to wrap my arms around her, but Candy raised her free hand. A powerful force pushed against my chest and arms, shoving me back. I fell to the ground and my phone flew from my hands into the grass. Already in photo mode, the flash went off and the artificial shutter clicked as the phone took a burst of photos.

Candy noticed the flash. As I struggled to stand, Candy stepped away from the sign and grabbed the phone. With jerky moments (as if fighting someone for the wheel of a car), Candy returned to the information sign. Candy illuminated the sign with the phone's flashlight. My wife continued speaking to someone I could not see.

"Read this sign, Eleanor. I am so sorry. Please, let me go. I have my own love, my own life."

From where I sat, Candy was waving the cellphone across the sign, reading it while also having a conversation with someone not there. Once the camera reached the end of the tourist sign, Candy let out a shriek that chilled me to the bone. I rose to my feet as she crumpled to the ground. I rushed over and held her in my arms, making sure we were far enough away from the water that we wouldn't fall in.

"Babe, babe, wake up," I said, gently kissing her and patting her face.

She remained cold to the touch but appeared to be warming up. She opened her eyes slowly. Her eyes were no longer dark. I could just make out their familiar greenish tint.

"I had the weirdest dream," she said.

We stayed there for a long time, laying on our backs and looking at the stars. Eventually, Candy felt well enough to get back to our hotel room. The memory of what just happened apparently wiped from her mind. I didn't tell her any details. We finally rose and were leaving when I broke away, saying I needed to take one more picture.

With her a safe distance from the water, I trained my flashlight on the same infographic sign Candy had. In large type, the title read '*The Tragedy of the Broken Harts*'. Below the headline was a French-Canadian translation. It detailed how Eleanor and Thomas Hart, two newlyweds who were married on that very spot in 1915, perished when the eroded ground beneath them collapsed under their combined weight. The current carried them down the river and over Horseshoe Falls. The sign then detailed all the lives lost over the falls over the years. I was speechless as I caught up to Candy, taking her hand, which had fully warmed. We returned to the hotel.

"Everything okay, babe?" she asked. "I'm so tired. I can't wait to get into bed."

"Yeah, I'm okay," I said. I was quiet for most of the rest of the trip.

Weeks later, I had put the terrifying experience behind me. Candy had no other experiences after that night. While we were still in Niagara Falls, I insisted Candy practice the protection words Marge had shared. I also made sure my wife wore the amulet during the rest of the trip. Candy remembered nothing, but I'd become a believer of things I once considered woo-woo.

When I finally uploaded the photos from our trip to Niagara Falls, I scrolled through, deleting duplicates and blurry photos. When I reached the power station photos, my blood froze all over again. Standing behind Candy in every photo was Eleanor Hart, soaking wet, wearing an antiquated dress covered in stark red stains.

Good People Coffee
WEST LOS ANGELES, CALIFORNIA

If I had to describe Good People Coffee in one word, it would be loud. Very loud. Okay, maybe alive is the better word. I ship books from a spot near here and visit other businesses nearby as well. Often while visiting those other businesses, I can hear music blaring from Good People coffee shop. It is a siren call for those who lie caffeine and a good time. (And Good People.) From across the street, it sounds like a party.

I guess this place is a party in a sense. The vibe is always upbeat and though the shop itself is cramped it opens out into a cool open-air patio in the rear. Once upon a time it used to only have seating on the front sidewalk, and unless you were a smoker it was tough to hang out there because so many smoked outside. But after the pandemic they opened the back patio as many restaurants did in LA.

That circumstance transformed the place. The wide-open space gave the loud music a place to breathe, and the diners space to breathe as well. The shop has an Afro/Latin heritage that shows in their sense of community. They welcome every-one with enthusiasm.

The food and drinks here are special. Breakfast, or "Brekkie" as they call it, options are fantastic. And the drinks are exceptional. This is where you may want to try something new outside of your normal drink.

Because the coffee shop is so fun and feels like a party, I ended up looking outside the coffee shop for inspiration for this story. The coffee shop is located right along one of the busiest streets in Los Angeles. Shop, sidewalk, traffic, right there. But across the street is a place that has been under construction seemingly forever. It was once upon a time a grocery store but for years has been fenced up so no one can see inside. It is a whole city block, and it sits opposite the coffee shop.

Late at night (the coffee shop sadly closes early now), dozens of massive trucks roll in like a convoy, enter a side opening in the construction site and then drive out soon after. It is an understatement to say how odd it is to see this late-night convoy. They were apparently hauling out dirt, but the regularity and the speed at which they arrived and departed felt surreal. It is as if the construction site is a quarry and not an old supermarket.

Another thing, since the shop is right on the street, buses go by all the time. And then while I was there one day, I heard the familiar grind of wheels on asphalt. A kid whizzed by on his skateboard. All those things came together to create this unique tale for a unique coffee shop.

DRINK RECOMMENDATION: They have a drink called *The Notorious Vanilla Bullshit*. I'm not here to give their menu secrets away, so any combination of vanilla and espresso where you get your coffee will do. Bonus points if you add a dash of cinnamon.

Rock Lobster

PAUL CARRO

An abandoned, haunted rock quarry awaited Tyler. Despite its sordid history and dangerous environment, he looked forward to visiting the place. He took the bus to get there which gave him the courage to face the haunted quarry. Tyler figured riding public transportation was fraught with more danger than any old ghosts, at least based on his experience.

He planned to meet his friends Judd and Frank there. Unlike Tyler who had to take public transportation, his friends' parents drove them to the quarry. Well, no good parent allowed their kids to play at the quarry, so they were dropped off at the public library. The routine was for them to go inside like they were interested in books. Once inside, they waited for their parents to drive away, then they walked from there to the haunted grounds.

Because Tyler lived too far away from his two friends, he could never hitch a ride with them. Tyler was not made of Uber money, so he had to take public transit to meet them.

The bus, always filled with interesting folks, stopped in front of a convenience store close to the quarry. From there, Tyler would skateboard several blocks before climbing down an embankment to a side street that led to the quarry.

Tyler preferred sitting near the front of the bus, looking down in his lap, earbuds in to drown out all the misery that seemed to love company. Often the rear of the bus smelled like the back of his school. Pot smoke made Tyler sick, and he wanted nothing to do with it.

Besides, his dad did drugs, and the man was no longer around. The man loved needles more than he loved his wife and kid. Then one day he loved one too many needles. *Kay ser rah, sir pa*, Tyler remembered a distant relative murmuring at the funeral. Though he had mostly gotten over the loss, it stung sometimes when he saw friends doing cool things with their dads.

People frequently engaged with Tyler on the bus (always older men, never cute women his own age). Tyler used the earbuds as an excuse to avoid talking to people, but sometimes riders still refused to leave him alone. Those times were scary because it meant someone refused to read signals, or worse, failed to recognize that he was only fourteen.

His current ride to the quarry remained uneventful for most of the trip until one stop where a man who smelled of pot entered. The passenger walked past and forcefully banged

Tyler's legs. It did not appear inadvertent, more of a body check.

Startled, Tyler glanced up. Big mistake. The man hovered over Tyler, waiting for a reaction. The man was prison lean with facial tattoos. He grinned at Tyler as if sizing up a meal. Tyler faced several dangerous situations riding the bus over the years and usually got by on his wits. Something told him there would be no getting by anything with this guy.

Thankfully, more passengers entered at the next stop which forced the man to move on. Tyler breathed a sigh of relief, but his hands shook with nerves. Not good. He needed steady hands for his favorite past-time—origami. Tyler unzipped his backpack, reached inside, and touched some paper. The contact gave him peace. He used to fold paper on the bus out in the open, making gifts for elderly riders, but too many mooks targeted him for enjoying such a nerdy craft.

When not high, Tyler's dad taught him origami. Tyler was young, so his dad taught simple shapes at first like planes and swans. His Dad was gone before he could teach any next-level origami. Like most things in Tyler's life, YouTube became both parent and educator. (His mom was nice but worked from dark hours to dark hours six days a week, so he rarely saw her.) It was through online tutorials and practice that Tyler improved his skills. Paper folding also calmed Tyler's nerves.

He needed to calm them after the confrontation. Something about the tattoo face passenger felt dangerous and frightening. Making precise creases took intense concentration. When Tyler bent paper to his will, the world vanished. Nothing existed, nothing mattered. When folding, Tyler found peace.

What started as a simple hobby had become elaborate. Gone were the days of only white paper. He had since added colored paper and markers to his repertoire. Green was good for aliens, blue for sea creatures, and so on. If he weren't afraid of being mocked, he would have pulled out paper and started folding right then to de-stress. There was something dastardly about the tattoo man.

"Hey, hey, hey!" someone in the back yelled.

"Driver!" Another yelled.

The yells were loud enough to hear over his headphones, so he yanked them off. Chaos engulfed the bus as passengers fled to the front of the vehicle. Tyler tried to understand what was happening.

"It's the man who kicked you," the old woman across from Tyler said. "The bad boy."

The old Latino woman often got on the same stop that Tyler did. The two rarely talked, merely shared head nods of recognition. Tyler always let her board the bus first while he waited patiently for her to dump her coins into the slot.

Alarmed by the events, the woman looked at Tyler and talked through the situation as it unfolded. The woman explained that the "bad boy" was the source of the chaos at the back of the bus.

Tyler caught a fresh look at the guy before the crowds of people blocked his view. The man had to be late twenties or early thirties. *So old*, Tyler thought. Tyler was already at the front and had nowhere to go. The bus was not in a safe place to stop, so whatever was occurring continued while the bus moved. More screams sounded at the rear and then banging as someone pounded on the door.

"Back door! Back door!" A desperate voice cried out.

The driver yelled back, confused, and finally stopped. The doors opened and whatever was happening spilled onto the streets. As quickly as it began, people retook seats as if nothing ever happened. Screams continued outside, where a man wailed in agony and cried for help. Tyler tried to see, but too many people returning to their seats blocked his view. Soon they were on the road again.

Tyler got off two steps later in front of the Mini Mart and something caught his eye. As the bus pulled away, he glimpsed the rear doors of the bus which had a set of bloody handprints on them. What happened on the bus? And why had everyone simply moved on when the person got off? It looked like someone needed help. But maybe that was how things were in the city. Everyone wore their earbuds like he did and blocked out the worst things, even if someone was in trouble.

Dropping his skateboard onto asphalt, Tyler kicked off. The quickest way to his destination was to brave the breakdown lane for a few blocks and hope passing cars avoided the crazy kid on the skateboard. (There were no other stops until well past the quarry.)

A guardrail appeared off the right ahead where the ground dropped precipitously. That was the spot. He hopped the rail and ran/skidded down an embankment littered with tossed road debris. Mostly fast-food wrappers, candy wrappers, and empty soda and beer cans as well. Once the steep hill bottomed out, he jumped a second guard rail, which led to a cul-de-sac of elegant homes. Back on asphalt, he dropped the skateboard and sped down the street. An unseen dog behind a fence alongside a home's carport barked at him as it always did.

"Good boy," Tyler yelled and kept going.

Soon he reached a dirt path where he had to walk again. The long stretch led to the base of the quarry. His friends Judd, and Frank came from another direction and would arrive at the top of the quarry while his path took him to its bottom. The guys had a short walk through some woods which led to the cliff top high above the haunted property. (No one had ever seen any ghosts, but everyone assumed the place was full of them.)

He neared the end of the path and entered the quarry. The massive landscape looked as if someone dropped a desert in the middle of an enormous forest. Once past the tree line, the ground turned to dirt and stone.

The open expanse was larger than many football fields combined. Stone cliffs lined one side of the quarry. Different footpaths offered passage from ground level to top side. At the center of the whole thing was a massive cave. It opened at the center of the cliffs and fed an underground mining facility.

Just outside the cave, boulders of various sizes dotted the landscape. Tyler and his buddies often joked about how stupid it was for people to mine rocks when they were already out in the open.

As cool as the cave looked, Tyler never ventured in, figuring if there were ghosts, that's where they would reside. Besides, it was too dark to navigate with his cellphone flashlight. The guys were determined to explore its depths at some point but had never ventured past the cone of sunlight cast across the cave entrance.

A wide dirt road ran from ground level along the side of the quarry and into the forest. Tyler heard somewhere that the owners designed the remote road to keep the massive trucks from disturbing locals. The road led through the forest to the interstate.

Midway along the dirt road rose a massive pulverizer machine left behind when the place closed. Though not quite Godzilla sized, it felt like it to the teens. Especially Tyler, who was relatively small for his age. Weeds and forest had reclaimed much of the land that the machine sat on. Part of the legend behind the haunting involved the old machine and its propensity to start on its own, especially if people were close enough to stumble into it. (That did not stop Tyler and his friends from climbing on it.)

Further up the road where the cliff levelled off to flat ground stood a huge water tank that served some purpose back in the day. Tyler took in the familiar sights while plotting what they might do when his friends arrived.

Still on edge and waiting for his friends, Tyler decided it was time to make some origami. He jumped up onto a large boulder near the entrance of the cave. Once his butt adjusted, he unzipped his bag and retrieved a brown piece of paper and creased it. The quarry disappeared, as did memories of the bus while he folded.

After some time of working on a bear, something broke his concentration. He found it odd because he rarely noticed the world when folding. Looking around, he saw nothing so he went back to work.

Every twist of paper brought the bear to life. If he had a better workstation than a rock, he would have fashioned teeth.

But that required a razor blade, which he only had at home. A bear foraging on all fours would have to do. Tyler placed it on the boulder and jumped off the rock.

As he hit the ground, he spotted something sparkling in the cave. It was face high. Eyes? It was only a flash that vanished as quickly as it had appeared. Did his friends arrive while he was folding? Did they sneak into the cave to scare him?

"Hello?" No answer. It had to be his friends. "Not funny guys. I already had a rough time getting here."

He gave his friends props for venturing further into the cave than they ever had before. None of them ever crossed the line from sunlight to mystery before but if they were in the dark, he knew how to find them. Tyler grabbed a rock and hurled it into the void.

Crack! The rock bounced loudly off another inside. The noise should have caused his friends to cry out in surprise, but they did not. It was his imagination. There was nothing there. He turned and eyed his bear that held court over its boulder when something thudded near his feet.

He spun and spotted a rock settling into place among others on the ground. Did it come from the cave? Was it the same rock he hurled? He did not pay enough attention to the one he threw to know for sure. It looked similar.

"Hello?"

Another flash of light appeared deep in the cave. Again, at face height. The sun shone over Tyler's shoulder, so there was every chance it caused the weird glare. Maybe a stray beam made its way through the curtain of darkness. Another rock landed at his feet, closer this time. He leaped and screamed, only to be met with laughter. High above, his friends stood there, ready to launch another rock in his direction.

Tyler shook his head and went to meet his friends halfway up the dirt road. By the time he reached them, he forgot about his bear and the rock that might have come from within the cave.

Because it was Sunday, the bus was nearly empty when he and the old lady got on. There was only one lone passenger seated in the middle of the bus. While fine with sitting next to the woman, Tyler was happier having a seat to himself, so he chose the back of the bus. The other rider wore a hoody and sat slumped over as if asleep. There were three exits on the bus: front, middle, and back. Tyler moved to the very back of the bus, past the last set of doors.

He sat and pulled a random piece of paper from his back-pack. Green. A Martian maybe? He had science fiction on his mind because he and his friends had a blast playing out their version of a post-apocalyptic science fiction battle the day before. They had such a good time they made plans to pick up where they left off the next day.

Tyler had just started folding the green paper when a voice sounded out loud enough to be heard above his earbuds. "Hey, don't ignore me. There's no ignoring me," an ominous voice said.

Tyler looked up and saw the sleeping man was no longer asleep, if ever at all. The man dropped the hoodie to reveal his tattooed face. It was the man from yesterday! Tyler looked down, stuffing papers back in his bag. He searched for his cellphone, hoping to bury himself in a game and wait the ride out. Wait the man out.

Except the man dropped into the seat next to him. "Think you can ignore me?"

Tyler froze, unable to speak. He shook his head.

"We can have a go outside. You want that?"

The man held a pack of cigarettes and made a stabbing motion toward Tyler's stomach. A double stab. The way the man moved his hands and where he aimed the cigarette pack felt like someone with experience. Tyler watched a lot of movies and films and YouTube. The motion looked like someone in prison using a shiv.

While the man motioned with cigarettes, his other hand went instinctively toward the waistband at his back. The man had a weapon. Tyler did not need to know details. He simply read the room. This was a very dangerous man.

"We can get off at the next stop and have at it. What do you say?" the man said.

Tyler said nothing. No, he did not want to get off on a stop and have a fight with an adult, especially one who knew how to stab people and had a knife.

"Either way, you're getting off on the next stop," the man said.

Tyler rose in a panic, but the man kicked his legs across the aisle, blocking Tyler's path. Tyler glanced at the front of the bus, which appeared so far away. But there was a bus driver and the woman who could possibly help before his bloody handprints ended up on the bus door.

The crazy guy hit the bell for the next stop. Tyler hoped the man intended to get off, but soon it became clear it was one more threat in his bag of tricks. Before arriving at the stop, the man moved to a seat just past the back door and spread his legs across the aisle again. When the bus stopped, the man gestured for Tyler to exit. Tattoo Face, as Tyler deemed him, did not move toward the exit himself, content to force Tyler into one option: get off the bus.

Maybe if Tyler exited, it might satisfy the man. But what if Tattoo Face got off and followed? The stop was in the middle of nowhere. There were no people around on Sundays. Tyler would be alone with the dangerous psycho.

Tyler moved toward the open door, which would close soon. The man smiled, happy to have control over the boy. But Tyler leaped over the man's legs and raced to the front of the bus. Without saying a word, Tyler dropped into a front seat behind the bus driver and across from the old woman.

The woman smiled at Tyler, but he could not muster a smile in return. His hands shook. His stop was nearing, he needed to make it that far and pray the crazy man did not get off as well. He was safe for now.

Or so he thought.

Seating at the front of the bus was three seats stretched sideways (so they could be lifted for wheelchairs when necessary). The rest were traditional twins running front to back on both sides of the bus. The man appeared and sat next to Tyler. He leaned in toward the boy. The woman frowned, unhappy with the man's sudden presence. The man paid her no mind, too busy focusing on his toy.

Tyler grabbed his cellphone and placed it to his ear, pretending to talk to Judd. But with every fake line of conversation (making Judd sound older and bigger, and waiting at the upcoming stop) Tattoo Face made a snarky retort. Tyler's stop was next, but he remained in danger. The man was clearly crazy. What if the Tattoo Face got off too?

"Leave the boy alone," the woman said.

"Shut up bitch, I'll cut two as quick as one," the man said and brandished an actual knife.

It was a steak knife, maybe stolen from a restaurant, but it would do the job. Dried steak sauce or blood covered the blade. The woman screamed. The driver yelled but fell silent when he saw the blade.

Through it all, the man stayed focused on Tyler. The man had chosen his victim that day. The stabbing victim would be the boy who liked to fold paper, the boy who wanted to play with his friends, the boy who wanted to go home.

The driver stopped the bus and threw open the door. It was as if the driver understood the danger would follow the boy. The woman scrambled to the back of the bus, the opposite scramble from the previous day. She had 911 on the phone but could not articulate where they were.

Tyler rushed out the door. The man exited as well. The bus closed its door immediately and drove down the street, leaving Tyler alone with the tattoo faced man. Turning to Tyler, Tattoo Face raised the blade.

With a quick spin and run, Tyler threw his board down onto the pavement and kicked off. The man gave chase and appeared as if he would catch up almost immediately. Tyler started crying but he kept kicking and riding. Soon, he left the man behind. Tattoo Face yelled every variation of the F-word known to man.

The bus had stopped in the distance. The bus driver opened the door. "Get in. Cops are on their way," the driver said.

"He's right behind me," Tyler said and kept going.

The bus driver was smart enough to do the same. The bus drove away. There were no other cars on the street, because why would there be when someone needed help? Tyler eventually reached the familiar fence and practically fell down the embankment. He could not go fast enough to meet his friends.

Tyler's phone had dinged while he was escaping the crazy man, but he was too busy staying alive to check it. Once in the clear he checked the message and cursed. The text said his friends could not make it. Tyler should have known. Because the library was closed on Sundays, the closest drop off spot they used as an excuse was the mall. That was much further from the quarry and required a long walk.

If their laziness wasn't the issue, it was probably the movies. His friends were likely having popcorn and soda instead of meeting him. Meanwhile, he was stuck running from maniacs and being alone with people in caves who throw rocks and have flashy eyes.

Tyler feared going back for the bus. The crazy guy would be out there waiting. Tyler had no intention of crossing paths with tattoo man again, which left two options: wait out the guy and chance a bus back or make the long walk to the mall and see if his friends' parents could drive him home.

The buses by the mall went to different parts of town, nowhere near his house. Those buses stayed on the more affluent side of town, while his bus line serviced the poorer communities and streets. There were transfer options, but they took forever and he could not afford them.

Mall it was, though. Tyler was too frightened to return to the direction where he might encounter the madman again. He texted his friends. *Are you guys at the mall? Can I hitch a ride?* There was no immediate response. Depending on the movie, he would have to wait up to two hours to get a response, so he decided he would fold for a bit.

It was then he remembered his bear from the day prior. He walked to the boulder to see if it was still there and was shocked to find something unimaginable. What sat in its place took his breath away. Tyler blinked, then rubbed his eyes. Sitting atop the boulder was a much different origami creation. A lobster.

A rock lobster!

It was enormous. Tyler moved closer and circled the elaborate creation. Compared to his work, the lobster was huge. It was four feet long and stood two feet high. Made of multiple stones rather than sheets of paper, it was not technically origami. But there was craft and care involved in the creation.

An oblong rock made up the torso of the lobster's body. The shape resembled the center of a lobster. To find something so close must have taken forever. But that was nothing compared to the tail and claws, which showed remarkable craft. The claws had open spaces between the pincers. There was zero chance that someone would find two stones that looked exactly like lobster pincers, not even in a quarry, so someone must have manipulated the stones in some fashion.

A closer inspection revealed twisted striations. (And handprints?) Markings like hands on Play-Doh covered the claws. How could someone twist rock? It was impossible. Yet, there it sat; two rocks formed into perfect lobster claws.

He looked around in search of the artist and spotted a glimmer in the cave again. The glimmer was face high if the individual was a child. And if it was, it would make sense. The legends behind the quarry haunting revolved around children. Decades ago, an explosion in the mine killed dozens of people. The rumor was that the owners used teens and kids for labor, and it was they who perished that day.

Were ghosts responsible for the lobster origami? Did they take his bear which was nowhere to be found? Inside the cave, the eyes did not vanish but moved gently, as if watching the outside world. Then its head turned, just slightly, and a ray of sun captured a clear image of orange eyes!

Orange was not a human eye color. That meant it was an animal in the cave. And child high for an animal meant it was massive. Tyler needed to get out of there. He turned to run and slammed into something. The smells overwhelmed Tyler. Pot, body odor, and blood.

It was Tattoo Face! The man waved the knife around and practically drooled like an animal himself.

"Well, well, well, what have we here? Come down here to party? Party of one? See all the used condoms around the place? None are mine because I refuse em'. Not going to sacrifice my needs for those of my victims."

Rather than stab Tyler immediately, the man reached for him. Tyler turned and ran, but the man grabbed Tyler by the backpack and yanked him off his feet. But youth was flexible. Gravity took hold and Tyler's feet hit the ground. When Tyler landed, he twisted, spun, and detached himself from the backpack.

The wild escape caused Tyler to stumble onto all fours. Mercifully, the weight shift caused Tattoo Face to stumble backward. The man growled and threw the backpack down near the skateboard. Tyler had hoped to grab the board as a shield against the blade, but it was out of reach.

"You little shit! Stay still, time to get what's coming to ya'."

Blood pounded in Tyler's head so hard that the man's words sounded distant. Tyler wished to get small, to hide, to go away forever. Since that was not an option, he needed to escape.

Darkness was the answer. It could be an equalizer. It was his only option because the man was coming on fast. Tyler scrambled to his feet and ran for the cave. Though there was an animal inside, there was one outside as well. He had to take the chance.

As Tyler booked it into the cave, the man cried out in frustration, a simmering pot boiling over. Rage on top of rage. The man would tear, slice, then spit into the open wounds. Though Tyler and his friends never ventured past the mouth of the cave, he now refused to recognize the imaginary border. There was as much danger lurking in the light as there was in the dark.

Tattoo Face closed the gap, pulling in so close that Tyler feared he would never make it into the cave. The boy rushed into the darkness and felt a hand brush his shirt. So close! Where Tyler kept running, the man stopped to adjust to the dark.

Water splashed underfoot up to Tyler's ankles. He didn't care where the ground water came from, he only knew he had to get out of it soon, because the splashing was giving away his position. After about a hundred feet, Tyler stopped and pressed himself against the cave wall. He was grateful and lucky that he had not run into anything. The area was pitch black.

The darkness frightened him, but less than the man did. Tattoo Face's feet splashed through the water and the already frightening voice grew more so when amplified by the cave's echo.

"Here, little piggy. Time to come out and splay!'

A face appeared in the darkness when the man, with practiced efficiency, flipped open and lit a lighter. A flickering orange glow demonized the already demonic face. One saving grace was that the man faced away from Tyler and the flame illuminated only a tight circle around the man.

Tyler crouched and found a rock. He threw it deeper into the cave where it pinged off the stone walls. The man smiled, never turning toward the sound.

"You think I will fall for that trick, dead boy? I know you are too afraid to go far in the dark. But I am the darkness. You are further from light than you can possibly imagine. I have all the time in the world, and I know you are about to sissy pee."

Tattoo Face sniffed the air. It was true, Tyler was close to peeing. He would not last long. If the man turned his way, that would likely trigger a deluge down his leg. The man would sniff him out quickly. The evil man turned toward the path that led deeper into the cave. It was then that Tyler saw something the man did not.

A glint. As orange as the flames. Eyes. The eyes of the other beast lurking in the shadows. The orange-eyed thing moved and splashed into the water. That drew the man's attention. Tattoo Face rushed toward the sound while Tyler rushed for the exit. The secondary splash of footprints caught the evil man off guard. He turned, confused.

"Hey!" Tattoo Face yelled, trying to figure out the simultaneous footsteps.

Tyler ran out of the cave. Once outside, the sun blinded him. That, combined with his wet feet on the rocky ground, caused him to stumble. The fall stunned him, but he was too frightened to care. Tyler could not immediately rise but rolled over onto his back so he could see the entrance to the cave. He expected the man to leap out. Instead, screams filled the cave.

"Hey! What? No! Let me go! What are you..." Tattoo Face shouted in between cries of fright.

The screams terrified Tyler. What could make such a man cry out in desperation? What was in the cave? He was about to find out. The screams grew closer. Tyler scrambled back along the ground, looking over his shoulder for his skateboard. Maybe he could hit the man with it. The boulder that held the rock lobster sat nearby and blocked the view of his board. He rose.

Then fell on his ass.

The orange eyes stepped out into the open. Along with other eyes that made no sense. Each set of "eyes" was made of quartz of different colors. Rose, crystal, burnt orange, and one with eyes so black they appeared to be made of coal.

They did not belong to animals, but to rock people. Rock boys, to be precise. Each one looked to be about Tyler's height and size, except they were not normal boys. They were boy shaped amalgamations of stones.

The combination of rocks was unmistakable. Head, a large, rounded rock. Neck, a slender rock. Torso, a massive stone. Arms, an assembly line of long stones with pebble sized rocks at the joints. Smooth, rocks with pebbles for fingers made up their hands. They walked on heavy stone feet that capped off legs made of thick stones. Two of the boys dragged Tattoo Face along with them. Blood dribbled from the man's mouth, obviously a result of the struggle of flesh against stone. The man continued fighting against his captors. Four other stone children brought up the rear.

Tyler worried. Now that they had Tattoo Face, was Tyler next? The man pulled one arm free of the stone children's grip. In a fluid motion, he reached behind his back, grabbed the knife, and raised it high.

"He has a knife!" Tyler yelled, suddenly concerned for the rock boys.

Tattoo man stabbed one in the exact spot he threatened to jab Tyler—straight at the liver. The blade snapped off at the hilt. Still fighting, Tattoo Face stabbed the handle into the eye of his captor. It made a cracking sound but did no good.

The man tossed the handle and punched the nearest boy in the face and screamed in pain. The crunch of the man's bones was loud. They exploded in a pop. His arm fell to his side, useless. The two holding the man reasserted their grip on him.

"Don't just stand there, kid, help me!" Tattoo Face cried out.

"I can't," Tyler said.

"You little shit. I was going to make it quick with you, but now I'll make it slow."

Even in the presence of something otherworldly, the man shouted threats. There was evil in the man, pure evil, nothing else, even while wrestling with something that should not exist.

Two of the rock children broke away and walked toward Tyler who prepared to run. But the boys walked past him, nodding their rock heads as they went. They headed toward the crusher.

Meanwhile, the two holding the man swung their arms and the tattoo guy went airborne. The rock people lifted him as easily as the evil man had lifted Tyler. With a crack, the man landed on the large boulder containing the rock lobster. The lobster split into sections and fell to the ground.

What a loss, Tyler thought. He never even got a picture. Tattoo Face fought to find the breath that was knocked from him. He turned to Tyler and cried out through a wheeze.

"Throw a rock at them or something, kid. We're human. You gonna let them do their thing? We need to stick up for other humans, right?"

"Let you know when I see one," Tyler said, surprised at how cold his own voice sounded.

Tattoo Face spit at his captors and tried to roll away, but they held the man firm. Then one of the other stone boys grabbed a sizeable rock and approached the screaming man.

The rock boy placed the rock in the screaming man's mouth! Tattoo Face's eyes went wide. He tried to spit the stone out, but it was too large and already lodged in his wide-open jaw. The rock boy pushed the rock further in. Tattoo man went wild, crying out through the stone, trying to kick, trying to move, but could not. The stone expanded the man's throat, then moved past it.

Tattoo man spit up blood but breathed in relief when the object cleared his airway. Then they fed the man another stone, slightly smaller, but it produced another round of agonizing kicking from the man.

Stone after stone, they fed the man. Partway through, Tattoo Face stopped struggling and simply took the punishment. Tyler tried to find sympathy, but the man had been intent on stealing Tyler's childhood from him. Tyler wondered if the stone boys had their childhoods stolen as well. Sometimes Tyler thought it would be cool to work in a quarry, but it was much different to come and play versus work there.

Tattoo Face went from screaming to groaning and his stomach had filled to pregnancy size. All the rocks had settled in one spot, making his distended stomach a mini quarry. The rock boys let the man go. Tattoo Man's eyes went wide when he realized they released him. He spun his legs, stepped onto the ground, and—face planted.

More like stomach planted. The man's rounded stomach proved too heavy for him to move. He floundered like an upturned turtle. One by one, the rock boys circled the man.

Tattoo Face noticed the gathering of feet. "No, please, no more!"

Blood spurted from his mouth when he spoke. The thin tattoo man was thin no more. Even his throat was distended by the rocks having been shoved down his throat. The boys picked the man up by each limb and lifted him off the ground.

"No, wait! What are you? Kid? Help me kid!"

Like pallbearers, the boys carried the man across the quarry toward another ghost of the past. The pulverizer. Despite his shredded throat, the man found his voice when he spotted where they were carrying him. The man's voice had changed. Whether from the damage to the throat or pure fear, the man sounded like a child.

One of the stone boys prepped various parts of the machine, pulling levers. With a sputter, the machine came to life, and soon roared like the T-Rex Tyler always imagined it to be. Long dormant lights on poles sputtered to life. Forces were at work, and it all related to the bad man.

The one who started the machine tossed a large rock into the machine's mouth to test it. It came out on the other side in pieces. One made into many.

"No. Kid, tell them. Tell them I'm a good guy!"

"I can't. I'm not a liar."

"Son of a bitch. I'll kill you all. I'll gut every last one of you. I'll tear this world apart!"

It was then that Tyler learned some men were beyond human, were something else, were only a physical shell. Underneath the skin where the real stuff happened, the man was walking evil.

The rock boys lifted Tattoo Man and fed him into the pulverizer. Tattoo Face managed a brief scream that quickly turned to a strange ugh, as the machine did its thing. The machine pounded and pulverized flesh more efficiently than it had the single stone. Rocks in the man's stomach offered minimal resistance. They crunched and spurted bloody dust as the machine did its thing.

What came out on the other side was the inside of the man. Evil in the form of blood, squished body parts, and quartz flakes spurted out the back of the machine. There were no tattoos left to see. No man either. The pulverizer had lived up to its name. The T-Rex had finished its meal.

The machine died, as did the lights, and the world fell silent except for the sound of stone footsteps crunching on gravel. The boys reentered the cave. Once inside, one turned back, Tyler saw the glint of orange quartz eyes for a moment before they receded into the darkness.

Tyler unzipped his backpack and went to work.

Though it took longer than expected, Tyler felt he owed his new creation to his rescuers. The boy folded like the machine on the road ahead—efficient, unstoppable. He used the entire color palette of his markers. He tore paper, reassembled it, folded it into angles so tightly it added stability to the work.

The sun had mostly set, and dusk settled in. Soon he would be unable to see, so he quickened his pace. It meant he would have to walk back to the bus in darkness, but he was not afraid any longer. He was not a boy any longer either. The day's events had changed that.

There on the spot that once housed a rock lobster, and hosted a man who ate stones, sat something new. Six child superheroes, complete with capes, stood in a circle. Tyler shaped the origami into boy superheroes. Real boys, not stone versions. Tyler felt it was important to show them he knew who they were. He knew the legends of the boys trapped in the mines.

Each superhero suit was a different color, matching the color quartz of each rescuer's eyes. Tyler hoped they would understand what the colors represented. Tyler lined the origami superheroes in a circle and in the middle, he placed another origami creation. A horrific, tall, tattooed man with steak knives for hands.

It was always important to have a big-bad to go up against. The rock boys had a variant of the Tattoo Man in a paper form wrapped as tight as a drinking straw. When playing with action figures, the heroes would always win against evil every time, no matter how dire the stakes.

Just like in real life, Tyler thought, looking back to the pulverizer one last time. Though it was dark, the machine's silhouette stood against the backdrop of the night sky. Tyler went on his way, heading home. Behind him, the lights burst to life. He looked back and watched the boys retrieve the origami.

Tyler waved and the boys waved back. The moment the boys took their gifts, the lights went out.

Lights came from another direction as cars drove down the dirt from above. Teens looking for a party. Some honked, some hooted. In the past, Tyler would have wished to be their age, would have wished to stay and try to join in. Once upon a time he would have felt left out, felt uncool, would have longed to be in their group.

But he now understood what mattered. Six boys had perished, but they stuck together, and they looked out for their own. Tyler had his own friends, his own family, as imperfect as they all were. But in the end, they were all that mattered.

Tyler felt no need to join the party setting up camp in the haunted quarry. He was ready to go home.

10 Speed Coffee
Sawtelle Japantown, California

I wrote a story at 10 Speed Coffee in volume one. This new location did not exist then, but it is a great new spot. Japantown is already a fun place to visit. There are many great shops. Tons of great food places and a nice vibe to the place. While there are a few other coffee places nearby, this one is always packed with good reason.

The staff is top notch and sometimes they bounce between the two locations. They are friendly, quick with drinks and always in a contagious good mood. I don't know if Thursday bucket hat day is still a thing with them but that was always fun to see when they did it.

Next is the coffee itself. It is darn good. They know me because I generally order the same thing every time because it tastes better there than most places. The pastries are top notch as well.

This location fills up fast with students so seating can be tough but there are lawn chair style chairs out front to lounge in while waiting for a seat. All Japantown is worth a visit, but a stop here is a must.

As this coffee shop caters to cyclists, there are bikes hanging throughout the shop, but I drove a different kind of vehicle to get there, my car. Nearby there is a printing shop I sometimes use. If I have orders to pick up, I like to write at the coffee shop first then get my print order. Since parking is tough in the area, rather than move my car, I will walk the few blocks to pick up my stuff and then return to where I am parked.

To get to the print shop though I must pass under a perilous street bridge under a very busy section of highway. That is what inspired this story.

DRINK RECCOMENDATION: My usual. A large cold brew, black. (If yours is not as good as theirs, feel free to add a splash of milk or something. But I take mine black here.)

Thumbs Up

PAUL CARRO

The DJ on the radio billed the rainfall as a once in a lifetime event, coming down so hard it swallowed the road ahead. Judy fiddled with the buttons on her dashboard, trying desperately to clear the fog off the interior of the windshield. She failed. No matter which buttons she pressed, or knobs she turned, the window fogged over. Not that she could see the road, anyway.

"Come on! Shit, shit, shit," she said, wiping the condensation off the windshield in small circles using the sleeve of her LL Bean chamois shirt.

Judy did not have LL Bean money and was not even from Maine, but she had dated a guy in college from there. He had a thick accent and a kind face. Last she heard Carl was married. She was not and was fine with it.

I'm fine. No really, I'm fine, was the overused mantra she shared with all her friends of a similar age. The *dirty thirties* were anything but so far for Judy, but at thirty-two, she still had time to grow into a bad-decisions phase.

Driving across country on her own was the start of such poor decisions. Eager for a vacation, she planned to drive somewhere where she could sit poolside and drink fruity drinks. Except she never checked the weather and ended up driving through a monsoon in Tennessee. She understood it was not an actual monsoon, simply a rainstorm, but from where she sat behind the wheel, there was no difference.

Traffic was non-existent. Because she did not know the area, she was not sure if there was never any traffic, or if the storm kept locals at home. Once, when she and Carl visited his family in Maine, they drove without spotting another car for almost an hour. And that was on the freeway. Country living was so different from where she grew up. Traffic equated life back in the big city.

An eighteen-wheeler and another car passed earlier, but both quickly faded from view they were moving so fast. Beyond those couple of passersby, she seemed to be the only one foolish enough to be out in the rain.

Judy drove in silence, enjoying the sound of the rain on the car. It was 1989, and she had made various mixtapes for her cassette player for the drive, but she felt it best to concentrate on the road rather than on *Huey Lewis and the News*. The car headlights' beams vanished mere feet in front of her vehicle. How the other drivers went so fast earlier, she could not fathom.

She was happy when the road went from winding into a straightaway. A deep, mountainous forest stretched all the way to the road's edges on both sides. Bridges periodically appeared overhead. She did not like the bridges because the water from the overhead street somehow found its way down to the street she was on. The collected runoff made puddles so deep that they swamped the sides of her car with such force that water dribbled through the edges of the windows. Maybe it was the water getting inside that made her windshields fog over so much.

Finally, she glimpsed taillights in the distance. A relief. Being alone on the road was becoming creepy rather than comforting. The eighteen-wheeler was nowhere to be seen, but she caught up to the other car that passed her earlier. If he slowed enough for her to catch him the roads must have gotten worse. That meant she needed to drive more cautiously, but she intended to follow the the other vehicle as closely as she dared.

Follow the red train, Judy thought. Just like her buzzed college years, *always follow the red train, not the white train.* A hell of a life hack. Sometimes it surprised her to have made it into her thirties. She lived through a much different poor choices phase back in the day. The car ahead would be her canary in a coal mine, giving her an idea of what to expect on the road ahead. For that, she was grateful because the road was an accident waiting to happen.

And suddenly it did.

The crash happened so fast. A loud bang that could have been a gunshot sounded as she passed under another overhead bridge. The car lifted as if it had struck something. *Don't be a body, don't be a body, don't be a body*, she immediately thought, even as she fought for control of the wheel that had slipped from her grip.

She never saw the object on the road, only felt the collision. In the Appalachia, the roads were striped by forests on either side, stretches of asphalt waiting to be reclaimed by the green. It was a nearby tree that finally stopped her vehicle with such force that the airbag exploded.

Judy's head pressed against the steering wheel. She moaned in pain and confusion. One moment she was driving, and the next she was parked. Everything in between remained hazy. The air bag, despite its role as a safety feature, had whomped the snot out of her. The collision with the tree was minimal, but the airbag did its job when she kissed the tree trunk. It was dark out despite the mid-day hour, too many clouds in the sky. That made the road harder to see. She looked back, trying to spot what she struck.

Was it a body? Did someone jump off the bridge overhead and land under her tires? She saw something fall, then thump when she ran over it. The idea of hitting a body creeped her out on many levels.

Tap. Tap. Tap. Already on edge, Judy screamed when someone tapped her window. A man pressed his face against the glass.

"Are you okay?" the tapper asked.

"Not really," Judy said.

"What? Roll your window down."

Judy checked her surroundings. Trees sat dead ahead of her car. Empty road and darkness loomed on the side where the man stood in the rain. Ahead sat a parked car, the one she had been following. She knew enough not to roll down windows for strangers, but she was also confused and worried about being hurt. Her face and head promised a headache was on its way. (Or did she already have one?)

"I don't want to get rain in the car," she said.

"Doesn't matter, your car's fucked," he said. "I hit it too."

Hit what? Judy finally rolled her window down, mere inches. The man raised his hands to show they were empty.

"I get it. Don't give the guy access. Smart. I taught my daughters the same. But I also taught them to recognize when they needed help."

Gripping the wheel, Judy assessed the situation. The man, bearded, tall, wet, nodded in recognition of her concern. He spoke through it, giving her time.

"Massive rock. Assume it came loose from the hillside above during the rain and dropped into the road. I ran over it but kept control of my vehicle. I went back to the road to move it so no one else would get hurt but could not find it. Either my collision knocked the rock away or the flowing debris field washed it off the other side of the road. Just got back to my car when I heard your collision. I feel gut-punch guilty if I missed it and you struck it."

Judy shook her head. She remembered seeing a rock fall from above. "Different rock. I saw one fall."

"Shit," the man said and looked back down the road. "Brings us back to are you okay?"

"I need to get out," Judy said.

The man nodded and stepped aside. She stepped out and stretched. Her anatomy felt mostly in place, but her head throbbed relentlessly. She had not had a migraine in ages but felt one coming on. If the headache hit full force, she could not drive, not that the vehicle was drivable. The man was correct, her car **was** fucked. Judy did not remember hitting the tree that hard, but the front end had crumpled. In the short time she inspected the damage, the rain soaked her clothes.

"Look, I can give you a ride. There must be a town up ahead," the man said.

"I don't know..."

Lightning flashed and thunder rumbled right behind. The sound struck her skull with concussive force. She was not okay. Lightning struck again, so close. They were in the thick of it. Staying behind was not a good idea. Maybe it was time for that poor decision making in her thirties. Deciding you only live once; Judy nodded and followed the man to his car.

He opened the passenger door for her first. A gentleman, at least. Forty, ruggedly handsome. She hoped his being a father to girls extended to his overall treatment of women. (If he really was a father. She did not know the man.) She settled in the seat.

"I'll be right back," he said.

She watched him run back into the road, searching. Because he was busy, she thought it a perfect time to check his registration in the glove compartment, but as she reached for it, pain struck her skull. She grabbed her head and cried out. Her vision sparkled. The world was going black. Her head throbbed and her sinuses burned as if on fire. She felt she might pass out when suddenly the man jumped into the driver's seat.

He noticed her condition. "Are you okay?"

She shook her hair out and leaned back into the seat, throwing him a smile and a nod. The nod caused her to wince as it amplified the throbbing. She did not want a stranger to know she was vulnerable.

"Just shaking my hair out from the rain. I know my car is screwed, but so is your car's interior. Sorry."

"Please, I have girls like I said. You think this thing hasn't been baptized in Kool-Aid? Besides, it's not as fancy as your car."

"Fancy?" Judy asked.

"Yeah. I don't know anyone with airbags. But then airbags are just hitting the market, huh? I read about them in the newspaper. Guess they work. We are almost in the nineties though and will probably see flying cars then. I promise to be careful driving. If I hit a tree, we wouldn't land so soft. Name's Frank, by the way."

"Judy."

Lightning struck, and both leaped before falling into laughter, a shared fright. Frank started the car, and they drove away. Judy watched the road, looking for the first opportunity to get out somewhere she could use a pay phone. The sky had grown darker if possible and her head demanded she get to a doctor soon. At least his vents worked fine. The road was still hard to see through the storm, but at least the windows were fog-free.

Frank turned the radio on or tried to. Static owned every station. Only bits and pieces got through. Fragments of songs and DJs and news flashed through in time with lightning strikes, but nothing came in clear. The intense volume of the static made Judy cringe.

"Do you mind?" Judy asked.

The man turned it off but looked confused. "My radio works fine. Weird. Must be the storm. Headache?"

"I'm fine."

"Listen, no offense to what I am going to tell you. One, you look like Jennifer Beals from *Flashdance*. Not because of the stripping, but because of the wet hair."

"Thank you," Judy said, not unhappy at the comparison.

"And second, you look like shit."

"Okay, I take it back. Plus, she was a dancer, not a stripper. Big difference."

"Big difference how?" he asked.

"Clothes."

"Yeah, okay. And she wanted to be a ballerina, right?"

"There you go, you're evolving. I thought you said you had daughters."

"Bella and Joy, seven and nine. Combined, that's sixteen. That's what it's like with the two, having one rabid sixteen-year-old."

Judy laughed. She remembered herself at those ages. Terror was an understatement.

"Love those buggers, though. Yeah, apologies if I say something stupid. I'm trying to do right by my girls but I'm a bit of a bull in a China shop where my mouth is concerned. What about you? Kids?"

There it was. The same question. She considered adopting just to avoid the questions in the future. "Single."

"No shit!" He eyed her like a newly discovered species. "You are hot. No offense again. I know a lot of guys at work I could set you up with."

"Are they as charming as you?" Judy asked, throwing shade over his many verbal miscues.

"Nobody's as charming as me."

He smiled and looked pretty. Only for a moment. A lightning strike made him look scary, and her head hurt again. His smile faded.

"That. That's the shit part. You look sick. Let's find a hospital. Do you know the area?" he asked.

"No. I'm passing through, going on vacation. You're not local?"

"Nah., I work at a lumberyard out of state. I'm transferring out here for a new job. I was here house hunting this week. Was on my way home."

"I guess we're both lost, then. Appreciate you not hitting on me since you're away from home."

"Who do you think I am? Married is married. My Marie is a keeper. I lose her and I'm a weeper. When I say you're hot, I mean nothing beyond that. Looks last only so long, but marriage, that's forever. Eager to get home, but I promise to get you somewhere safe first."

"I appreciate it."

Judy squinted. There was something up ahead in the rain. Not something, but someone. A hitchhiker. He was in his fifties, soaking wet, with his thumb out. It took Frank longer to spot the man. He was going too fast and passed by. Judy locked eyes with the hitchhiker. There was something in the man's gaze that worried her. The hitchhiker appeared excited to see her, all in a split second in the rain.

Frank hit the brakes gently, not wanting to skid. He pulled off the road. The hitchhiker trotted toward them.

"What are you doing?" Judy asked.

"We can't leave him out in this rain," Frank said.

"Why is he out here to begin with? Who hitchhikes in a storm?"

"Someone who needs a ride."

"Then let me out," she said.

"What?"

"I refuse to ride with a stranger."

"I'm a stranger."

"I refuse to ride with two strangers. Would you expect your daughters to?"

Frank gripped the wheel and raised his shoulders. He viewed the man in the rearview getting closer. Seemed harmless enough. Frank rolled down his window, waved, and yelled. "Sorry." Frank drove off, hunched over the wheel, upset. "That wasn't right. Let's get you somewhere, and maybe I can ask someone to go pick that guy up."

"Maybe he will already have a ride by then," Judy said.

"Do you see any other cars?"

She looked both ways. None to be found. Frank tried the radio again. News, DJs, music, only fragments. He turned it off, obviously frustrated. She grabbed her head while he was consciously looking away from her. The headache had not subsided. They drove in silence for some time before something appeared in the distance.

"Hey, a diner," Judy said.

"Oh no. I have seen the Twilight Zone. We stop there and we are stuck in a booth telling stories and unable to leave for some unknown reason.

"We must stop. Directions. These are locals."

Frank nodded and pulled in. It was an old-school diner with a large, paved driveway. The place was dark. Frank pulled up near the entrance.

"Looks closed."

"We have to check," Judy said.

"We?" When she reached for the door handle, he waved her off. "I will check."

She watched him go. Even though they were close to the door, Frank vanished into darkness. (When had it gotten so dark?) Lightning and thunder struck simultaneously, and Judy grabbed her head. She needed that doctor, or some medicine at least. Frank startled her when he leaped back into the driver's seat.

"Closed. Let's go."

He tried the radio again. In a blip of a signal, she thought she heard a DJ announce it was 3AM, part of a night program. Impossible, Judy thought. It was 3PM at most. The static rode up her spine and throbbed at her temple. Frank swore and gave up again on the radio. Judy was about to ask him if there was a town in their future when she saw the man in the distance. Impossible.

The hitchhiker?

Yes. No mistaking him. The man looked on with those sorrowful eyes and a raised thumb. Frank noticed as well.

"How did he get past us?" Judy asked.

"We stopped, remember? He got a ride with someone else, and they passed us when we stopped. I get it, but I feel guilty from before. Shouldn't we stop?"

"Why did someone ditch him so soon? There must be something wrong with him."

Frank nodded and drove, shaking his head as they passed the man, never slowing this time. They drove in silence for some time. Judy realized she spent all her goodwill with Frank by refusing to pick up another stranger. It was horrible to leave the man out there, but she did not dare to ride with two men she did not know.

The Appalachian Mountains coalesced around their car. Nothing but mountains and lightning strikes and darkness settled over the valley road they traveled on. Judy longed for a town, longed for a bar and a fruity drink. It surprised her she had not needed a bathroom break yet, especially with the rain pounding down.

Then something loomed ahead in the distance. A car off the side of the road. Frank maneuvered and pulled over. The car was a wreck. Front end mangled into a tree and the windshield smashed.

"Terrible storm. Let's see if someone needs help," Frank said.

This was unnegotiable, unlike picking up hitchhikers. Judy nodded. But her eyes shot wide when the headlights fell on the vehicle. "No way. That's my car!"

"Wait, what?" Frank asked, confused.

Before he could protest, she was out of the vehicle and checking her car. Right where she left it. (But was the windshield always smashed?) Rain soaked the interior.

"What happened? How did we get back here?" Judy asked.

"We took a wrong turn out of the diner!" Frank yelled, trying to be heard over the storm. "Look, more debris flowed down and hit your car. There are mountains everywhere. We need to get back on the road. At least we know which way to go now."

She nodded, and they got back in the car. Something was wrong. They should have seen someone on the roads by now. "I am not a bad person," Judy said.

"Did I imply that?" Frank asked.

"Yes. The hitchhiker. I don't want to die today, Frank. I have plans to get to a beach, have some fancy drinks and..."

"And meet your future husband?" Frank asked with enthusiasm.

"Meet a guy. Let's start there."

"So, you will not ride sober with a person in need in the rear seat? But you will get drunk, which will inhibit good common sense, and then hookup with a total stranger?"

Judy looked out the window into the omnipresent rain. Her new friend was correct. That was the plan. Hookup with a stranger. Or two. Shame, nothing was ever safe. Guilt settled in the pit of her stomach. The man had helped her. He was seemingly a good man and husband, and she forced him to avoid someone else in need. It was just...

What? She could not pinpoint it, but something in the storm unnerved her beyond the violent weather. Her headache kept her from remembering details, like where they had driven, and how long. Had the hitchhiker been excited to see her? She felt they recognized one another but Judy could not place his face. Soon they passed the diner again. If the hitchhiker had not caught a ride, they would see him soon.

They did. Frank pulled over well ahead of the hitchhiker. The hitchhiker did not move, probably afraid to offend the ride gods. Frank did not say a word, just let it idle. Judy sighed.

"Okay," she said.

Frank smiled and rolled slowly until stopping alongside the hitchhiker. The door opened immediately, and the drowned rat of a man leaped into the seat.

"Thank you. I was giving up hope," the man said.

"The first or second time we passed you?" Frank asked.

"Both."

Judy caught sight of the man in the rearview mirror. She moved slightly to allow a better view. Fifties, scruffy, too thin for a man of his age. Graying hair but at least still had some. He looked sad, Judy thought. Then he caught her looking. The man met her gaze and frowned, upset.

Judy looked away. Frank adjusted the mirror, so he had a clear view. "I'm Frank, this is Judy."

The man nodded and leaned back in the seat, trying to avoid the driver's gaze. Frank adjusted the mirror again. "And you are?"

"Lost."

Frank and Judy exchanged a quick look. Frank shrugged, and tried to make light, but concern washed over Judy's face as heavy as the rain. Judy found a knob that adjusted her side mirror. Not worrying if Frank needed it for driving, she focused it on the man so she could watch him.

Frank, meanwhile, glanced between the road and the rearview mirror. "Pick someone up, and you have to worry if they are worth worrying about."

The passenger leaned his head against the window and looked out into the storm. "Don't have to worry about me hurting anyone."

Frank shared another look with Judy. She nodded. A relief.

"Not anymore," the man said.

Bad answer. Frank and Judy stiffened in their seats. Lightning struck again and Judy cried out.

"Are you okay?" Frank asked Judy, suddenly forgetting about the passenger.

"The lightning. It made your face scary. Sorry, I don't know why I am on edge," she said.

"I do." Frank pulled to the side of the road. He turned around to face the man in the back seat. "Hey buddy, tell us your name, where you're going. Something. I picked you up. Saw that you needed help."

"I needed help a long time ago," the man murmured.

"See? That's the kind of shit that makes me think I should have listened to Judy and left you back there."

"I am so sorry Judy," the man said.

Judy turned around as well and looked straight at the man. He looked familiar, but not really. There was nothing that jogged her memory as to why she initially thought she recognized him when they drove past him on the street. The man wore jeans and a Joker tee-shirt, not exactly rainy weather gear. "Sorry for what?"

"Everything. I never thought I would make it to fifty," he said.

"You go out in the rain dressed like that, you won't make fifty-one," Frank said. "Where are you going?"

"I don't know Frank. I have a general idea. My name is Boyd. If I don't seem like good company, please don't take it as my being ungrateful for the ride. I am not a danger to anyone anymore."

"You keep saying that. So, you were? How long ago are you talking? Yesterday?"

"No. Thirty-some years"

Judy smiled. Finally, a suitable answer. "Pleased to meet you, Boyd."

"Don't say that," Boyd said.

"Look. I am not starting the car until I know what the deal is here."

"The deal is you all are going one place, I'm going another."

"Judy and me? We're not together. We're just both trying to get home. Where can we drop you?"

"I'll know it when we are there."

"Who did you hurt?" Judy asked.

"Judy!" Frank said, as if worried about the answer.

"Melody-Ann, sweetest thing this side of the river. She is an influencer now, with that smile of hers."

"A what?" Frank asked.

"A model." Boyd locked eyes with Judy. "Yes, she is still around. I didn't hurt her in that way. I broke her heart. Tried to be a better man for her and failed at every turn. Left me almost thirty years ago to the day. My friend Brad was there for me, but then he was gone as well. As for where I am going, I will know when we get there."

"Good enough for me," Frank said and started the car. Soon they were on the road.

Lightning struck again. Judy held back a scream, but something about Frank again. She could not put her finger on it. It was like a flashlight under a face in summer camp. Her head hurt so badly that she could barely stand it. She knew the man in the back but could not place from where. He was so familiar.

Another flash of lightning, and this time it was the car that bothered her. Something about the windshield. Bright lights could trigger her migraines. She turned to look at the man again, mostly to keep her headache at bay.

"You said your friend was gone. In what way?"

"Suicide." The man looked away from Judy, back out the window. When he spoke again, it was as if the conversation took place with his own reflection, not with the other passengers. "He was stabbed to death."

"That's murder, not suicide," Frank said, never taking his eyes off the road.

"Nah. Taking on five men in a bar. Suicide. He was crazy with guilt over what we did when we were kids. After we got out of prison, he was never the same. Yes, I was in prison. You don't need to ask. Five years. Not long enough. The both of us. Maybe if we had stayed in longer, Brad would still be around."

"Are you from here, because we need to know where we can drop you off and get her to a mechanic and a doctor, maybe not in that order," Frank said.

"Yep. Local. Live here in town. Never left."

Judy lit up and unfastened her seatbelt. She practically leaped over the seat. The storm was not subsiding, and the lightning frightened her more than ever. "Is there a hospital? Can you direct us there?"

"Yes, and yes. But we need to go somewhere else first."

"Listen, buddy, you haven't asked about us, but we're both tourists passing through. We don't know the area and we had an accident."

"I know who you are. Everyone does."

"What?" Judy asked.

Lightning flashed over and over, filling the cabin with light. Frank hit the brakes, stopping in the dead center of the road. Judy flew forward into the dash. She grabbed her head. That was it. The pain grew worse. She looked down and noticed water in the seat between her and Frank. Water washed in through the front windshield and soaked the front seat.

"Water?" she asked, confused.

"I don't care about that," Frank said.

"The lightning. It's bothering you both. You're seeing things. Please, if you drive, we will be there soon."

"Where?" Frank asked.

"Drive," Boyd said.

"Frank, there's water getting in the car," Judy said.

"I don't care." Frank drove. Ignoring the storm, he hit the gas.

They hit a bump at the same time lightning struck. Judy flew in the air and saw both men at once. She cried out in fright. But when she landed, everything was okay. Judy grabbed her seatbelt and strapped herself back in.

The car roared down the road, as if trying to outrace the rain. Thunder fought to drown out the engine, but the car sped toward its upper limit and the engine whined above even the storm. Inside, Judy screamed, pressing her hands against the dash, bracing herself.

"Take a right up ahead," Boyd said.

A dirt road appeared ahead but it was muddy from the rain. Frank took the turn at an unsafe speed. Mud splattered the side windows. Judy screamed for him to slow down. Frank refused, kept his hands on the wheel and his foot on the gas.

"A left up here!" Boyd yelled to be heard above the worsening storm.

"Don't listen to him, Frank. We're in the middle of nowhere. Who knows where he is taking us?"

"I can't drive anymore. We need to get there. We need to get out of this storm. Can you promise me we will get out of this storm?" Frank eyed Boyd in the rearview mirror once again. Frank squinted. "I know Jack Nicholson was the joker. The Batman movie just came out. That's not Jack Nicholson on your shirt."

"It's Heath Ledger."

"Is that another of your friends?" Judy asked.

"No, he's a famous actor. Take a right up ahead."

"Please, Frank, no."

He took the turn onto another dirt road that was half washed away. Frank sped along until finally hitting the brakes. He looked at Judy. "I'm tired. But if you want me to stop, I will."

Lightning struck, and the two looked at one another. Truly looked at one another. Sorrow overtook their faces, and they gripped hands for the first time. But it was Boyd who was crying. His eyes dripped like the deluge outside.

"Let's drive," Judy said.

Frank put it in gear once again, taking his time, no longer in a hurry. Both looked out the windows, taking in the scenery, trying their best to see the world through the rain. Beautiful trees accompanied them on their journey. The water made the world green.

A metal arch rose high above the road in the distance. The gate was open under the arch, providing entry to an immense cemetery. They drove under the metal arch at the front, which was connected to a metal fence circling the property. They drove a short distance inside before the road split off in two directions. Grave markers of all sizes stretched out farther than they could see. Frank idled the car.

Boyd wiped his nose. "I'm so sorry. Me and Brad thought it would be fun to throw rocks. So many come down during the rain. Each of us threw one off the bridge. We never meant no harm. At least the kind we caused. We were only seventeen."

Judy pointed at the windshield. It was mostly gone, smashed to smithereens. Water poured into the car.

"Frank..." Judy said and pointed.

"I know. Saw it about a mile back. I get it."

"We did our time. Brad, though, could not deal with the guilt. He drank a lot and got into fights in bars. Two weeks after our release, he was stabbed to death in one such fight. My girl had already left me by the time I was out. I lasted almost thirty years until I couldn't take it anymore. Today I jumped off the same bridge I threw the rock from."

Lightning flashed and those in the front seat saw Boyd clearly. His neck was twisted nearly around, clearly broken. His head spilled red from the contact with the pavement. Boyd's wrists both showed exposed bones where he tried to stop his own fall. He was a corpse, but only when the lightning flashed. When it stopped, he was himself.

"They told stories of a ghost car driving around for thirty years. Every time someone mentioned it, I felt guilt all over again. I threw one rock, Brad the other, never knowing we would score direct hits. What were the chances of two cars so close together in these parts, anyway?

"I was lost in the storm. I was following Frank's car," Judy said.

Boyd nodded; a piece of the puzzle solved. "Bella and Joy are doing well. One is a veterinarian, the other a schoolteacher. I discreetly sent money from time to time."

Judy looked at Frank, confused. He smiled at her wistfully. "My girls."

"I am so sorry." Boyd reached for the door handle. "This is where I get out."

"Are you sure? We can give you a ride."

"Like I said. We are going to different places. Been a day for me, a long time for you. Do me the favor and finally go home? Please. I have done my time. The start of it. I have a feeling that things are about to get much worse for me."

Boyd exited the car and headed down one branch of the crossroad. Judy finally remembered where she saw him. On the bridge when he was seventeen. The last face she saw, at least before meeting Frank. It was not long before the storm swallowed Boyd whole. Frank and Judy sat idling.

"Teacher and veterinarian. Boyd took so much from us but gave me that gift," Frank said, beaming over the career path of his girls.

Judy reached her hand through the smashed front windshield and waved her hand around in the rain. "I feared the storm so much, but the rain is beautiful, isn't it?"

"Yes. And you are too. You would have made a wonderful wife. I am sorry you never got to meet Maria."

"Or your single friends?"

Frank laughed. The pair could see one another now without waiting for lightning to strike. Half of Judy's face was gone, ripped away in a massive chunk near the top of her head. Her brain drooped over the side of her exposed skull. Frank, however, still had a rock lodged in his face. Only half his face remained. He looked out at his passenger through his one good eye. The other half of his face was smashed, gore held the stone in place.

"Where do you think this road goes?" Judy asked.

"I guess we will find out together."

With no sign of the storm subsiding, the two drove off into the unknown.

Café Donuts

WEST COVINA, CALIFORNIA

I was born in West Covina, grew up there until I was seven, then moved back a few years after graduating high school. Only a block from my home, there is a coffee and donut shop aptly named Café Donuts. When Paul explained the premise of this anthology and asked me to contribute a story, it was obvious where I would go for the inspiration needed.

The building that houses Café Donuts has been there as long as I can remember, although it hasn't always been a coffee and donut shop. Several businesses have passed through that location, though the exterior has remained mostly the same, save for the updated names of the businesses there and the resulting ghosts of previous names indicated by faint black marks on the outside walls.

The Café is a curiously squat, weathered building of white brick with a partly sloped roof and large arched windows. The entire thing looks like architecture out of some bygone era. Inside, however, Café Donuts is a completely contemporary space. Bright electronic monitors that display the entire menu hang above all the donuts resting behind glass cases fit for displaying jewelry. The open kitchen is filled with modern appliances that make all the delicious donuts, coffee, teas, boba, smoothies, and even sandwiches. Patrons can grab a treat and a hot or cold beverage, then have a seat at one of the polished wooden tables to relax and enjoy the peaceful ambiance.

The last time I stopped by Café Donuts, the juxtaposition of trendy interior and aged exterior got me thinking. Here was a modern business using an antiquated structure, as so often happens. What if that were reversed? Something ancient using something modern? The ideas began to form and coalesce as I played around with these notions. And eventually those ideas blossomed into this story.

DRINK RECOMMENDATION: Since part of this tale takes place in Yucatán, Mexico, how about going for something cold to stave off the heat? Try a nice cool frappe mocha with a dash of caramel. Enjoy.

Hymn of the Brine

S. Alessandro Martinez

Dante's legs flailed as he kicked the covers off the bed like they were on fire. An angry, primal scream wanted to burst from his throat. He always tried to resist the awful crawling sensation that invaded his muscles. Every single time, he tried to ignore that damn building, creeping white noise prickling ache.

But it could never be denied for long. If he didn't kick, his muscles would explode with the pent-up energy that seemingly came from nowhere. It was torture. A torture his own body inflicted upon itself.

Lying in bed, staring at the vague designs on the popcorn the ceiling, Dante's brain tried to find patterns where there were none. His eyes were dry and grainy. And while his lids felt heavy as lead, they refused to stay shut, no matter how much he ordered them to do their jobs.

With the damn insomnia exacerbated by his restless legs, he couldn't remember the last time he had gotten a good night's sleep. Had he ever?

Dante filled his chest with a deep breath, held it until his lungs couldn't take it anymore, then let it out in a long whoosh. Forcing his eyelids down, he told himself to fall asleep.

Like a snot-nosed kid who would always do the opposite of what you wanted, Dante's eyes sprang open. Anxiety and frustration burned inside his ribcage. That scream really wanted to come out. He was this close to hitting himself in the head with a frying pan to knock himself out like some cartoon character.

With a defeated sigh, Dante sat up in bed, swinging his feet out and onto the floor. The glowing red numbers on his bedside clock told him it was already past three in the morning. Zoe stirred beside him for a few seconds before she stilled, her breathing returning to its soft snoring. He turned to look at her. The bright moon cast its silvery beams through the window, illuminating the gentle rising and falling of Zoe's chest.

Must be nice.

Dante watched his girlfriend for several minutes. The moment she'd gotten into bed and graced the pillow with her head, she'd been out like a light. How did she just fall asleep like that? It made no logical sense to him. Why could her brain power down for the night while his brain couldn't?

Dante felt like he had already tried everything under the sun—doctors, drugs, reading, yoga, meditation, acupuncture, hot baths, exercise. Every solution that worked for someone else failed to work for him. Years of unrelenting insomnia were grinding him into the ground. Every night it would sneak into the bedroom just as he closed his eyes, just to rough him up like some assailant, although never having the courtesy to deliver a knockout blow that would leave him blissfully unconscious.

Standing up, Dante shook out his legs, then strode over to where his phone was charging on the dresser. Clutching the phone, he plopped himself back in bed. There was one thing that sometimes helped. It was a bust more often than not, but he might as well try it. His alarm would go off in a couple of hours. He needed even the tiniest bit of sleep before he would drag himself into the office.

The phone's screen lit up as Dante unlocked it. He opened the YouTube app and searched for "relaxing ocean videos." A list of hundreds of videos popped up, offering a plethora to choose from. Lots of underwater videos of fish, a playlist of gentle wave sounds, several ten-hour loops of calming beach ambiance. Everything an ocean sound enthusiast could hope for.

Years ago, Dante had discovered how relaxing listening to those types of videos could be. The seaside ambiance often induced a state of tranquility. That was, if he only listened to them every once in a while. If he put on the videos several nights in a row, the effect turned into the complete opposite. It was as if his brain became afraid of the sea sounds and put itself on high alert. There'd be zero chance of sleep then. It was weird, but whatever. Dante had accepted long ago that his body was stupid.

His thumb swiping up on the screen, he scrolled through the list of videos. Dante was pretty certain he knew the reason he found the ocean videos so calming. Growing up, he and his parents traveled to Mexico every summer to visit family in Progreso, a beach town on the Yucatán Peninsula where his mom and dad had both grown up. A lot of fond memories were created during those summers: swimming in the warm waters, playing with cousins, night-time beach walks, singing songs with his grandparents. Damn, how he wished he could remember those songs. Even if he could recall the tunes, there was no way the words would come to him. His Spanish had gotten so bad over the years. His dad would be appalled.

If his dad was still around. He passed away when Dante was sixteen. That was when Dante stopped going on the trips. It was too painful. After his dad's death, Dante never returned to Mexico, much to his mom's great disappointment. Especially when she moved back there once Dante moved out on his own.

None of the videos that popped up as he scrolled caught his interest. The most popular channels were always the ones listed first. And, like most everything else, the most popular ones weren't that great, so Dante filtered them by date. Maybe someone uploaded something good recently. Some hidden gems.

As soon as the filter re-listed the videos, the very first thumbnail caught his eye. It depicted an empty beach at what he was pretty sure was dusk. The golden sun had sunk more than halfway down into the black waters of the horizon, and a few purple clouds dotted the inflamed red sky. The image filled him with warm nostalgia.

The twenty-minute video had been uploaded a few days earlier and attained a whopping two views. Dante grabbed his earbuds from the nightstand, popped them in, and tapped on a thumbnail.

"Sure, why the hell not?"

No ads played before the video started. The image of the beach at dusk immediately appeared on the screen. No fade in from black. No intro from whoever was recording. The camera was mounted on a tripod because it didn't move or wobble at all. The video was a bit grainy, and Dante wondered what it had been filmed with. Though the sound was wonderful. Water softly breaking against the shore came through on the earbuds with a little fuzz like a 90s home movie. Each miniature wave vied to see who could make it farthest up the shore in a lazy and languid competition.

After about two minutes into the video, Dante realized his chin had dropped to his chest and his eyelids had been drooping. There were no burning pins and needles in his legs. *Nice.*

The unintended excitement at feeling like he was going to fall asleep woke him further, and he swore under his breath.

Settling deeper into his pillow, Dante closed his eyes and focused on the audio. Something had changed. Nothing major but there was something else he detected. Beneath the sound of the small, splashing waves was now... a thrumming? That was the best word that came to mind. A thrumming that came from somewhere far from the camera. It didn't interfere with his growing relaxation, though.

In fact, it added a pleasant quality to the whole thing. There was a certain rhythm to the thrumming that complemented the waves. It filled his ears and seemed to work its way into his skull, into the bone itself, and resonated.

Wait, were those words mixed in?

"Dante?"

"Hmm?" he rolled over to see Zoe shaking him. "What? What's wrong?"

"You're going to be late if you don't get your ass in gear soon," Zoe said with a grin. "I was worried you weren't going to wake up. Looks like someone finally slept well." She kissed him.

As he pulled his lips away from hers, Dante noticed the sunlight outside the windows. After wiping a line of drool from his cheek, he checked the phone resting on his chest, still held in one hand. It was almost 7:00 AM.

Never in his life had he fallen asleep so fast. That had to be what happened, right? He didn't get suddenly transported forward through time, passing four hours in the blink of an eye.

"I don't hear a man meat getting dressed and ready," Zoe called from the bathroom in a singsong voice.

"Yeah, one sec." Dante forced himself out of the comfortable bed.

He made it into the office and to his desk just in time. All throughout the day, he couldn't help but marvel at how energetic he felt. Reports that weren't due until the end of the week he finished by that afternoon. He answered all emails in his inbox and even helped a fellow cubicle drone with a spreadsheet.

"You're looking peppy today," Diane, his manager, told him. "You still get those restless legs? My sister gets them and told she me about this new supplement she found online that helps her."

Dante couldn't remember how many times Diane's sister had sent along "helpful" information.

"Yeah, email me the info. I'll take a look."

He wouldn't.

By the time he got home that evening, Dante's energy hadn't diminished. He wasn't wired or hopped up or anything like that. It was more of a nice alertness. A there-ness. He hadn't trudged through the door as usual, drained of any semblance of vitality, only to plop himself down on the couch and stare at the TV for the rest of the night.

No, Dante felt good. So good that since it was his turn to make dinner, instead of going out to grab fast food, he decided to actually cook something. Zoe wasn't home yet, so he ran to the store, returning shortly after with a big grouper fillet. His recipe for pescado frito had been passed down by his grandmother, who used to make it all the time for him.

The fish came out perfectly, and Zoe's face lit up when she arrived home and saw the food on the table. After dinner and after washing the dishes himself (he had insisted), Dante suggested they break out a board game.

"Okay, what the hell is going on?" Zoe asked, giving him an exaggerated side eye. "Are you trying to butter me up for something? Did you do something bad? You did something bad, didn't you? Did you kill someone and need me to help you hide the body? Fine, I'll do it."

Dante laughed. "I think you watch too much true crime crap. Look, I just had a good night's sleep last night and I've been in a good mood today. Go get Scrabble."

"Mmhm, if you say so." She ruffled his hair as she left to go get a game from the closet.

When they went to bed later (Dante had let Zoe win every round of Scrabble), he felt like sleeping. It wasn't the usual dead exhaustion that fogged his brain and turned his muscles to useless jelly. No, this was a sleepiness like a puppy lying on a soft blanket, tuckered out after a long day of playing.

But an hour after lying down in bed, listening to Zoe mumbling nonsense in between snores, Dante's brain and legs were back to their usual bullshit. Eyes not wanting to stay closed; legs kicking like he was playing hacky sack with the comforter.

Screw it.

He grabbed his phone, went to YouTube, and popped in his earbuds. Maybe the ocean videos would work a second night in a row. One could only hope. Today had been such a good day. He couldn't remember the last time he had felt as good and refreshed. It had to work.

Finding the video in his watch history, Dante tapped on it and settled down into his pillow, waiting for the soothing sound of the waves to carry him off to sleep on their gentle current.

The video played, and the same grainy yet calming sound came through, but nothing happened. His ears didn't tingle. Nor did his brain slow and relax. His legs became twitchy.

No drowsiness, only frustration. Instead of throwing his phone across the room, Dante gave a defeated sigh. He should have known better than to hope this method would work again so soon. When had he ever been so lucky?

Wait, there was that rhythmic thrumming in the background again. Now that it hadn't made him fall instantly asleep, Dante focused on the sound. Just as he thought the previous night, it sounded like the thrumming morphed into language after a minute. He couldn't discern any particular words, however.

Raising the volume, Dante strained his ears, desperate to hear more. While concentrating on it, the sound had become like an injection of dopamine. It made him want to listen to more of it. He *needed* it. That breathy, almost flute-like voice saying (singing?) those unknown words. It calmed his legs and scratched an itch in his brain he never knew had existed there until this very moment.

Whatever the source, it had been too far off for the camera's microphone to have picked up any more clearly. No matter how loud he put the volume or how hard he pressed his earbuds into his head, the distant words were incomprehensible gibberish.

Wanting to see if this person had any more videos, Dante tapped on the account name, *elmarsant0*. There wasn't much info on the user's profile other than the number of followers (four) and an email address. There were dozens of videos, however. Oddly, all the thumbnails showed the same sunset covered beach from the first video, though each from slightly different angles. Scrolling through the list, he noticed the posting dates. For at least ten years, the account uploaded a video once a month.

Dante selected a random video and played it.

It was almost identical to the first video. The sun in the flaming sky sank below the dark ocean as the sound of waves hitting the sandy shore came through the headphones. About a minute in, the thrumming began. The rhythm was slightly different, but Dante thought the voice belonged to the same person. Again, however, the words came from too far away to be comprehensible.

After fifteen minutes of intent listening, the video ended. Dante chose another at random. It was more of the same, except this video had the black silhouette of a palm tree frond against the red of the sky, peeking in from the top left corner of the frame. There was the sound of waves, the thrumming, and singing. Yes, it had to be singing. He was certain now. This song had an altogether different cadence and tone from the other two but originated from the same voice.

And ahhh... the beautiful sounds, the music vibrating into his eardrums, filling him like the empty cup he now realized he'd always been.

He selected another video at random and played it.

He needed more.

Then another.

More of that heavenly music.

And another.

Each showed the same angle of the beach at dusk, give or take a few inches in either direction. All possessed the deep thrumming and the flute-like singing of unknown words.

What were they saying?

One more video.

Oh, how the sound burrowed deep into his ear canal like some divine worm, scratching better than any Q-tip ever could. Stimulating the membrane of his eardrum and all those tiny little bones that made one hear. Scratching that itch in his brain and cleansing his soul with its cosmic touch.

Next video.

Yes. Ocean waves to sound waves to waves of dopamine coursing through his body, making him want more. They penetrated his head, his brain tissue, the jelly in his eyes, the marrow in his bones. He could taste the salt air on his tongue. He could smell the sea water, and feel it splash against his skin.

Something flashed across the screen just as the video ended.

Replaying the video, Dante fast-forwarded to the last few seconds. Right when the video was about to end, something moved across the screen. He tried to pause at the precise moment, but no matter where he froze the video, the image remained blurry.

He brought his phone closer to his face, squinting at the screen. With the setting sun behind the mysterious object, most of its features were in shadow. Was it a head? Could be, though it looked strange. Was that because of the blur? Now that he studied the grainy pixels, Dante thought he could make things out. That line there could be a mouth. And if that was an eye, it sure was a small, beady eye. He moved the video forward one frame. A patch of skin that wasn't in shadow reflected the deep red of the sky. It looked wet and—

"You're up early."

Dante jolted, almost falling from the bed. *What the...?*

Zoe yawned, snuggling up to him. She smiled with sleepy eyes.

"Oh... yeah." Dante checked the time on his phone, then looked out the window at the brightening sky. "I, uh... wanted to hop in the shower first." Had he really stayed up all night? How many videos had he watched? With a weak smile, he kissed Zoe on the forehead before stumbling out of bed toward the bathroom in a daze, as if he had been asleep, and woke up mid-dream.

The rest of that morning at work, Dante could focus on nothing other than the image of that blurry shape that might have been a face, and his strong desire to watch more of the videos. Or more precisely, to listen to that strange singing that, so far, every single video contained. The more he thought about it, the more the need—the craving—ate away at him like an acid eating through the armor that was his willpower. When he realized he'd been staring at the same spreadsheet that he opened forty-five minutes ago, Dante gave in and pulled out his phone.

The screen came to life, and he navigated to YouTube. The app was still open to elmarsant0's account. So many videos still to watch.

But he wasn't allowed to watch them during work hours.

Who was going to notice?

No, no, no. Diane could walk by any second.

A few seconds of video wouldn't hurt.

He would get in trouble. A so-far stellar track record at this company was not worth the risk.

An undeniable static ache coursed through his legs, which kicked and spasmed under the desk. The sleepless night last night wasn't doing him any favors. And now he was getting restless legs during the day? Great.

Dante massaged his eyes. How had he gotten so wrapped up in those stupid videos? Those stupid, wonderful, glorious videos.

God, I need a vacation.

Hmm, a vacation?

An idea sprang to Dante's sleep-deprived mind. Going back to his phone and elmarsant0's account, he tapped on the info section and found an email address. Opening his email app, Dante composed a new message.

Hi. I'm a new watcher on your YT channel. It doesn't say in any of the vids I've watched so far, but I was wondering if you could tell me where these are all filmed? The beach looks beautiful. Thanks. -Dante

After copying and pasting elmarsant0's email address into the recipient bar, Dante hit send. When five seconds had lapsed, he hit refresh.

Refresh.

Refresh....

No new emails.

He wanted to laugh at himself at how ridiculous he was being. Although he feared that if he allowed himself that emotional outburst, it wouldn't be laughter escaping his mouth, but sobs. What had gotten into him? It was like he was hooked on some drug. What had the videos done to his psyche? Maybe someone planted them for him to find. Crazy conspiracy theories zipped through his head: subliminal messages; mind controlling signals; hypnotic notes and tones.

Ah, none of that mattered. He needed to know where this beach was. A desperate need had spread through his nervous system, spreading roots like some invasive weed. If he could just get there. Get to that unknown beach and....

And do what?

His phone pinged with an email notification.

An actual gasp emanated from Dante's throat, almost choking him. His sweaty fingers fumbled with his phone, dropping so that it thudded against the soulless-gray office carpet. Grabbing the phone like it had personally insulted him, Dante straightened up, only to smash the back of his head against the edge of his desk. A passing coworker stared at him with concern.

"I'm okay," Dante said through gritted teeth, and waved the guy away.

When his vision returned to normal, he opened his email. There was one new message. He had gotten a reply from elmarsant0.

Hello Dante. Thank you for enjoying my videos. The stretch of beach is Uaymitun. It is near the village of Chicxulub. It is quite beautiful.

Chicxulub? That sounded Mayan. A quick Google search brought up the info. Chicxulub Pueblo, a town on the Yucatán Peninsula, lay within the Chicxulub crater. The crater was the site of the asteroid impact that was believed to have caused the mass extinction of the dinosaurs. Blah, blah, blah.

While that was all nice and fascinating, what grabbed Dante's attention was the precise location. Apparently, this town and beach were a brief car ride from Progreso, the town where he used to vacation with his family and visit his cousins.

The town where his mom lived.

Now *that* was interesting. He wondered if he'd ever gone to this beach or maybe even just driven by it when he was little?

Setting his phone down, Dante's fingers found the nearest pencil and began tapping it on the desktop. Ugh, how he wished to hide in the restroom to listen to more videos. They called to him. That itch in his brain urged him on as if it had a consciousness of its own.

Ideas and plans formed in his mind.

Wouldn't it be even better to listen to everything in person?

Think, think, think.

Yes, that would be amazing....

Did he dare? He needed to listen to that thrumming, that singing, in person. There was a ravenous hunger in his ears. In his very being. And it demanded intimate indulgence in that ethereal hymn!

The pencil snapped in his grip.

He had to do it.

Ignoring the work he was supposed to be doing, Dante remained on his phone. He didn't care if his manager caught him. All that mattered right now was the thrumming and the singing.

Since it was the off-season, travel options to that part of Mexico weren't too expensive. Not that the cost would have stopped him. Money was of no concern now. He worked as quickly as he could, planning his journey and purchasing tickets. A flight to Cancún left in three hours. From there, a bus would take him to Progreso. Then he'd walk to Uaymitun if he couldn't get a taxi or someone to take him. If he left now, he'd have just enough time to drive home and grab his passport.

As soon as Dante pushed away from his desk and stood up, Diane stepped into his cubicle.

"Dante," his manager said. The smiling older woman was a head shorted than he was, yet her coffee breath wafted up all over his face. "I'm going to need you to look at these files. Can you get back to me in two hours?" She held a thick folder out for him to take.

"No, I have to go," he replied in a harsh tone. He tried to step past her. "Get the fuck out of my way."

"Excuse me?" She blocked his way with her diminutive frame. Her over-plucked eyebrows furrowed. "Who the hell do you think you're talking to, Dante? You better sit your ass down and get back to work."

Without a second thought, Dante placed both palms on the woman's shoulders and shoved her backward. The force sent her careening into the side of another cubicle, toppling the fabric wall into the computer behind it, smashing the monitor. Papers floated lazily in the air as eyes from every corner of the office stared in shock at the scene.

Dante ripped off his tie and threw it on the ground. He'd always hated that necktie. Stalking out of the building before anyone had the chance to call for security, he hopped into his car and sped out of the employee parking lot, heading for home.

He was there in no time, having flown through the streets and surprised no cops had pulled him over. Zoe was still at work, so he zipped inside, grabbed his passport from his underwear drawer, and was back in the car like a bolt of lightning. The airport was about forty-five minutes away, thirty if he didn't let up on the gas. Dante sped off.

A groan burst from his chest as soon as he turned onto the eastbound on-ramp and saw traffic.

"What am I doing?" His fist slammed against the steering wheel, sending a shock of pain through his hand. "What the fuck am I doing? I've gone out of my mind. Absolutely batshit."

Dante dug his phone out of his pocket. He had to call Zoe and tell her what he'd done before someone else did. But when he unlocked his phone, the video was on the screen. The big play button waiting to be pressed.

Up ahead, he spotted the cause of the traffic congestion. Construction, of course. As his car rolled closer, the racket of all the construction equipment permeated the car, bleeding its terrible noise into the cab like a boat taking on water. Car horns blasted every few seconds with their angry screeches. Enraged drivers yelled out their windows as someone cut them off. A news helicopter chopped its way through the air above, its whirring, thumping blades slicing Dante's last remaining nerve.

"God dammit!"

He connected his phone to the car's Bluetooth and played the video. The thrumming and singing soon came through every speaker, filling the inside of the car with blissful music. The audio washed over him as if the ocean waves themselves were flooding in, anointing his body with their salty touch. His vision blurred as that burning itch in his brain was oh so deliciously satiated.

Before he knew it, Dante was at the airport, settled into a space on the second floor of the parking structure. He had no memory of the drive after putting on the video. He felt that should have concerned him, but more important matters were at hand.

Leaping from his car, Dante made his way into the airport. He checked in with minimal fuss and no bags to check. Security took an excruciating amount of time. The only items he had to put through x-ray machines were his wallet, keys, passport, and his stupid shoes.

"And your phone, sir," the TSA agent herding everyone told him. "Put it in the tray."

Dante realized he still gripped his phone in one hand like a life preserver. The only thing keeping him afloat. It surprised him, the amount of willpower it took to pry his fingers from the device and deposit it into that gray bin on the conveyor belt. He snatched it up as soon as he exited the body scanner, then jogged over to a bench to put his shoes back on.

He pulled his boarding pass out of his pocket to check the gate, then looked at his phone for the time. The flight would depart in about an hour. He noticed two missed calls from work. Like he was ever going to communicate with them again. They didn't understand his priorities. No one did. The only thing that mattered was getting to that beach and listening to that beautiful, transcendent music.

"Crap!" Dante saw that the phone's battery was in the red. He'd forgotten to grab the charger at the house. Heading toward his gate, he stepped into one of the airport's many overpriced shops. He picked up a charging cable and new earbuds, costing him triple what they would have at a normal store.

But he didn't care. Money meant nothing any longer. The only value those slips of green paper and those numbers in his bank account had was what everyone agreed they were worth. Well, Dante didn't agree any longer. They held no value for him. He'd give it all away if it got him to his destination any faster.

Sitting in the terminal, waiting for the call to board, was torturous. He dared not listen to the video, as much as every fiber in his being craved it. What if he was lost in blissful serenity when they began boarding the plane? Disastrous.

Dante sat there, legs bouncing, arms crossed, and chewing the inside of his cheek. His phone was plugged into an outlet underneath the seat. Every few minutes, he would check it, only to see the time crawling forward at a pace slower than a fucking sloth with two broken arms.

God dammit!

What he screamed in his head almost exploded from his mouth. That sort of outburst was not something Dante could afford. It might worry the people around him. Someone might call security about the crazy guy yelling at nothing, even though he wasn't crazy and was yelling about something appropriate. Just because they didn't understand what he was trying to do. Where he was trying to get to. But of course, they didn't understand. They hadn't heard the euphoric hymn from the beach videos. He should play it for everyone to hear. Maybe then they'd get a fucking move on and get this flight in the air!

No.

No, no, no.

He couldn't play the music for them. Share this sacred gift with all the assholes and shitheads surrounding him? These filthy masses of undeserving trash? No damn way. This was all meant for him! No one else.

A ding came over the PA system, and a woman's smooth voice informed people that boarding would commence.

"Thank Christ," Dante growled. After ripping the phone cable from the outlet, he leapt from his seat and raced over to the line, even though his last-minute ticket purchase meant he was in the very last boarding group.

Dante had always hated gate fleas—those people at the airport who stood right next to the line when their group hadn't even been called. All they did was crowd around and get in everyone's way.

This was different, though. He *needed* to get on that plane.

"Screw this," he mumbled, and cut in front of an elderly couple.

"Excuse me, sir—" the gate agent began.

Dante cut her off. "Listen, I'm absolutely terrified of flying. If I could just get in and sit down, it would really help me out, you know?"

The agent looked him up and down before her face softened, and she nodded. Dante had no idea what he looked like, but his appearance seemed to convince her. She scanned his boarding pass and smiled. "Go right ahead, sir. Flight attendants inside the plane will check to see if you need anything. Okay? You're in excellent hands."

Without another word, Dante practically sprinted down the jetway until he caught up with the people who boarded before him. Airline employees were helping a man in a wheelchair to his seat, while a lone mother was buckling in two young children in a row further back.

Dante's seat was in the last row of the plane. Taking his spot at the window, Dante popped in his new earbuds and pulled up the video on his phone. Hopefully, no one would bother him as he slipped into that nirvana of ocean waves and sublime melodies.

Dante hit play.

Every inch of Dante's skin broke out in goosebumps as soon as the singing poured into his ears. The world around him faded into a hazy murk of unimportance.

A gasp caused Dante to bolt upright in his seat. He could tell his mouth had been hanging open by the stale, offensive taste on his dry tongue. Looking around, he spotted a small child standing in the aisle, staring at him with parted lips and huge, misty eyes. It was the boy he'd seen earlier.

When Dante unbuckled his seatbelt, the kid ran back up the aisle, presumably back to his seat and his mom. Standing up, Dante saw that while his row and the row across from him were empty, the rest of the plane was about three-quarters full. In fact, they were in the air, and the roaring drone of the engines filled the cabin.

"Are you okay, sir?" A flight attendant had appeared beside him. "You look pale."

"I'm okay," Dante croaked, his sandpaper tongue scraping against the roof of his mouth.

"Well, if you need to use the lavatory, use it now. We'll be starting our descent soon. Are you sure you're alright? Let me get you some water."

"Thanks."

As she walked away, Dante noticed a small face peering over the back of the seat several rows ahead. When his gaze locked onto the child's large, fearful eyes, the face immediately hid itself.

What's that kid's problem?

The flight attendant was back as soon as Dante had buckled himself back into his seat. She handed him a bottle of water, which made him realize just how thirsty he was. After chugging half of it, there was a ding overhead and the pilot's crackling voice announced that they would land in twenty minutes.

Checking his phone, it surprised Dante that he hadn't received any more calls or messages. Then he realized he had no network connectivity in the air. Of course.

With nothing to occupy his mind save for his own thoughts, accompanied by the racket of the jet engines, a sudden swell of lucidity smacked him in the face. What was he doing? What he insane? He had to be. No one with functioning brain cells would hop on a plane with no luggage or plans whatsoever except to get to some random beach they saw on a video.

Stupid, stupid, stupid!

Dante wanted Zoe there to hug him, to comfort him. He wanted his grandpa there, his grandma, his mom...

His mom.

He was on his way to Progreso. If he contacted her as soon as they landed, maybe she could meet him in town and prevent him from making more of a mess of things. Send him back home to face the consequences of his manic episode. Yes, he'd call her as soon as he could.

The inside of Dante's cheek was hamburger by the time the plane landed and taxied to the terminal. His phone buzzed the entire time as the network reconnected and messages that couldn't get through before now started pouring in. He was too scared to look.

"Local time is 10:04 PM. We thank you for choosing to fly with us today," the captain said over the speakers.

Everyone stood up to crowd the aisle. Dante remained seated with his leg acting like a bouncing spring. By the time the people ahead of him could move forward, he was on the verge of a panic attack. The collar and armpits of his work shirt dripped with sweat, and his lungs refused to take in enough air. But once out of the plane and in the terminal, he calmed himself, letting his heart return to its normal rhythm.

The phone clutched in his hand buzzed again with dozens of missed calls and text messages. Most from Zoe. He read a few.

where r u?

i called ur mom, ur scaring us

dante!

theyre saying u assaulted Diane????

answer ur fucking phone!!!

His finger hovered over the call button next to Zoe's name. He wanted to push it.

Didn't he?

That thrumming and flute-like singing floated through his mind. But he didn't have his earbuds in. How was that possible? His brain reverberated with the music. It was in his head. He didn't need the phone any longer. The music was inside him.

It had chosen him.

Walking over to a trashcan, Dante snapped his phone in half and dumped it. It was useless to him now that he carried the beautiful hymns inside his head and could listen whenever he wanted. No, he was not going back to his old life. No need to call Zoe and reassure her. There was no reason to call his mom to meet him and talk him out of anything. He would get to Uaymitun. The beach called to him.

"That's him."

"Don't point at people like that."

"But that's the changing man!"

Dante turned to the kid from the airplane who had been watching him. The child's mother tried to wrangle him and his brother.

The mom looked up at Dante and gave a weary smile. "Sorry."

Dante smiled back and waved at the kid, who cringed.

"He was a monster," the kid whisper yelled.

Once outside, Dante found the bus that would take him to Progreso. So close to his destination. So close to his destiny. Dante boarded and took a seat. The music played in his head during the entire three-hour trip. No one sat next to him.

It was well past 1:00 AM when he arrived in Progreso. One taxi loitered outside the bus station. Dante hustled over, waving at the driver leaning against the cab and smoking a cigarette.

"Hey, excuse me. I need to go to—"

"Uaymitun?" the taxi driver finished for him, flicking the cigarette butt onto the ground and putting it out with the bottom of his shoe.

Dante understood the response should have surprised him, but it didn't. Quite the opposite. It comforted him. Here was the answer to any lingering doubts he might have still held. The universe itself was guiding him to where it knew he should be.

"Yes, there," Dante said as he got into the back of the cab.

The men did not speak as they drove. Dante caught glimpses of the driver in the rearview mirror when they passed under the odd streetlight. There was something off about the man that Dante could not quite put his finger on. The man's skin, while brown like Dante's, had a washed-out quality to it and his eyes seemed overly beady and wet, as if they were constantly tearing up.

"Here," the man said after they had driven past the town of Chicxulub and out into what seemed to be the middle of nowhere.

The cab driver pulled into the driveway of a simple house made of white stone. Standing at the front door, illuminated by the beams of the car's headlights, was someone Dante knew.

Dante stepped out of the car. "Mom?"

Again, he wasn't surprised, so much as assured. The hand of fate had guided him here.

"You got here so quickly," his mother said, striding over to him. Her skin possessed the same washed-out quality as the driver's. "I'm glad Zoe called me. Maybe we can get her out here soon as well."

She took his hand and guided him around to the back of the house, to where a narrow path snaked its way through a wall of palm trees and brush. When they emerged on the other side, Dante sucked in a quick breath as a glorious and spellbinding beach opened before him. The waters were obsidian black, and a bright moon hung high in a star-filled sky, but he was certain this was the same beach as the one in the videos. He knew it in his heart.

"Everyone's been waiting for this day," his mom whispered from beside him as they walked hand in hand toward the water.

A strange thought occurred to Dante as he looked out at the endless sea. A mild breeze ruffled his hair and clothes. Gentle waves lapped at the shore. Yet the vastness of the ocean itself appeared immaculately still. So still, in fact, it was like a mirror, reflecting the large moon and all the stars. As above, so below.

"I followed the music, Mom," Dante said, unable to take his eyes off the ocean.

"I know," she answered. "I knew you'd find your way back to us some day."

She then hummed. Dante's head snapped in his mother's direction. A rhythmic thrumming emanated from deep within her throat. He knew that sound. He had listened to variations of it so many times over the past few days.

An answering thrum came from the water.

"Look," his mom said before beginning to sing in a soft, flute-like voice that filled Dante's flesh and soul with theophanic tones and melodies. He didn't understand the words she sang, but he would. He would.

Out in the perfect glass ocean, the reflections of the stars moved, swaying this way and that. They then rose to break the surface. Silhouettes of misshapen heads now bobbed above the water, the starlight hovering just over their faces, offering vague glimpses of beady black eyes, gray translucent flesh, and wide mouths open in chorus. More stars appeared under the water.

"Your grandma and grandpa are eager to see you," his mom remarked.

"But I thought..."

His mother looked at him with love. "We live a long time. Generations still live in the deepest trenches."

The song emanating from those out in the ocean coursed through Dante. He felt every single mystical, cryptic note journey through each wrinkle in his brain. Notes that no human tongue ever had produced. The otherworldly music consecrated Dante's blood and spirit. Euphoria crackled like lightning through every nerve. His mother no longer had to guide him. He stripped off his clothes and waded into the water, zealous and eager for his baptism.

"You will be remade as I have," his mother called out, stepping into the water behind him. "As we all have."

Dante swam out into that dark ocean of night, the numinous singing fueling his muscles and his will. As he neared the swimming figures, he realized the lights grew out of their heads on spindly, fleshy stalks. Strong hands then pulled him below the inky surface where, by some miracle, he could breathe.

Stars. Hundreds of luminous stars growing from the figures' heads filled the endless black underwater, each attached to an alien face. There was a moon down there as well. Giant, glowing, hallowed. The hands pulled him farther out to sea where the water grew deeper and deeper, bringing him closer to that sunken other moon that was not a reflection after all. He now realized it was another light springing from the forehead of something titanic. Something that must have lived for eons.

A familiar hand grabbed Dante's arm. Though the skin was no longer brown, but gray and translucent; the fingers were no longer soft, but webbed and bony; Dante knew his mother was by his side, shepherding him, supporting him.

"It is time for communion with our sire," she whispered, perfectly audible despite the water between them.

The mouth behind that colossal moonlight let loose a rejoicing melody that penetrated the fibers of the universe that made up Dante's consciousness. He marveled as the behemoth loomed closer. A reverence and exultance like nothing Dante had ever experienced before overflowed his physical being. His imagination ran wild as he pictured this profound deity receiving him, chewing him up to rid him of his human shell, and spitting him back out, reborn. Remade into what his true blood called him to be.

His mother embraced him, followed by the many arms of his family.

"Be what you were meant to be," she whispered.

Dante let them all push him into the mouth of this briny, abyssal god.

"Welcome home."

Ministry of Coffee
WESTWOOD, CALIFORNIA

This wonderful coffee shop has fantastic food and incredible coffee. One can order from a tablet out front or the host who always has a cheery smile. Located blocks from UCLA, the place is often filled with college students. It also sits next to a Trader Joe's so perfect for going out, getting coffee or lunch, then doing grocery shopping after.

This area is the newly developed part of Westwood and sits block away from the main street that has long been the core of the college town. The coffee shop is Australian based and has a laid-back vibe. They have cool movie posters plastered all over the bathroom walls. This place is definitely worth a visit if you come to Westwood.

Now I must add up front that this day I was interacting with a certain Facebook group called Books of Horror. That group has a fondness for spicy material and bloody material. I did not realize at the time how much they were influencing me this day, but I was checking updates from the group while I waited for an idea to form. When the idea came to me, I was in a spicy and bloody mood so be warned this and one other story in this book are a bit more graphic than other volumes in the series so far. (And the other volumes get pretty graphic.)

Where this story came from is from overhearing two students. One was studying nearby where I was writing. Eventually a friend arrived to join her. The new arrival looked around as if expecting a third. As she set up her own laptop, she asked where their other friend was. (Apparently, she was expecting her to already be there.)

The woman who was already seated mentioned how their friend had a short notice call from her "sugar daddy." They laughed, talked about it a bit and moved on to studying. Meanwhile, I Googled sugar daddy websites (author browser histories might someday be used against us) and this story was born.

The biggest thing that struck me was that though such a relationship is transactional, there are two parties involved. What if they have very different goals? Settle in and ~~listen to~~ read *The Symphony*.

DRINK RECOMMENDATION: Something fancy seems appropriate. Though this coffeeshop is Australian based they make a great Spanish coffee drink known as Cortado. That is my choice for this story. If you have never had it, now is the time to try something new.

The Symphony

PAUL CARRO

Neville knew she was in love the moment Martin pushed her off the cliff. "You asshole!" Neville screamed as she plunged forward. Her screams echoed across the canyon. She closed her eyes in terror, unable to look at the ground so far below.

She tried to remember her training (all ten minutes of it). *Starfish, wasn't there something about a starfish?* She spread her arms and legs in the starfish formation and finally opened her eyes. It was amazing! The zipline had not failed, and she was rocketing across a canyon towards a staged platform. Once she landed, there would be several more trips on the zips until she reached the beach far below.

The view was amazing, with the ocean in the distance and mountains in the other directions. As great as the view was, the speed is what made the ride. She loved it more than she expected. A platform loomed ahead. She lifted her feet at the end as instructed and came in for a landing. The waiting zipline guide jerked her to a halt and unhooked her.

Neville raised her arms and screamed in triumph, looking back to Martin and others back in the zipline queue. Her date, Martin, rode over next. He might have been fifty to her twenty-one, but the age difference vanished when she watched him zip over. He was fit and fierce.

Martin did not default to a starfish position (which controlled descent speed). He streamlined himself for minimum wind resistance and maximum speed. Martin lifted his legs at the last second and landed perfectly. Of course he did. Money did the man good, Neville thought. Once the guide unhooked her date, she leaped up onto his waist and gave him a big hug.

He flashed his epic smile as he set her back down. "That wasn't so bad, was it?"

"It was almost shit my pants bad," Neville said and burst into laughter.

"Only four more platforms to go before we reach the beach," Martin said.

Neville looked down toward the next platform and gulped. It was a much longer zipline than the first, but she was ready. They had to wait for the others first before going onto the next round. Two married couples from New York had signed up for the same zip tour. The two men bragged on the van drive up the mountain about how easy it would be, but once they arrived at the top and saw how far down it was, they voluntold Neville to go first.

Soon everyone had landed, and Neville lined up for the next stage. She kept her eyes open the rest of the way down to the beach, loving every minute of the new experience. She was not a woman of means and had signed up on the sugar daddy website just for some financial relief for her college bills. The man turned out to be more than a financial lifeline. *Martin was a butt-rub full of fun*, Neville thought.

Never on her own would she have been able to afford a weekend getaway to Catalina Island. Neville did not care that he was married. Because she worked so much in college, she never went out. That left her single, but with no time for commitment. The boys at college who showed interest were clingy from the start.

Besides, despite his age, Martin was fitter than most of her classmates and smelled better to boot. Plus, with no dad in her own life (and mom since passed) she was not above recognizing she had some daddy issues. They had checked into separate rooms of a two-bedroom bungalow, but she decided mid-air that they would only need the one room that night.

After the zipline and a botanical garden tour, it was time for dinner.

"Now that we have gotten to know one another better, we can officially call this an elucidate," Martin said, before bursting into laughter.

Elucidate? The word led Neville to fear she had something in her teeth. Failing to understand the word, therefore the joke, Neville squirmed in her seat. Neville could not tell if he just told a dad joke or not. If it was, she felt she should roll her eyes and bat at him playfully. Such a good-natured response would confirm her comfort level with their age difference.

What she was uncomfortable with was the setting. Never had she experienced such fancy dining. The discomfort and his laughter made her worry that he laughed at her, not with her. Using the back of a spoon, she checked for remnants of grilled artichoke in her grill. (Lord, there was so much silverware.) She used plastic utensils and paper plates in her one bedroom back home. Who had time to wash dishes every day?

Nope. Teeth clear. Now Neville had to respond to a joke that went over her head. Up and to the right, off to wherever highbrow jokes went to die. Assuming it was not a dad joke, Neville laughed, but her laughter started as his stopped. *Awk-*

ward, party of one, your table is ready, Neville thought but kept giggling.

Martin gestured to the waiter, who refilled both their glasses with a red that she could only sip, not gulp. It was too exquisite, like silk on her tongue. She was an alcohol connoisseur, if not an alcoholic outright, but the bottle of wine before them was special. She moaned uncontrollably after the initial sip.

Her response perked Martin up. For such a composed man, it was as if she found his weakness. The promise of youthful sex. She was into it, even if he was not sure if she wanted him. He probably knew, though. He was whip smart. Neville could tell. She returned to the food.

"Oh, this is the tits!" Neville said as she took another leaf from the artichoke and dipped it in melted butter, then a dipping sauce she could not identify. And this is only the appetizer?"

"Indeed," Martin said, studying the student as if she were a newfound species.

All the diners dressed to the nines except Neville. Neville wore her nana's (may she rest in peace) best crocheted top. In a black and white world, the only color in the restaurant was that of Neville's orange and pink top. Oh, and the red wine. The food/wine combo kept Neville from focusing too much on standing out.

"I grew up around a farm, but never had artichokes before. How am I out of the loop with this?" Neville asked.

"Foods grow in different parts of the country, different parts of the world. There are many such delicacies out there: Chioggia beets, Goji berries, and durian. None of it matters in the end. The elevation of any ingredient depends on the chef."

"Well, bravo to this cook." Neville slid another rough leaf across her teeth after dipping it into the lemon aioli dip (she finally remembered what the waiter called the fancy sauce). To impress her date, Neville tried to eat sexy, but scraping leaves against teeth was a hard look to pull off.

"Those are simply leaves. You have yet to consume the heart," he said, smiling dentist-proof teeth.

"Well, you're winning mine pretty fast."

"Oh, no, please, do not misunderstand this date. I have no desire to sleep with you."

"What? It is a sugar daddy dating site. I thought…"

He raised his hand to stop her. "Neville, you are lovely. Prettier than your pictures. If you think people in the restaurant are staring because of your societal status, you are partially correct. But just as many are staring because you have the bosom that they begged their surgeons for. Rare to evoke envy in the wealthy, but your genetics are a rare gift."

"I would thank you for the compliment, but seeing as how you stewed it in a slam, I think I'll pass. Your word salad could use a better chef."

"Well said. As intelligent as you are, beautiful. You just started college at your age?"

"Community, yes. I needed time after high school to work and save money. Speaking of that, the point of this date was to engage in a financial situation that might benefit my abilities to further my education."

"That is all I am interested in. Your education. But of a different type. I promise to help with both. Do you ever watch reaction videos online?"

Neville shook her head. "Nope. Animal rescue vids and new dances. I don't have much time to watch because I make my own content. Tasteful."

Martin nodded. "Yes, I've seen your site. You undercharge by a great deal."

Neville turned red, both surprised by meeting someone who knew her naked work, and by such a compliment on the fees. "Need to build an audience first. Besides, not everybody is a moneybag like you. You are a moneybag, right?"

"I am. And as such, reaction videos bring me great pleasure. In them, I can witness the joy of people discovering movies, songs, and places for the first time. I am partial to watching people react to hearing older songs for the first time. My wife is partial to people reacting to food."

Neville bristled at the mention of the missus and discarded a leaf atop a growing pile on a bleach white plate. "Saw the white line around your ring finger and thought you were hiding her."

"Hardly. I am not that careless. The ring is being cleaned."

"Where does your wife fit into all this?"

"We seek similar things in life; therefore, we have certain agreements. She is a successful businesswoman and does not need my money, nor I hers. Everything else we share."

"Everything?" Neville asked and went back to the wine.

"Dear Neville, I can offer a price that would entice you to join us both, but as I said, I am not interested in you in that way. I have no idea what my wife is up to tonight, nor do I care. She is her own woman and can do as she wishes. I assure you neither of us has an interest in you beyond your experiences. Your online presence intrigued me, and I sought you out. Now, as for the reaction videos, to hear someone respond to Journey for the first time as an example..."

"Is Journey a band?" Neville asked.

Martin laughed. Neville melted under the perfect smile and the infectious nature of his surprised laughter. He did not snort like she was prone to. Neville enjoyed seeing the man let loose. She had inadvertently brought him joy, and it was a good look on him.

"Yes, Journey is a band. And it brings me great joy to see people discover them for the first time. As with all things, watching videos only goes so far, and with my resources, why not watch people react in real life, in real time?"

"Are you going to take me to a Journey concert?"

"No. Those days are over. But I intend to take you on a journey. But that will come later. For now, let's experience this restaurant together. Enough with the appetizers. Have you ever had sea bass?"

Neville shook her head. Soon after, the chef rocked her world again.

It was when they returned to the bungalow that things got hinky. Neville was drunk and leaned on Martin more than she needed to. She pressed her tits against him at every chance, hoping to get him warmed up to the idea of having some after dinner fun.

The bungalows faced the beach and were fancier than most places Neville had stayed in before. More like a mini apartment than a hotel. Though she flirted with people online and made money from her sexy sites, Neville had never gone out with a man on the sugar daddy site until Martin. They met briefly for coffee back in LA and it was there they set the date for a weekend getaway to Catalina. The trip was exceeding Neville's expectations.

Martin stopped at the door and pulled his key card for the door from his breast pocket. Neville leaned on him, not as drunk as she pretended to be. She kept her body pressed against him with her arms around his waist. The contact was enough to warm anyone's engine, or so she thought.

He stiffened at the door, turned to her, and looked down. (He was tall, Martin was.) "I mentioned my desire to witness people experience things for the first time. Have you ever killed someone?"

"What?" Neville asked, suddenly sober.

"If during dinner I had arranged for someone to be delivered to our bungalow bound and gagged, would you participate?"

"Participate? In what?"

"The perfect murder. We are here for a weekend. No one would know. By the time they discover the body, we would be gone."

"Ah, that would be a fuck no!"

"Wait here, then. It will only take a minute."

Martin swiped the key card and entered the bungalow. Neville looked around, seeking help. Stars and lights from boats in the bay sparkled, but people were scarce. She prepped her cellphone to go live if necessary then rushed inside. Someone had to stop him.

A cloth sat draped over something in the middle of the room that could have been a body. It was definitely not there when they left the bungalow. Martin yanked the cloth away to reveal a champagne cart. Fresh cut fruit filled a spiral around the bottle sitting on a riser in the center. It was fancy-pants stuff.

Martin shrugged. "Confession. I only arranged champagne."

"Jerk," Neville said and rushed to check each room. "Just making sure."

Martin popped the top of the champagne and poured Neville a glass. She noticed he did not pour one for himself.

"Aren't you going to join me?"

"No. As I mentioned, I am not interested in you beyond sharing new experiences with you. Our date for tonight is over and we will pick up tomorrow. Have a good night."

With that, Martin exited their bungalow. If the champagne wasn't so amazing, Neville would have been ready to kill someone. She cradled the bottle to her chest, went to her bedroom and settled into bed to watch TV.

The sex had gone on for two hours. Neville felt her roomie's sexual antics like a low-level earthquake. Whoever the woman was, she had banshee lungs. Martin had stamina and a willing partner. Earlier, Neville had champagne and watched reality TV until she dozed off. It was the sound of a couple in heat frolicking around the shared living room that woke Neville.

When Martin put his things in one room and hers in the other when they arrived on the island, she thought he was being a gentleman, and not assuming anything. Neville did not speak up because she was her own bathroom kind of woman. But to discover he planned all along to keep separate rooms after sundown surprised her. But Martin meant it because he returned late at night with a giggling woman. The two bounced around the common area before they retreated to his room and started having sex.

Despite the distance between the two rooms, Neville felt the world bounce and heard the cries of passion. (And the spanking, there was a lot of spanking.) After a ridiculously long time, Neville creeped out into the living room to get a better listen. She was angrier than turned on, but she could not grasp why his escapades bothered her. The man was married and had never promised sex. Still, it felt like a rejection, even though an offer had never truly come to the table.

The woman's perfume (something expensive) lingered in the air. Her dress was on the floor, a fancy thing, but obviously she could not get out of it fast enough. Finally, everything went silent. Neville was leaning on the couch with her ear against the wall dividing Martin's room and the living room, when his door opened.

It was too late to get back to her room. She leaped to her feet. Martin appeared, fully nude. The man was in ridiculous shape, because of course he was. Martin crossed over to the small kitchen and filled two glasses with tap water. When he turned around, Martin spotted Neville. Busted and embarrassed, Neville went on the offensive.

"Care to explain yourself?" Neville asked.

"My date with you ended when I dropped you off. From there, I walked about the island, met someone and returned here."

"To have sex with someone other than me?"

"To have sex with someone who has never cheated on her husband before. Experiences, remember? I will never see her again, but it is rude for me not to bring her water. I respect the choices she made tonight. She decided on pleasure, and I enticed her with financial incentive. I am generous, as you would know if you had checked your phone."

"Yeah, well, I don't see a future for us. Poor manners and all that. Maybe I should bang an islander just to even things out. How does that sound?"

Martin laughed, as close to a snort as he might ever get. "I cannot overstate how little that matters to me. I do not care if you hook up with someone. You could hook up with my date based on some fantasies she shared with me. You could hook up with the young couple in the bungalow next door. There's always the doorman. Ah, the chef. Show your appreciation and all that. None of it matters to me. I do not care if you retreat to your room and masturbate with some toy in a drawer."

Neville went red. "Stop."

"Point is, I do not care how you relieve yourself. I hope in whatever manner you enjoy the experience, but otherwise I do not care. Your sex life means nothing to me, and I have no interest in the details. If you choose to share them with me, I will listen patiently, but you will not turn me on. You will not seduce me. There is only one thing I want from you."

"What's that?"

"For now, a second date."

Martin let the subject drop and turned to bring the water to his guest. Worse for Neville, the man's backside was as enticing as his front.

"Ass," she said, meaning it both ways.

Having never checked the app, Neville returned to her room, grabbed her phone, and opened the dating site's page. Martin had been her first connection on the app that she responded to. There were dozens of offers from other men. None were as handsome as Martin, and most were downright creepy.

She never intended to sleep with any of them. Her profile was simply to be their date, some eye candy. Neville was not vain but understood the way people looked at her. It was a lifelong thing, and she was not stupid, only played it up on dates occasionally. That she even considered sleeping with Martin was based only on physical attraction. Yes, she expected payment for the date, but never planned to hook up. Which was good because it never happened.

It took Neville a moment to find the payment page. The app danced a fine line between escorting and dating. But tips were allowed. She checked the tip and dropped onto her bed. The amount was outrageous, beyond what she would have expected, even for sex.

Fuck yeah, there will be a second date, Neville thought. Her anger faded even as she heard the cheater escort the other cheater out of the bungalow.

Neville never thought to notice if she was prone to sea-sickness on the initial ferry ride to the island. She was too excited to consider such a thing. But their cruise on the glass-bottom boat confirmed she had sea legs. Despite the warm temperature, the ocean breeze chilled her enough that she leaned into Martin during the cruise. They travelled around a distant side of the island, lined with yachts and pleasure boats. Below their feet, through the glass, swam sea life of every type. She wondered if any were the incredible sea bass that she so enjoyed.

A mother and her two children sat near the front of the boat while Neville and Marting sat near the back. An older gentleman in a Patagonia vest and silver hair took up the middle. Neville got the sense the man only feigned interest in the fish at their feet when what he really wished to view were her tits. She kept them covered in her hoodie, zipping it up soon after she noticed the man's gaze.

As annoying as it was, she was used to such attention, so let it go, figuring she was a tourist, and the gross dude was one as well. She would never see him again, so it was pointless to make a scene.

Besides the scenery, Neville thought about her updated bank account. Martin had tipped her an entire semester's worth of tuition. Right to the penny. College bills were odd in that they never rounded up or down. Nope, the bills ended in seventy-two cents or some such (while the dollar amounts were frightening). Or used to be frightening before she met Martin. That he knew the exact amount meant he did his homework.

Which begged the question? What did he really want from her? It was easy to figure out what the Patagonia guy wanted, but Martin remained a mystery. He was fun, dashing, a word she never thought she would use for a dude. Most of all, he was a mystery.

They finally returned to shore and had a little time to kill before catching the ferry back to the mainland. As they departed the glass bottom boat, the older man in the vest nodded at Martin. The old man then vanished into a sea of people just arriving on the island on an adjacent dock.

"Do you know him? What was that nod?" Neville asked.

"He approves." Martin said.

"Of what?"

"My choice in women, I suppose."

After a brief stop for breakfast and another amazing meal. The couple took the ferry back to the mainland. On the way, Neville stood at a rail near the rear of the ferry watching the island grow small in the distance. She had left Martin inside talking with someone on the phone.

He finally joined her. She wanted him to embrace her. Grab her from behind, shield her from the wind, but mostly to make her feel okay. Back in the real world, problems awaited. Yes, she had a burst of financial relief, but she still held multiple jobs just to get by, and she needed to study.

He did not embrace her. He leaned onto the railing alongside her. "Did you enjoy your time?"

"It has been a bang her."

"Nice word play. Does my sleeping with whom I choose to offend you?"

"While on a date with me, yes."

"Well, I apologize. Opportunity arose."

"Along with something else," Neville said.

"I had a wonderful time. You were everything I hoped for. If you are wondering if I think you are beautiful, the answer is a resounding yes. Would I jump into bed with you? In a heartbeat under different circumstances."

"For the record, I had an amazing time. It's just, I assumed the sugar daddy app would lead to a certain transactional relationship. It is a plus that you compensated me without my having to put out. And while I am attracted to you, you are married, so I'd rather not make things messy by sleeping with you."

"Charlotte wouldn't care. She thinks I'm crazy for not sleeping with you."

"OMG! She knows about me?"

"Absolutely. She doesn't know about Paris from last night."

"Paris? You slept with someone named Paris? Cancel your tip to me and end this date right now. I can take you screwing someone other than me, but not with someone named Paris. Kidding! Don't take the money, please."

Martin smiled. "Fake name, I'm sure. She was the wife of one of the New York couples on our zipline tour," Martin said.

"The one with the fake everything?" Neville asked. Martin nodded. "Well done. She was hot."

"I suppose. Not nearly as attractive as you."

"This is where you lose me. I do not understand you."

"You will come to understand, I promise. For now, I hope you enjoy our dates. I promise to expose you to new things each time."

"Multiple dates? That means multiple payments? Because if I divide the very generous amount you already tipped by, say, three more dates, I'm slicing down your generosity."

"Yes, multiple payments. You will want for nothing. I am ready for a coffee. Join me inside when you are ready," Martin said and headed toward the interior of the ferry.

Neville watched the man go. He stopped in the ship's doorway and turned back.

"Oh, and Neville, I believe my research is accurate. But have you ever been to the symphony?"

"No," Neville said.

Her answer prompted a grin from Martin. He turned and entered the ferry. Neville stood on the lower deck. There was an upper deck as well that sat further from the water than the lower. Neville loved looking out onto the ocean and the island in the distance. It was calming.

More than even the scenery, the financial boost of the weekend gave her a sense of peace she had not known in a long time. There was a saying that money did not make people happy. Neville declared that saying bullshit.

"Yes!" Neville yelled out to the sea.

She took a deep breath and felt a weight lifted off her back. Neville never realized how heavy that burden was because she bore it so long that she grew accustomed to it. She did not understand exactly what floated her date's boat and certainly did not understand the sexual politics involved with the older man. But removing the sexual component freed her in a way different from how the money did. She could choose who she wanted to be in a relationship with. With a financial cushion, she could go out more and meet someone from college.

A chill overtook her. The brisk wind whipped hard out on the ocean and tossed her hair about but it was a warm day. She crossed her arms and felt goosebumps rise on her arms.

Watched.

Neville felt watched. There was an upper deck that sat further away from the ocean than the lower deck, which she stood on. There, high above but not far away, she saw Patagonia vest man. He stared down at her. This was more than just her tits. The man was leering in a way that felt predatory. She rushed inside to join Martin, but mostly to get away from the creep on the upper deck.

Neville sat strapped into the seat on the slingshot ride at the state fair. Martin stood by, watching with glee as Neville battled her building fear. The weeks since the island had changed her life more than she could imagine. She immediately quit one job, and the others were on the way.

On the second date, Martin paid off a month's rent at her place. (They went motorcycle riding up the coast, with her seated on the back, holding onto him the entire time.) On the third date he paid another month's rent, and on the next, he paid another semester of tuition. It was insane the amounts he paid. All she had to do was spend time with him and let him watch her enjoyment about new experiences.

Their fourth date was the most daring and unique they had been on. And the nastiest. Martin took her to a late-night body suspension festival. He explained this was unrelated to religious ceremonies in some countries. They were entering an underground bacchanalian festival that was entirely hedonistic. He made sure that Neville was okay with it before they entered.

The event took place in a warehouse that opened out into a field with tents. Music and weed filled the air. Bodies hung by suspension wires throughout the grounds. Most who were hanging were naked or mostly naked. Dicks and tits were on display everywhere and people were having sex in the open.

Neville thought she was prepared, but the scene surprised her. It was unnerving to see flesh stretched to its limit. Hooks attached to wires and ropes pierced people's skin. The ropes ran to ceilings or counterweights nearby and kept the people dangling in the air. It was a truly unique sight.

Based on how daring the event was, the crowd was larger than Neville would have expected. Martin led the way, holding her hand. He wore leather gloves, a leather vest, and leather pants. The vest was open and displayed his rock-hard abs. His bulge was impressive, but there were many impressive ones on display from those who dangled naked from hooks as well.

The women were equally enticing. Many had tattoos covering large portions of their bodies. Lots of the women wore leather or PVC cutout tops, leaving their breasts bare and sticking out through the holes. Neville wore a simple black party dress that barely dipped below her hoo-ha, and yet after seeing the other women, she felt overdressed. People in the crowd reached out and groped both her and Martin as they walked through the event.

It freaked Neville out at first, but it was so brief each time that she did not bother to identify the culprits. The place was lit to keep most of the activity in the shadows. Intense music blasting through the venue and ambient crowd noise drowned out Neville's frequent cries of surprise each time she witnessed something new and lewd.

Makeshift beds, cartons, cots, and various items served as beds where people had sex in various combinations. One naked man masturbated the largest cock Neville had ever seen. The man simply walked through the crowd, masturbating vigorously and showing off to everyone. He turned to Neville as he passed and stuck out his tongue in a licking motion. But he never slowed, never stopped, just took his junk on a world tour of the facility.

"Did you like that?" Martin asked over his shoulder, shouting to be heard above the noise.

"I don't know how to answer that or any question right now. I am not a size queen though, if that's what you're getting at."

Martin laughed and led Neville forward. It was as if he had a destination in mind. Soon they arrived at a spot where a woman tatted from head to toe dangled from hooks. Men and women circled her and touched her all over. Martin made his way over and people cleared the way. Martin positioned himself behind the woman. He caressed her body for some time and spanked her tight ass. The crowd cheered Martin on. If he knew the woman he never let on. After the brief foreplay, Martin unzipped and slid inside her.

Neville had only heard Martin having sex on the island, but now she got to watch him as he screwed in front of everyone. The woman cried out in pleasure as Martin screwed her and other attendees, both man and woman, rubbed and touched her elsewhere. Martin grabbed her by the waist to keep her from flying away. (She was wired to a ceiling after all.)

Other hands from the assembled crowd reached for Neville as she stood and watched. Part of her wanted to let them explore but each time she flinched. No one pushed anything. Once she showed she was not interested, they moved on. There were plenty of willing participants to be had elsewhere.

Moans and groans filled the air. There were people having sex everywhere, not just her date. The sights and sounds made

Neville dizzy, not to mention all the pot smoke they had passed through. She felt fuzzy, warm, and horny. When a woman dressed in a leather cat outfit stepped from the crowd and approached Neville, she did not shy away.

The woman was stunning, toned, hard bodied. She wore leather boots to her hips and a bustier that crossed her ribcage and held up her large, uncovered breasts. She wore a tiny leather G-string that barely covered anything. But the sexiest part was the partial face-covering. It covered her head like a comic book super villain, exposing only her emerald eyes and pink, pouting lips. The woman had a single tattoo, a line of Latin right above her G-string. It read: *In fine autem cenamus et morimur.*

Cat woman walked toward Neville, each leg crossing over the other as she strutted toward her. Somehow, the crowd had cleared. There was only the cat woman and Neville. Everyone else faded away.

The woman reached out and ran a hand along Neville's stomach and breasts before circling around her. The woman positioned herself behind Neville and pressed their bodies together. The feeling of a woman's breasts against her back was not unfamiliar. She had friends who she goofed around and played with all her life. Bodies collided with bodies all the time, no big deal. But this was different. The way she hoped to entice Martin on the island was being used on her and she was warming up.

It felt sexy, and the woman's scent was intoxicating. Like Martin, she reeked of money. The woman wore a scent that eluded Neville. Something only those with means could afford. Reaching around, the woman moved a hand up Neville's dress and slid it into Neville's panties. Neville gasped with excitement. The woman breathed softly into Neville's ear and kissed the side of her neck. Neville had been without sex for a long time, and it surprised how quickly urges consumed her body. The woman ran another hand around to cup one of Neville's breasts through the dress.

The woman's fingers felt as if they were everywhere all at once. The woman knew what she was doing. Neville tried to turn her head to kiss the woman but the woman released Neville's breast and grabbed her face, forcing her to watch Martin. Once Neville locked on him, and watched him have sex while the crowd cheered, the woman added the second hand to what she was doing below. Neville moaned and felt like it came from someone else. Once again on a date with Martin, Neville was experiencing something new, but this time he was oblivious, too focused on his own pleasure.

"Do you like to watch him? Your boyfriend?" the cat woman asked.

"Yes," Neville hissed.

It was the words as much as the expert touch that finally pushed Neville over the edge.

Neville screamed.

Her body had warmed in the chilly night air while thinking back to that suspension festival night but the building fear as she sat by herself in the launch position on the Slingshot ride quickly overrode the sexy thoughts. She tried to focus on that night to calm her nerves. she was excited for the ride but scared as well.

The ride operator who had been chatting her up non-stop finally hit the button with no countdown or warning. Neville rocketed into the air at an intense speed. Like the zipline it was terrifying at first. She screamed for some time before falling into laughter as the ride reached its peak. She spun in the seat, looking down on the world below. A world in which she was no longer financially desperate.

After the human suspension festival, Martin paid off her rent for the remainder of the year. Neville screamed again from her bouncing seat in the sky. It was a primal scream, one of release, one of freedom. And comfort. Even in the hedonistic warehouse where flesh ruled, Martin never touched her other than to take her hand. And she never touched him.

That night of the festival they established themselves as partners, not lovers. Any signs of jealousy on her part disappeared. She enjoyed looking at the man the same way she would an actor on TV, but she no longer felt any urges for him. The suspension party (*come on, it was an orgy*, Neville thought) established them as partners of excess, not flesh. That dynamic was freeing. And turns out Martin knew the woman he banged was going to be there. He had already slept with the woman's twin. This was one of his new experiences moments, sleeping with twins.

After being lowered back to the ground, Neville rushed to Martin, and they hugged. Martin shared how he heard her screams above the overwhelming noise of the fairgrounds. With sex removed from the relationship they acted as lovers. The two walked hand in hand, played some carnival games, and ate deep-fried cucumbers and deep-fried Oreos. Both were disgusting and glorious, Neville thought.

"I grew up near a farm but never got to go to the fair. My mom could not afford it," Neville said.

"Do anything you want while we are here."

"I think I am done. Not sure I can surpass the Slingshot. don't you like the rides though?"

"As a child. I have moved on. I prefer my speed behind the wheels of vehicles or planes."

"Well, look at you, Mr. Snooty," Neville said, laughing.

Martin appeared to take offense. He dropped her hand. Neville cringed. Had she said the wrong thing? She was so content in their mutual agreement that she never sought to censor herself for the benefit of her date. Now she might have made a faux pas.

He would have been right to take offense. Despite their luxurious dates, he never flaunted his wealth. He always dressed for the occasion. Now at the fair, he wore jeans, a flannel shirt and Timberland boots. Neville wore Daisy Dukes that showed off just enough ass, and a sleeveless tee with a button-down top tied off at the waist. The top remained un-buttoned, covering her arms but not her chest.

She looked at Martin. He appeared upset. She realized it was all mere calculation as he grabbed her under her armpits and lifted her into the air. With a thump, he dropped her into the back of a passing hay wagon that she had failed to notice. Other people were already on the hayride. Martin gave chase and Neville cried out as if in a dramatic movie, begging him to run. He had to make it, just had to.

Martin caught the railing at the back of the wagon and leaped up. The other riders clapped with glee at his "rescue." Martin took a seat among the hay bales and pulled Neville against him, her back against his front. He strapped his arms around her waist, and they rode around the park, taking in the sights. Neville rubbed her arms over his and thought about how wonderful life had become.

Unlike most of their dates, they attended the fair early in the day. It was odd to end the date at midday. A normal couple would have moved on to something else, or faced reluctant chores together, or retired to a bedroom together for the rest of the afternoon for sex.

It surprised Neville when, instead of going home, Martin drove them to Beverly Hills. He had various cars, and the one he currently drove was a convertible. (Neville always dreamed of convertibles, but the truth was it totally messed up her hair.) One more thing off her bucket list, though.

Martin pulled up to one of the many fancy shops lining the street. It was a loading area only. A stunning woman in sunglasses and yoga attire stood curbside. When Martin pulled into the spot, the woman came around to his side of the car and passionately kissed him. She then crossed over and opened Neville's door. Martin gestured for Neville to get out.

"Neville, dear," the woman said and pulled Neville into a hug.

The woman's scent was familiar. She lingered in the hug, pressing her body close to Neville, who grew flushed. And confused.

"I am sorry. Who are you?"

"Charlotte. Martin's wife."

Neville went pale. "I'm sorry, I..."

The woman placed a finger against Neville's lips. "Hush. I know all about you. Martin did not lie to you when he said that I know everything. I think he is crazy for not sleeping with you, if you were willing, of course, but he has his quirks Martin does."

"Honey," Martin protested, slipping on his own sunglasses.

"You do. All those YouTube videos of people listening to songs for the first time. Please." Martin smiled even as Charlotte turned to face Neville. "I prefer repeating experiences once I find things that excite me."

With a tap of the horn, Martin pulled away. Neville looked around. "Where is he going?"

"It is my turn to play with you. We are going shopping."

Neville looked around at the bustling streets. People looked fashionable and hip. Even tourists travelling in groups looked reasonably dressed to be out in public. Neville felt naked in her Daisy Dukes.

"I am not dressed for this," Neville said.

"Oh, please. Let's have our *Pretty Woman* moment, shall we? Let them drool in the meantime."

Charlotte took Neville by the hand and led her down to a shop. Unlike the movies, the saleswoman in the shop greeted yoga clad Charlotte and Neville with great enthusiasm. The clerk and the woman kissed. Neville waved to the clerk, who complimented Neville and said she would absolutely hook her up.

It was a formal dress shop, not a stylish contemporary retailer. Neville did not recognize the name of the store nor the brands of dresses inside. Everything looked expensive, and a chandelier dangled from the ceiling.

Before long, Neville was in a fitting room with several dresses to try on. Charlotte stood in the fitting room with her, and Neville wondered if she was supposed to dress in front of the woman. She had established comfortable boundaries with Martin already, but not with Charlotte.

Charlotte moved in close and lowered her yoga pants. Surprised, Neville gasped. But the woman only lowered them so far. Just enough to show off a tattoo. It was a line of Latin script. *In fine autem cenamus et morimur.*

"But in the end, we dine and die. We have already met Neville. It is so good to see you again. Now I will leave you to try everything on. We need to ensure you dress properly for the symphony."

Charlotte exited the fitting room, leaving Neville stunned. She thought she understood her relationship with Martin, but now everything was different.

Stretch limos lined the block. The dress and circumstances weighed heavily on Neville. She had spent hours in a chair, having her hair and makeup done. She enjoyed being pampered and even had fun talking to Charlotte, but she failed to understand why a symphony was so important.

Yes, the dress and services were paid for by Martin and his wife, but it was Charlotte who oversaw everything. Neville saw other dresses that she fancied more, but Charlotte made it clear there were very specific guidelines. The dress could only cover one shoulder, for example. And the shoes had to be open toe. Strangest of all, she needed to wear fishnet stockings.

There were no universes Neville could think of where fishnets went with open toe shoes and a formal evening gown. But it was not her money. She followed directions. From inside her stretch limo, she looked out at all the other stretch limos lined up before a massive symphony hall. She knew of the concert hall but had never ventured inside. It was a classical place, which was not Neville's jam.

None of the other attendees wore fishnets as near as she could tell. None even exposed a single shoulder. They were formal, bottom to top.

"Neville? Neville darling?"

Neville turned back to Charlotte and Martin, who sat together across from her inside the stretch.

"What's wrong?" Martin asked.

"She feels underdressed," Charlotte said.

"In a two-thousand-dollar dress?" Martin asked.

"Ten, honey. Ten thousand."

Neville choked on her champagne and spit some of it back in the crystal champagne flute. "No one else is wearing fishnets."

"Oh, honey, it might surprise you how many are going bare underneath. These crowds like to play that they are above all of that, but in the end are we not all bags of walking skin. Fornicating walking skin bags. No sense denying the pleasure built into our bodies. I know you enjoyed our night together."

Neville blushed and looked back out at the assembled crowd. It helped calm her nerves to know proper people went commando in their fancy clothes. As Neville settled and relaxed, Martin asked an odd question.

"What do you know about string instruments?"

Besides electric guitars, Neville knew nothing about them. Her I don't know list was growing. *I don't know why I am wearing fishnets; I don't know why I must expose one shoulder; I don't know why in Hell the dress cost ten thousand dollars and*

weighs a shit ton. And I know nothing about string instruments.
Neville simply smiled and shook her head.

"The violin goes back to at least 1530," Martin said.

"But the harp, well, it goes back much longer than that. The harp predates modern human record keeping. Except…" Charlotte said, sounding giddy. Rather than finish, she tossed it back to her husband.

"There are paintings of a tall man playing a violin for Zeus himself."

"He's a Greek God," Charlotte said.

Neville nodded. She knew that much. She had seen the movies, maybe studied something about it in class.

"Zeus was known for his excesses, and he sought stimulation constantly. It was only the other gods who could influence him and keep him occupied. Servants lost their novelty quickly, for their flesh was too weak for the man. Legend is that one man, in a bid to win the hand of a woman he fancied, promised the gods that if they would make the object of his affection love him, he could help them. The mortal announced he would collect the powers of the other gods in his instrument. With that, he could entertain Zeus and leave the other gods free to pander to their own excesses rather than live to mollify the All father," Charlotte said.

"Nikias Pyramus was his name. Now, the legend has it that the gods accepted the offer and bestowed powers upon the instrument. Three heads appeared on the scroll of the violin," Martin said. He noticed Neville's confused look. "That is the end of the violin. The trio of heads created unique sounds and emotions in the All Father."

"Pyramus played for Zeus and legend has it the music brought tears to Zeus who cried for so long it formed all the oceans on earth. Other songs brought such rage that Zeus cast a plague on man. But Pyramus wished to play for Zeus and then return to his love. But Zeus' excesses did not allow the man a break and his symphony lasted one hundred years. By the time the composer returned to earth, the woman he loved was rotting in the ground," Charlotte said.

"That is so sad," Neville said.

The story fascinated Neville and took her mind off the crowds outside. For a moment, she got lost in time. Martin held up his phone and showed a painting of a man playing the violin for Zeus.

Martin pulled the phone back, looked at the image, and smiled. "Whatever one thinks of the stories, there are paintings from ancient Greece showing Pyramus playing a violin. That would make it thousands of years before the first violin as we know it."

Neville snorted, holding back laughter. The couple eyed her, unsure of what prompted Neville to laugh. She turned to

Martin. "You love seeing people experience things for the first time. You're taking me to a Journey concert. Of sorts."

"I suppose. But it is more than that. This is new for me as well. Pyramus plays only once every hundred years. He plays a symphony for his lost love. The notes carry all the way to the afterlife."

The limo finally stopped. Neville tilted her head, confused. "You mean an orchestra plays a Pyramus symphony every hundred years."

Before the couple could answer, the driver arrived at the limo door and helped Neville out. All heads turned as she exited the vehicle. People climbing the stairs into the music hall stopped and turned, looking down at the woman.

Unlike Neville, who stood alone while people stared at her like a zoo animal, well-wishers swarmed Martin and Charlotte. Sitting on the sidelines, Neville clung to her clutch purse like a life preserver. It was the only thing keeping her occupied while her personal benefactors made the rounds.

Once Charlotte finished greeting everyone, she brought people over to meet Neville. Concert guests hugged Neville and conveyed how wonderful it was to see her at the symphony. Neville, who earlier felt improperly dressed, suddenly felt like a rockstar.

The inside of the concert hall was grand. The entrance alone had such high ceilings dotted with chandeliers and soft lighting that Neville felt as if she had stepped back in time. Towering columns of marble rose from floor to ceiling and looked as if they belonged in ancient Greece.

The floor was marble as well, a checkerboard of black-and-white tiles. (Chessboard, Neville corrected herself silently. These people didn't play checkers, she thought.) Three stark white staircases rose from the floor to balcony entrances above. A coat check and bar sat off to one side of the enormous lobby. The familiar male/female restroom insignia hung just past the bar. Neville took note. If she yawned too much from boring classical music, she could escape to the restroom. Velvet curtains hung partially open across the half dozen doors leading to the concert hall. Ushers stood alongside every opening.

Martin gestured to Neville, and they headed toward one of the concert hall doors. As they neared the entrance, Neville felt as if she were being watched. Looking up on a staircase so white they could have formed from clouds; she spotted a man in a tuxedo. He grinned at her. It took Neville a moment, but she finally recognized the man. It was the creep from Catalina. Though he cleaned up well, he still leered. She shuddered, but soon the crowd swept them along into one of the curtained alcoves.

An usher at their door checked their tickets and complimented them on their seats. He then handed small ring-size boxes to Martin and Charlotte. Neville reached out for hers, but Martin shook the usher off. The young man looked embarrassed over denying Neville.

"You don't need this, dear," Charlotte said, and they stepped into the hall.

Neville looked back and saw that the people behind received the boxes as well. WTF? Neville felt cheated, but she forgot everything when they stepped inside. The concert hall took Neville's breath away. Looming before here was a place of timeless architecture. As she took in the grand scale of the hall, she felt it carried the weight of history.

Despite throngs of people heading to seats (which flowed from the entrance to the stage in a smooth decline), the place was preternaturally silent. It was as if the hall sat inside of a pressurized plane cabin. Except Neville's ears didn't pop, they just felt muffled.

Grand artwork lined the ceiling like something from the Sistine Chapel. Balconies high above seemed to float and appeared as if they rested in the clouds. More pillars rose from floor to ceiling along the perimeters of the massive space. Marble carvings of robust cherubs and ropes of ivy spiraled around each pillar.

The rows of seats, cushioned in burgundy velvet, looked as old as time. Curtains of the same fabric were drawn closed just past the edge of the stage. Soft house lighting revealed a stage floor made of polished wood.

Martin and Charlotte led Neville toward center view seats near the stage. Spectacular seats. The auditorium was a thing of grace. Neville felt the ghosts of concerts past, of crowds, dressed to the nines from different centuries gathering to experience that which she was about to for the first time.

The symphony.

Soon everyone settled into their seats and gentle music rose from behind the curtains. Soft notes danced around as if coming from somewhere other than the stage. Neville was not sure what to expect, but it surprised her that the only instrument was a piano. Where were the strings? Where was the orchestra?

With a sudden whir of movement, the main curtains pulled open to reveal a series of other velvet curtains hanging at angles across parts of a much bigger part of the stage. The velvet drapes fluttered as if a torrential wind blew them about. Within the cyclone of fabric, a lone pianist played to the crowd. The music was classical but intense and appeared timed to accompany the dance of fabric on the stage.

The pianist was young, wore a tuxedo, and had long hair that swished in the air as he tossed his head about while striking the keys. It was a wonderful, lively performance. And as the storm built to a crescendo, other instruments filtered in. (Was that a flute? A French Horn?) Drums sounded like thunder. Cymbals crashed as stage lighting emulated lightning. Neville leaped in her seat and fell into laughter at having frightened herself over stage gimmicks. Charlotte smiled at the young woman and grasped her hand.

As the song came to a climax, all the curtains flew open, revealing a full orchestra. The audience clapped, delighted by the excitement of the first number. Strings took center stage in the next song. A conductor stood in the middle of the musicians and waved his wand like Harry Potter, Neville thought, stifling another laugh. Taylor Swift got by fine without a wand waver. Neville was not sure what conductors did exactly.

Music filled the night. Neville enjoyed the show despite having little knowledge of classical music. She followed the lead of Charlotte and Martin, clapping when they clapped, gazing straight ahead when they did. Neville tried not to fangirl out, but she had since noticed celebrities and prominent figures were in the audience. Some sat nearby. It struck Neville as odd that she had the best seat in the house. She already knew her sugar daddy was rich, but now she wondered how rich.

Plink.

Neville jerked her head back. She looked around. Something had sounded directly in her right ear.

Plink.

She shook her head and touched her ear. It was right there. Martin was to her right. She looked at him, but he appeared oblivious.

Plink.

"Stop!" Neville yelled at Martin.

The entire audience looked her way. Several people shushed her. The conductor on the stage coughed, trying to get everything back on track even though the music had never stopped. The stupid music.

"You shush!" Neville yelled back to the crowd.

Plink.

She growled and stuck a finger in her ear, trying to dislodge the horrid sound that landed there like an errant fly. Charlotte tightened her grip on Neville's hand. She tilted her head, trying to calm the woman down.

"Neville, dear..."

"Don't call me that. And don't touch me. Everyone wants to touch me. I don't like being touched. I can't believe I let you do those things to me that night."

"Seems to me you were all too eager. Especially since my husband is too disgusted to touch you himself. You were my pity case."

"Pity?"

"Ladies," Martin said.

"You shut up," both women turned their heads and yelled at Martin simultaneously.

Plink.

During a gentle flowing string section on stage, someone banged a drum, louder than when it substituted as thunder earlier. The sudden noise threw off the ongoing piece, and the conductor took great offense.

"Alvin, you stupid cow, there is no drum in this piece," the conductor said.

Alvin answered with a drum solo that threatened to drown out all the other instruments. So annoying, Neville thought. Why, after all the cool dates, did Martin take her to a boring ass symphony? Especially one with so many freaking guys looking at her. Who cared about classical music?

Plink.

Members of the orchestra turned on one another and began to fight. It started with shouts and taunts, but soon the musicians drew battlelines. They struck one another with fists and instruments. One woman sprung from the string section, knocked the conductor down onto all fours. The woman rode him like a horse around the stage, choking his neck as he fought to escape.

Plink.

Neville turned her head and glimpsed a man looking at her from the same row but a few chairs down. He looked angry as well but leered at her the way the man on Catalina had looked at her.

"What are you looking at?" Neville asked.

The man grabbed the non-existent boobs on his own chest and squeezed.

"Son of a bitch!" Neville yelled.

She was out of her seat before she knew it and glanced at Charlotte. Charlotte and Martin were arguing about one another's philandering. Charlotte looked away long enough to encourage Neville. People in the row shoved at Neville and cursed her out for bumping them as she charged toward the man. He remained seated. He was in his thirties, handsome, well-dressed, and someone she would normally consider dating. And she wanted to kill him.

"You like looking at my tits?"

"You like showing them off?"

Neville balled her fists and struck the man in the face. His head jerked back, and he came back frowning and red-faced. He balled his hands into fists. She punched his face again. Blood poured from his nose. He called her something, but she was not listening. Neville pulled her arm back as far as she could and punched him one more time. His nose cracked.

He covered the nose with his hands to capture the blood and looked at her with raging eyes. "You're lucky we are not allowed to touch you. How a bitch like you got to sit at the head of the table. I'll never know."

Plink. Plink.

The note in her ear changed. Neville was confused and decided it was time to go back to her seat. On the way, as she made apologies to those she brushed against with her flowing dress, she looked up to the balcony and saw the man from Catalina looking down from his mountain. Neville was not fully over her anger. She flipped him a middle finger. The man broke out into laughter and tipped an invisible cap in recognition.

She dropped into her seat, exhausted. Her hair flipped over one air, so she blew it out of the way. Martin looked at her.

"Are you okay?"

"Yes. It's not my blood," she said.

On stage, the woman riding the conductor composed herself and helped the man to his feet. The man massaged his throat and then waved his hand toward one wing of the stage.

"Ladies and gentlemen, in honor of this once every hundred-year event, please welcome Pyramus," he croaked to the audience.

A man of thin build and intriguing character took the stage, stool and violin in hand. He set the stool down on center stage and set his bow on it. Then he cradled the violin and with his fingers plucked a few strings. The audience fell silent.

Plink. Plink. Plink. Plink.

Neville was not sure who the actor was playing the ancient legend, but she wanted to ride him. The man was so attractive and talented. With just a few strings, he moved her more than the entire orchestra had earlier in the evening. The notes were joyous, beautiful, melodic. And strange. They did not sound like any violin she ever heard. She looked over toward Martin and noticed a bulge in his pants. He too was feeling moved, apparently. As he should, she thought.

Then Pyramus picked up the bow and slid it sensually across the strings. There were no words. Neville suddenly longed to touch the man. He had such noble eyes that appeared as if they looked back in time. In him, she saw a world as it could be, not as it was.

But the feelings did not last. He swept the bow across the strings once again and fell into a song of such melancholy that she lost all the hope and lust that had just visited itself upon her. A great weight fell across her as she listened to a beautiful song she had never heard before. There was no melody, it was merely odd notes from a strange violin that had three heads carved on its scroll. (Were they moving?).

The song was so powerful that Neville wept. The audience sobbed along as well. Musicians on the stage hugged one another and cried into one another's shoulders, trying not to interrupt the most beautiful composition any of them had ever heard.

Feeling watched again; Neville looked up to the balcony. There sat the man from Catalina who wept as well, not immune to the rapturous swell of sound. Despite the tears, he met Neville's gaze again and nodded. She felt bad that she had ever been angry at him. Surely the stranger felt her pain. That was it. Each touch of the bow to strings cut a hole in the hearts of those in the audience.

Every note he drew from the violin revealed a delicate truth. Sad memories from childhood to adulthood rose to the surface. Every terrible thing one had ever done came home to roost in the listener's mind.

Neville was too young to remember her father leaving. Except now she remembered it clearly. Before he left, there were constant fights between her parents. He said cruel things about her mother opening her legs and said he did not believe Neville was his daughter. The notes the man played grew deeper and richer until she could remember what happened next, after her father left for good. Neville's mom picked up the phone and called someone. A strange man's voice sounded through the phone.

"He knows," Neville's mother had said. "He left."

But Neville understood she was too young to remember such things. They were merely auditory hallucinations brought on by the melancholy of the master violinist's song. Life went on with her and her mom, and a man Neville called uncle. One early morning, Neville climbed down the stairs, eager to greet her mom.

Halfway down the stairs, Neville stopped. Her mother did not know Neville was there. Neville saw her mother sitting on the couch, head in hand, smoking a cigarette. The ashtray was full. Her mother did not smoke. Her father did, and she always hated it. (How did she remember all that? She was too young.)

The scene played out in her mind with clarity. That was it, the moment her mother broke, the moment she was never her lively self again. Soon they would be alone with only Nana to help. Neville wept over having never forgiven her mother for being defeated. She never understood what it was her mom had gone through.

She couldn't take it anymore. Neville let out a wail and realized she was not alone. People cried out in despair as they too remembered things long ago buried for the sake of one's sanity. The music stopped, but the crying did not.

The weeping conductor announced there would be an intermission before the big show to treat any people who needed medical attention from the earlier "unfortunate" physical altercation. Neville rushed toward the bathrooms but passed the man with the broken nose on the way. Her heart burst when she saw him.

He reached out and grabbed her arms. "I am so sorry I stared at your chest. I am a horrible human being. Because I am an utter and gross fool, I have lost three wives. All women deserve better. I am ashamed and I apologize to you."

Neville hugged him. "I forgive you. And I am sorry I so enjoyed breaking your nose. It made me delightfully happy to do so and for that, I ask forgiveness." She broke from the hug.

"Of course. Someone had to, right?" he said, smiling through the tears and dried-blood nose.

Neville made it to the bathroom and found a stall. She wiped away tears while she composed herself. Outside the stall, Neville heard several women consoling one another as they waited for a stall to open. One despondent voice belonged to Charlotte.

"We paid the rent and the tuition and other bills for a year. By the time anyone notices it will be too late," Charlotte said.

"Please. I would give anything to be in her place. Wouldn't you?" the unknown woman said.

"Yes. That saddens me the most. How did she win the lottery?"

Neville emerged from the stall. She wanted to ask the woman what she was talking about, but Charlotte looked so beautiful that Neville burst into tears. They both started crying again and hugged one another. The woman Charlotte had been talking too bawled as well and got in on a group hug. The threesome cried until there were no more tears.

Once the intermission was over, everyone settled back into seats. Pyramus who never spoke a word gestured down to the row Neville sat in. Martin and Charlotte escorted Neville to the stage. The conductor from earlier pushed a chair across the stage, spinning it in dramatic fashion like a magician in Vegas trotting out a box designed to cut someone in half. The conductor positioned the chair. Martin and Charlotte helped Nevile sit.

They each kissed her on the lips. "You are so lucky," Martin said. "You get an experience few ever will."

With that, he pulled out the small box and lifted golden ear buds from within. He placed them in his ears, and the entire audience followed suit. The couple returned to their seats, and the lights dimmed. A cone of light settled on Neville in the chair and a second cone of light settled on the nearby violinist.

*P*link.

"Ooh!" Neville exclaimed as something akin to an electric shock snapped her legs.

*P*link. *Pli*nk. Plin*k*.

Neville's legs shot open, giving the audience a view between her legs. She could not help it. Something had jolted her muscles apart. It felt... weird. She giggled at the odd sensation and felt she should be embarrassed, but she could not find it in herself. The fishnets were stockings only. For underwear, she wore a G-string per Charlotte's request. At least the dress still covered her lower regions.

Until it didn't.

*Pl*ink. *Pl*ink. *Pl*ink. *Pl*ink.

The fabric tore away. It was the oddest thing. With each plink, the hem of her dress ripped at some invisible seam near her waist. The bottom half of her dress fell away. Never had she thought of a dress as a two piece, but now it was. She wore the top half from the waist up but was bare from the waist down for all the world to see. Only the G-string remained in place.

Then Pyramus lifted his bow and played. She looked at the audience, who watched her with great anticipation, but soon she could no longer see them. The world fell away. She was on display. They were watching her. She was the instrument as much as the violin. To watch the man play was to forget there was an outside world. She was swimming on the current of every note.

Neville began laughing. She understood suddenly. Everything all at once. The world opened up to her. She psychoanalyzed Martin, understood his faults, weaknesses, kinks, his darkest secrets. They were there in the man's countenance. One only had to know where to look. She could sense everything about everyone in the audience. People pretending to be so many things they were not, afraid of not fitting in, not belonging to a certain society, despising many of their so-called friends. For all the assembled wealth, they were the weakest humans on the planet.

And then she gained awareness of other worlds and realized how small the earth was. How futile that humans fought over dirt on the smallest and least evolved rock in the solar system. Neville laughed at the futility of man. She could not stop laughing as the music guided her on a journey.

The carved faces at the neck of the violin moved so that a new face took the center position. Pyramus changed his strokes as well, launching into a furious burst of wide swipes of the bow. The notes struck a chord with Neville, who cried out in surprise and pleasure.

Neville was suddenly in bed with every lover she ever had. The round bed spun in a gentle circle as all her lovers at once set out to give her pleasure. They were inside her one at a time, all at once, not at all. Some simply apologized for the many lies they told to get her into bed. Charlotte was there as well.

The woman knew how to drive Neville over the edge. Charlotte was experienced and beautiful, and a guide to pleasure, but it was the words she whispered in Neville's ear that caused Neville to tremble with pleasure until she felt ready to burst.

Neville moaned in time to the furious swiping of the bow on the strings, and the music brought her closer and closer to the edge. Soon Neville cried out in pleasure unlike anything she had ever felt before.

Neville experienced an orgasm there on the stage that contorted her body. She lost her breath for some time. The audience clapped and cheered, clumsily assuming they understood. The sexual feelings were beyond anything they would ever understand. And then she understood what was next.

What had driven Neville over the edge was the lesson Charlotte whispered in Neville's ear. The sole purpose for those born of flesh was to experience pleasure... AND pain. Let the rest belong to the gods.

Neville looked to the balcony and saw the man from Catalina Island. She never noticed his long, flowing hair, the white beard, the bare chest. It was Zeus on the cloud, and this was his symphony. This was his way of understanding what normal mortals felt. She was his flesh instrument for the evening. He felt her pleasure, and now.

Let the pain begin.

Plink. Plink. Plink. Plink. Plink.

With each plink, the fingernails on her hands popped off and flew into the air. The biological confetti rained back down on her. The audience went wild with applause. She could see the crowd again. She looked directly at Martin and cried out as the pain finally struck. That was simply the start.

Something twitched in her eye. It bothered her, but worse was the itch at her feet. She curled and uncurled her toes or tried to. She looked down to find they were swelling. The violinist continued to pluck the violin strings and suddenly the dress tore at the exposed shoulder, causing the fabric to fall away.

That was why I had to dress that way, Neville thought. The audience went wild with applause. The torn fabric had released one of her breasts. All the men who had leered now had their full view. The other breast remained encased in the remaining part of the dress.

Neville gasped. she felt a tingle in her chest. An odd sensation, one that did not bring pleasure, only discomfort. Her breast grew there on the stage, turning red, bloating, filling. Her exposed breast jiggled. Neville gripped the armrests of the chair and breathed deep, trying to hold back the discomfort growing in her chest.

Pop! Her breast exploded. Blood squirted across the stage. The audience rose to their feet, giving a standing ovation as Neville screamed in pain, crying out for mercy. Her breast was split into quadrants where it had come apart and fleshy strings dangled on her chest.

Plink. *Plink*. *Plink*.

Neville gasped and held up her right hand. It had bal-
looned to an absurd size. Like water filling a latex glove. She
was afraid to move. Just lifting it brought agony. It too exploded. A strange note from the violin and her hand twisted and
popped, sending more gore across the stage. Neville's screams
synced with the music. The skeletal hand remained attached
to the wrist, but she had been de-gloved.

She cried out in pain and loved the odd sensations as much
as they threatened to shut down her systems. She looked at the
violinist and thought she saw actual notes fluttering in the air.
That could not be. Something was wrong with her eye. She
reached with her one good hand and rubbed her eye. When
that did not help, she placed her fingers around her eyeball,
pushed forward and grabbed. She needed the itching to stop,
and the music was guiding her along. She yanked and pulled
her eyeball out.

She threw it toward Martin, but it only splatted near the
front of the stage. He gave her a thumbs up. Her groin itched,
and she heard a rip, small at first. It was the dress. The remaining part of the fabric was no match for Pyramus. The clothes
tore and fell away. She had not worn a bra, per Charlotte's
request, so her other breast was now exposed to the audience.

The audience had at some point sat back down, but they
cheered at the sight of her almost fully naked. She still wore the

G-string and fishnets, but the itch near her crotch worsened. She felt movement between her legs, and, with a slight tearing sound, her G-string fell to the floor. The fabric should not have made any sound, but it did.

Neville felt a fiery immense pain between her legs and noticed a line of red where part of her vagina had torn away. The bloody mess was stuck to her G-string on the floor. Neville cried out in pain and looked to the violinist, pleading with her one eye, hoping he would stop.

P*link*. P*link*. P*link*.

With those few new plucks, one of her ears slid off the side of her face. Half of her scalp separated from her head and dangled to one side, held in place by the remaining part of her scalp and hair. Blood poured down her face. Her stockings tore open at the front of her feet and the nails of the toes shot into the air in another celebration of sound and pain.

Then one by one the toes fell off and rolled across the stage. Blood shot out like mini geysers, and she grew dizzy. But then her legs quivered. They trembled, and she wondered if the musician intended to bring back pleasure. He did not.

Neville screamed as her legs expanded and pressed against the fishnet stockings. Her skin pushed through the round openings and strained her legs. Her flesh poured out in long round strings like the Play Doh toy she had as a child. The legs continued to push through the leggings until the skin was ropes of spaghetti. What remained were legs of nothing but bone and blood, a partial skeleton below the waist.

She cried out martin's name, begged him to make it stop even though she understood it was her destiny. Her tongue failed her anyway. It broke off, and she started to swallow it before spitting it out. Her good eye moved in circles within her orbital socket, but as it spun faster, the eye fell out and landed on the stage. She was not sure where. Her other hand exploded, and though startled, she knew soon there would be no reason to be afraid.

The pain had brought more pleasure than the earlier tune. She understood she could not take much more, was not meant to, for that much pain was left to the gods. She looked up with empty eye sockets and saw Zeus sitting in his cloud above the audience, looking down at her with pride. She could see him more clearly than when she had vision. Then her other ear slid away. She could still hear the music, but from somewhere else, somewhere far away.

Neville stood on her skeleton legs and bloody mass of a body and the crowd went wild. They rose for another standing ovation. Suddenly she could see and hear the adulation even as her world swam in the dark. She reached her arms out, willing to share her pain with any who were willing, but the crowd proved cowardly. Neville's face had since slid halfway off her skull, but in the dangling slush of a face, she grinned.

She had finally attended a symphony, and it exceeded all her expectations. But more than anything, after living in their world, Neville learned one thing. She was better in nothingness than the affluent were in life. And like that, she was no longer on stage. She was merely a song called Neville.

<u>Starbucks</u>

MANCHESTER CENTER VERMONT

Being an anthology inspired by and/or written in coffee shops, of course it's inevitable that there would be a Starbucks or two within these pages. However, having worked for Starbucks for 14 years, I can say that this location has been one of the quirkiest I've ever worked at.

Located In Manchester, Vermont—a rich little town full of artists and patrons alike, full of history and commercial retail outlets—this Starbucks sits in the shadow of nearby Mount Equinox. At noon every day, without fail, a tornado siren wails exactly at noon.

I asked both customers and fellow employees what the noontime siren was for, and most just shrugged and said, "It's for lunch." This led me to start forming my original idea for the story.

Why was the siren sounding? Were there people in the town waiting for it to go off every day for a specific purpose? I wasn't sure about the answers to these questions, but my idea solidified when I learned from a co-worker that Manchester had its very own vampire legend. Thus, the story was born.

Over time, I began writing bits and pieces of the story on my breaks at work. When I told everyone that I was writing a story set in Manchester, in a coffee shop modeled after Star-bucks, two of my coworkers asked if they could be victims in the story and I obliged. Maybe you can figure out who they are. Anyway, I hope you enjoy this story because it was super-fun to write. Drop by Manchester sometime and say hello! (Might want to do it before noon, though...)

DRINK RECOMMENDATION: Since the story re-volves around the fictional coffee chain called Java Junction that may or may not serve a readily available base drink you can modify how you want to fit this drink recommendation, I highly suggest Starbucks' Mocha Frappuccino with strawber-ry puree.

For one thing, a chocolate-covered strawberry is just the thing to symbolize the opulence of Manchester, Vermont. Sec-ondly, the coffee and mocha are a nod to the name of the fictional coffee chain—Java Junction. Lastly, whether you mix in the sweet red strawberry puree with your Frappuccino or top your stark white whipped cream with it, its blood-red color is the perfect nod to the legacy of the Manchester Vampire. Enjoy!

Shadows at High Noon

JOSEPH CARRO

Liam Frost stood behind the counter at Java Junction in Manchester, Vermont, as the first rays of morning light streamed through the massive bay windows of the coffee shop. An old train station stop served as the shop's shell and foundation. Liam breathed in the aroma of coffee and fresh pastries, a daily ritual (and delight) while waiting for peak business hours to hit. At six in the morning, he'd already been working for two hours when most people hadn't even woken. Luckily, he lived only a mile away, so the commute wasn't bad.

The house Liam rented on Depot Street looked horrible from the outside, with its cracked and peeling yellow façade. The street was so named because it was once upon a time a massive railway route and depot nestled amid the scenic mountains and valleys. His rental was an old Victorian (emphasis on old), but despite the questionable exterior, the interior was surprisingly cozy and well-kept. Thinking of his new place, it struck Liam how much his life had changed.

Just a year prior, Liam had been living in Cambridge, Massachusetts, working at Java Junction in Kendall Square. He had hoped to manage the place someday. Everything was on track. Liam became an assistant store manager and was next in line for his own store. However, his landlord sold the building he'd been renting for the past decade at the worst time imaginable.

Rents had spiked, leaving him unable to afford a place in the area any longer, even on a manager's salary. Thankfully, his district manager offered a new location in their Manchester, Vermont store. The move came with a promotion to manager.

Liam was unfamiliar with Vermont. As a New England state, for him, Vermont was the most mysterious of them all. A Mainer most of his life, he made brief forays into New Hampshire and Rhode Island before a longer stay in Massachusetts after grad school.

When he arrived in Vermont, he counted only a handful of stop lights in the town and wondered how a Java Junction would even stay in business. He was used to the hustle and bustle of a city. As Liam settled in and got to know the area, he learned Manchester was a small town because nobody actually lived there. Or few did. Manchester was a pure tourist town.

That's why it surprised Liam to learn the town board had aggressively objected to the chain being brought in. There were protests, angry town meetings, and glares from the locals.

It seems the train tracks and depots were federally owned, rather than state owned, so the town had no say over the cafe setting up shop. Java Junction purchased the land from the government, not the locals.

Liam did his best to let the locals know he was one of them, a New Englander, through and through. But he spotted the resistance, the doubts, the glares. He occasionally offered a free cup of coffee to win over the locals but had little success in warming them so far. The front doors swung open and Diego, one of his shift managers, entered with a cheerful wave.

"Morning," Diego said, briefly disappearing through a door to the back room to set down his bag near the employee lockers, before re-emerging, tying his apron as he clocked in for his shift.

"Morning," Liam replied, going over some scheduling on his laptop, which he had propped up on the front counter. Now that Diego was on, Liam could focus on his own work and let Diego run the shift.

"What's on the agenda today?" Diego asked, checking the daily schedule.

"I'm doing my admin stuff for the next hour, then I have a Zoom meeting with Pat whenever she calls to go over some stuff with the store. We'll have our shift meeting at eleven when everyone else arrives. Bianca, Jason, and Ellie are on today."

"Got it," Diego said, already marking in times on the schedule when he'd be sending the baristas on their breaks.

"Bianca is out back making a few backups," Liam said, moving the laptop to a table. "Jason is on a break and should be back soon."

Diego nodded and went about doing his shift supervisor duties while Liam moved to a table. It relieved Liam that his shift supervisor had not requested an update on their missing employees. Ever since one of his closing baristas, Atticus, had disappeared without a trace almost a week prior, there had been multiple incidents at the shop.

Liam worried about Atticus, but had no updates and could not answer his employees' questions when they asked. This was the first morning since the disappearance that no one brought it up, though surely it remained on everyone's minds.

Atticus was a newer barista, trained mere months ago at another location before transferring to Manchester. Atticus was short, had multicolored hair, and loved art and music. His music appreciation came from his parents which helped the barista to appreciate lots of "older" music. Liam bonded with Atticus over such music.

The barista's disappearance was already unsettling, but when the sheriff came on the scene shortly after, it made everything more real. Liam worried for his staff, who had to go through not only missing their coworker but answering questions from law enforcement.

A few days prior, the Sheriff (Tom, he insisted Liam call him) entered the café with a deputy and took the employees one by one, into the break room for questioning. Tom had been antagonistic during the questioning. Poor Ellie ended up crying. Liam let her go home early that day and couldn't help but feel a spark of anger toward local law enforcement. Liam's own interrogation had been equally unpleasant.

"Could we step into your office and chat a minute? Liam, was it?" The sheriff smiled broadly, uncovering a set of Chicklet-like teeth that instantly instilled in Liam a sense of unease. "You can call me Tom."

"Sure, yeah," Liam said, following the sheriff's hand gestures toward Liam's office desk. Liam sat down, a pit growing in his stomach. Such unease made little sense, especially because the sheriff was trying to help find their missing employee.

"We're here to talk about your employee. A young Mr. Atticus Spalding. Tell me a bit of what you know about him, and anything you can recall that might help."

"Okay," Liam said, twiddling his thumbs, attempting to recall the days and moments leading up to Atticus' disappearance. "Atticus was reliable, was always here on time, never really called out. He's a talented artist, knows a lot about music.

The last time I saw him was when we closed together the day before he missed his next shift."

"You're aware that young Atticus never made it home that night?" Tom said, raising an eyebrow.

"I'm aware," Liam said. It was something that Liam had beaten himself up for since Atticus' disappearance. "Atticus was waiting for his parents to come get him the last I saw him," Liam said, his voice quavering.

"And what time was that?"

"It was around 7:35 PM. I needed to run to the convenience store to grab something to eat since everything closes so early around here. I had no food in the house. The store closes at eight, so I had to get going faster than I'd have liked. I wouldn't normally have left Atticus or any other baristas by themselves."

"And the convenience store cameras will show you shopping if we went and checked?"

"Yeah," Liam said, his heart hammering inside his chest. "Of course. Probably was about 7:45 PM when I arrived at the store, give or take."

"Well, I believe you, Liam," Tom said. "When his parents arrived at Java Junction, Atticus was nowhere to be found. Of course, you weren't, either," he said, letting the last part of the sentence hang. "Now, you rent that big old yellow house up the road, from what I understand?"

"Yeah."

Tom laughed softly. "I used to play in the yard there as a kid. Used to belong to a prominent Manchester family back then, but they all moved away to New York by the time I was a police officer. But that's neither here nor there. Would you mind if we paid you a visit sometime this week?"

"Yeah, I mean sure," Liam said, his throat suddenly dry. Did Tom suspect him of Atticus' disappearance? Why else would he wish to come out to the house? Liam wondered.

The man leaned back against a storage rack used to store large bags of coffee beans and big boxes of syrup. Tom made eye contact with his deputy, a small man in his twenties, who stood watch over the office entrance door to make sure nobody interrupted the conversation. The sheriff lifted his hat a bit, exposing a portion of wrinkled forehead and graying hair.

"I understand all of you are concerned," Tom said. "We're looking into it, as we do. However, I need you to be straight with me, Liam. Has Atticus ever mentioned any problems or concerns about working here at your coffee shop? Anything unusual?"

"Not really that I can think of," Liam said, furrowing his brow. Atticus had made jokes about customer service, and things like that, Liam thought, but nothing out of the norm for anyone in the service industry. "I guess, like me, sometimes the locals can get to us. They've been very aggressive lately.

Plus, a siren goes off every day at noon. No one in town will tell me what it is, so I ask you. What's that all about? I can't ever get a straight answer. Anytime I ask someone who might know, they just tell me it's tradition, or that it's a lunch bell of sorts because it's noon. That can't be it, can it? It's so loud."

"Is it? Don't notice so much anymore. I've kept watch for over twenty years. This is a small town, you understand. And your employers, Java Junction…well, they went and found a sneaky little loophole that the town board wasn't any too happy about. I can tell you that for a fact, because I'm the one getting all the complaints. Did you know that the local judge is my neighbor? Anyway, before I go off on a tangent, locals aren't happy with this big ol' coffee shop sneaking in. You've got to give them time to adapt. If you last that long."

The sheriff let the sentence hang for a while, increasing the pit in Liam's stomach. (Had that been a threat?) Before Liam could reply, Tom flashed his Chicklet smile once more.

"The business, I mean, of course," he said, flashing Liam a wink. The deputy smirked. "Now, me? I make my coffee at home, so I don't have a horse in this town versus chain race. But if I were to bet on one of those horses, I'd bet the folks in Manchester are going to protest with their wallets more than anything else. So, if one of them gets too aggressive, feel free to call, but just understand you're in their home, Liam, both you and Java Junction. And you people are not invited, despite how nice you all seem from my interviews."

Liam cleared his throat, trying to stifle his immense unease and growing frustration. "Aren't you here to ask about Atticus?" Liam asked.

The deputy stopped smirking and moved his hands to his belt. The sheriff seemed to stare through Liam's body to his very soul. Liam imagined Tom's two eye sockets as loaded shotgun barrels, ready to release their barrage into his body and tear him apart. Tom crouched down, bringing himself to Liam's eye level, flashing his Chicklet smile and pulling the brim of his hat back down over his eyebrows. The man did not blink once.

"Of course, Liam," Tom said. "Of course." He placed a large hand on Liam's left shoulder and squeezed, a bit too hard. Liam tried not to show his discomfort before the sheriff finally took his hand away. "Manchester is a small town, like I said before. People come and go, sometimes without notice. Life on the rails and all that. But I'll keep you updated on the investigation second in line after his parents." Tom stood up and motioned for his deputy to open the door. "For now, make sure your staff stays alert and reports anything suspicious."

The deputy walked out ahead of the sheriff. Just as Liam was trying to exhale and collect his thoughts, Tom stopped in the doorway and spun around.

"Oh, and Liam? That town siren? It's just tradition. Just a lunch bell of sorts."

Liam stiffened in his chair. There was something about the way the sheriff inflected his words that made it sound like a warning. Liam's palms began sweating when Tom pointed at Liam with his thumb and finger in a gun shape, and "fired" before blowing on the imaginary barrel.

"You have a nice day now. This is a nice coffee shop you got here!"

Tom left whistling a cheerful tune Liam had never heard before. Then again, Liam wasn't paying much attention because the siren went off and filled the café with its dreadful sound, just as it did every single day at noon. For the first time since Liam moved to town, the siren felt ominous.

The meeting with Pat, his district manager, went about as well as he expected. Pat seemed fair and mostly balanced but had never come to the store in person except one time. Their meetings were via Zoom calls after that. Liam got the feeling that Pat was purposefully avoiding their location.

During the meeting, Pat asked the usual things about sales numbers and shared with Liam the sales projections based on their current business models using a similar store volume for reference, since Liam's location was new and didn't have anniversary numbers to go on. Pat spent almost no time on any of the problems stemming from the locals that Liam and his staff had had to deal with. When Liam had brought up the meeting with the sheriff, Pat told him to "be positive" and continue helping law enforcement.

"Go over the Java Junction safety protocols once again with all your baristas and shift supervisors," Pat said, never betraying a single emotion in her features, "and make sure you have them all sign off on the sheet before you send it over to me in your monthly packet."

"Sure thing," Liam said, amazed at the apparent lack of concern for Atticus or the other baristas. Liam held his tongue. Perhaps he was reading too much into things and overreacting.

"Okay, Liam," Pat said. "Anything else you have for me before we hang this up? I know you've got your shift meeting soon, and I've got more paperwork to do."

"No," Liam said blankly. "I'm good. Have a good weekend."

Liam couldn't help but spot something on Pat's face—a flash of relief. Her smile broadened as the call ended. "You too. Keep up the great work, Liam! I'll talk to you soon!"

Pat disconnected before Liam could say goodbye. Liam stared at his own reflection on the darkened screen of his work laptop. Finally realizing he had yet to eat anything, he informed Diego and his baristas that he was going to lunch. Liam grabbed a bagel from the pastry case and walked outside to sit in the sun for a while and think.

By the time the shift meeting was about to begin, the store had had its first real business peak of the month and Liam had had to jump on the floor to help. It looked like old sheriff Tom might be wrong after all about his dire business predictions. Locals were giving Java Junction the cold shoulder, but the tourists sure weren't. Autumn was the hiking season in Manchester. The scenery was glorious, with colorful leaves, and tourists flocked to town. Soon, winter would set in, and tourism would shift to skiers.

For now, hikers it was. Tourists appeared happy to discover an honest-to-God coffee store on the way to the wilderness instead of the podunk convenience store with its lukewarm coffee that dripped out of an old rusty machine. It was a no-brainer that the tourists would flock to the last vestiges of civilization before giving themselves over to nature.

Java Junction was a national chain, after all, and locals aside, people enjoyed the comfort of brands they knew and loved. During the height of the rush, Liam manned the front register and helped on drive-through when he could. Diego did a great job of keeping the other baristas on an even keel. When the rush was over, Liam congratulated everyone before announcing it was time for the shift meeting.

Liam and Diego sat at a long table in the middle of the café and waited for the other shift supervisors to arrive. They made small talk as the others trickled in and took their seats. Liam went over all the business of the store that they were facing. Labor, the upcoming winter sales, rules about safety that Pat suggested he review again. And finally (although it pained him to do so) the discussion around hiring another barista.

The shift supervisors handled it well enough. Kaiden, Joseph, Kristen, and Sophia sat and listened attentively without blurting out anything about Atticus. It was on the team's mind though, and they spoke up at the open floor part of the meeting. Joseph went first.

"I'm going to be honest, Liam," Joseph said, folding his hands on the table and looking around at everyone. "I don't feel safe. Not here in this store, not here in this weird town."

Joseph was a good kid, still very young but polite and with a good head on his shoulders, a good work ethic, and a positive attitude. So, it pained Liam to hear that the employee didn't feel safe.

"Yeah," Sophia chimed in. "There have been so many crazy things people have been doing. I had handprints all over my car windows yesterday. They weren't from me."

Liam nodded, allowing them to speak without his interruption, until he was sure they said their fill.

Kristen chimed in. "Atticus disappearing like that? I worked with him a lot and the way he always talked about his parents; I don't believe he would have just run off."

"Which makes it even scarier," Sophia added.

"That reminds me," Kaiden said, sitting up straight. "We've been getting a ton of prank calls on my shifts. I just hang up most of the time now, but they just keep calling and calling and won't say anything. There's just, like, heavy breathing on the other end."

"Oh, and that sheriff guy was something else, wasn't he?" Diego said. "He was giving everyone the lead paint stare for, like, minutes when he was questioning everyone."

"I'm glad I wasn't here," Sophia said. "I heard he made Ellie cry. Is that true, Liam?"

Liam nodded. "Yeah, it's true. I sent her home early. Now, listen, everything you guys are saying is on point. It really is. The whole thing with Atticus is scary, and I really feel sad about it. I hope for everyone's sake that he just ran away and will be back in a few days, but obviously none of us know. The sheriff really is pushy and has a weird vibe, so you're not alone there. But the base sentiment I got from our old friend Sheriff Tom is that the locals pretty much hate us."

The entire group nodded in recognition. Some murmured sentiments of the 'no kidding' type. Liam continued.

"It's not my fault, it's not your fault. They've just had things a certain way for decades and then here comes Java Junction, sprouting up in their town, and they didn't really have much of a say in it. To be honest, I at least understand where that anger is coming from. But saying I understand it does not mean that I condone it. We're just here to work serving tourists and locals whenever they get their sticks out of their butts. We're just doing our jobs and are not in charge of company policy, so give yourselves some slack. I realize you guys have come under fire in a huge way, but you're still performing well, and our numbers haven't been too bad, especially with all we have going against us. I am proud of you all. The sheriff will pay me a visit this week and I will update you if I hear anything. Are you guys good?"

They nodded and looked around at one another. Liam wasn't sure if he'd made them feel better at all. It was hard to tell sometimes in a corporate setting what people really felt. At the end of the day, Liam was their boss and no matter how available he made himself to them, there would be a gulf of trust that could never be fully bridged. All he needed was for them to come halfway and he'd extend his hand, metaphorically.

As the meeting wound down, the front door to the café slammed open, causing a loud bang to reverberate throughout the space. A wild-looking man in his fifties stood in the doorway, legs wide apart and hands balled up into fists. His hair was close-cropped, and he wore Coke-bottle glasses. a flannel shirt, black jeans, and black work boots.

Liam instinctively stood and placed himself between the wild man and his employees. "Whoa, whoa, whoa," Liam said, holding his hands up defensively. "Is everything okay? How can we help you, sir?"

"Help me?" The man sneered. "You can help me by getting the hell out of this town. We don't want you here! Why can't you just leave?"

The shift supervisors all rose silently from their chairs. Sophia walked quickly over to the other baristas standing frozen behind the counter. The man noticed Sophia using the phone to call the police.

"Go ahead. Call the Sheriff for all the damned good it will do you. Every single one of you is trespassers! You're nothing but outsiders who don't belong. If you think just one of you disappearing is bad, wait until every single one of you has a missing poster. What do you think of that?"

Liam heard Sophia calmly talking on the phone to the police dispatch. His heart pounded with a mixture of adrenaline, fear, and anger. He'd never seen the man before and here he was threatening them about ending up missing like Atticus. Had this man been responsible for Atticus' disappearance? Then the strange man pulled a handgun from his waistband.

An icy chill creeped up Liam's spine. It had happened in a thousand neighborhoods just like this, but it had never happened to him. Until now. The man continued ranting as if unaware that he had pulled the firearm.

"Stay calm, sir," Liam said. His voice and words felt and sounded hollow, as if spoken through a straw into the wind. "Please, let's go outside, you and me, and we can talk about this without all these people here." Liam motioned with a hand behind his back for his employees to go away and move toward the counter. He hoped they understood what he meant.

"You have no idea what you're dealing with you absolute fuckwit! This town has rules! This town has traditions! You're upsetting the balance. Most of all, you're upsetting HIM."

"Listen, man," Liam said, licking his lips. His mouth felt dry and full of cotton, and his hands shook slightly as he held them aloft. "We're just doing our jobs here. Not trying to hurt anyone. We're just trying to run a business."

"Problem is," the man said, cocking the pistol. "Business is what we all want you to stay out of. Business is what we all want you to MIND YOUR OWN KIND OF. Noon comes every day, you'll see. He'll show you. Then you'll see. Or maybe you'll never see anything again. How'd you like that?"

The man leveled his gun at Liam. Liam felt his knees slightly buckle, but he held onto his stance for dear life lest he make any sudden movements that would cause the man to pull the trigger reflexively.

The Java Junction training was useless in this situation. In the training, the module offered hypothetical scenarios featuring active shooters and what to do in each case. One solution was to run and hide, the most obvious answer. Another scenario was to fight back

As Liam stared down the cold, steel barrel of the handgun, he knew there was no scenario in which he could fight back against a gun pointed at him at point blank range. He'd be dead before he so much as flinched. That's when Liam heard a familiar voice.

"Eli," said Tom. "Drop the gun and come on outside. Now, don't do anything dumb."

Eli turned and saw the Sheriff looming behind him. Liam felt like he could breathe again. When Eli turned, Liam slinked slowly behind the counter where the others were crouched.

"You guys go out the back," Liam said to them. "Here are my keys, so you don't set off the door alarm." He handed Diego the keys. "Meet up in the convenience store parking lot.

Don't make any noise and stay out of sight until you see the Sheriff driving away."

"What about you?" Diego asked.

"I'll be fine. Once Tom arrests this guy, I'm going to give him my statement, which I'm sure he's going to want after this."

Diego said nothing more and nodded. The baristas and shift supervisors crouched out of sight and made their way to the back office, where they opened the back door with Liam's keys and slinked out one by one until they were all out and the door closed softly behind them.

Tom's and Eli's voices had been rising steadily, but Liam had been busy instructing his staff and so he'd missed the last bits of the conversation between them.

"Now you know damn well this isn't the time for this, Eli," said Tom. "It's actually a bad damned time for this, Eli. It's almost noon. I'm going to give you to the count of three before there's no turning back."

"What'll happen, do you think?" shouted Eli, waving his gun around. "Do you think he'll come here personally and bleed these outsiders?"

"Shut. The. Fuck. Up." Tom said. "Last warning."

"Or wh..." was all Eli got out of his mouth before gunshots erupted throughout the café.

Eli's head ripped apart, sending red ochre viscera of blood, bone, and brain matter all throughout the café. Liam screamed involuntarily, covering his head with his arms as he shielded himself from the exploding glass from the pastry case, which was torn apart by bullets from Tom's gun. After what seemed like forever, the shooting stopped.

Tom's voice sounded clear and concisely through the café over the juxtaposition of a Taylor Swift song droning on through the empty and blood-spattered shop. "Liam, I'd like to have a word with you. I heard you carrying on back there behind the counter just now."

A pit opened in Liam's stomach, and he felt at a crossroads. All logic suggested Liam do as Tom suggested. After all, the man was an officer of the law and should be trusted. The sheriff likely wanted to question Liam about what the man had shouted and ask if everyone was okay.

However, the way Tom blasted Eli's head apart so violently filled Liam with a fear previously unknown to him. That, and the detached way in which Tom had asked Liam to come out from behind the counter, made him want to do the opposite. Liam crawled over to where the door was still ajar out back, his keys still hanging firmly in place in the lock.

Liam decided he'd had enough of the job, and mentally quit on the spot. He took his key from the lock so that after stepping out, the door would lock behind him. If the Sheriff opened it, it would set off an alarm. Once outside, he ran to join his employees gathered at the convenience store lot.

They all waited outside the store. The convenience store owner stood outside blocking the entrance and watching the going-ons. Once Liam arrived, the store owner locked his door and put up a closed sign. Liam looked frantic and had to be prompted by one of his staff to update them on what happened.

"What happened?" Joseph asked Liam. "We heard shots."

"Please, listen to me, all of you. I quit. This place isn't safe. I don't trust the sheriff. He just blew that guy's head off," Liam said.

"Oh my god," Bianca said, placing her hands over her mouth in surprise and fear. "Are you for real?"

"Yes. Get in your cars and go. Just go. Even if things were going to be normal after this, we'd be closed for days, anyway. Just drive. Fast. Don't worry about getting into your own cars, just carpool and get out of here before the Sheriff gets here."

A couple of employees did as he asked. But several lingered. Liam did a head count and found one missing. Ellie.

"Where's Ellie?" Liam asked. "Guys?"

Justin, on his way to his car, said, "Oh, we forgot to tell you in the meeting, but she never came in."

The employees continued their exodus. Liam hoped Ellie was simply out sick. But as the others got into their cars, he spotted Ellie's vehicle.

"Shit," he said, under his breath. "Shit, shit, shit."

Then the biggest shit of all. As his employees drove out of the parking lot, speeding away, a long line of townies walked toward the café. About thirty of them, men and women, stone-faced and solemn as a funeral procession. It was time for him to get out of there as well.

A click sounded and the cold steel of a gun barrel pressed up against the side of Liam's head. His body went stiff. A powerful hand grabbed his shoulder and spun him around. It was Tom.

"Maybe all that grinding coffee made you a bit deaf, Liam, but I said I wanted to have a word with you."

"Look, Sheriff, I..."

"It's Tom," he said, flashing his Chicklet teeth smile. "Like I told you before."

"Okay, Tom, listen. That guy you blew away seemed crazy. He was going on and on about us being trespassers and out- siders and how we were making 'him' mad. Hey, I didn't mean to make you mad, if you're who he was talking about."

Tom grabbed Liam by the shoulder and started laughing. Despite how fearful Liam was of the sheriff, he had to admit the big man's laugh was infectious. It began putting Liam at ease, despite everything. When Liam tried to turn to see if the townies were still where they had been, Tom's grip tightened immensely on his shoulder, preventing him from moving.

"No, you haven't made me mad, Mr. Java Junction. However, it's almost noon so I'm sorry for this. It's just tradition, you understand."

Tom whipped Liam's head with the barrel of his pistol. Liam cried out in pain and stumbled backward onto the pavement. His vision blurred, he crawled a few feet on his knees and elbows. The force of the blow made him vomit all over the tar of the pavement, and in his blurred vision, he saw the townies had all gathered behind him. Many were laughing.

"Damn, Tom, did you have to shoot Eli?" Liam heard one voice say.

"He was gonna shoot me on accident or maybe even try to shoot me to scare those kids off before we could get out there to block them. Speaking of, did you all block Route 9 in case they try to get to Bennington?"

"Yep. Kyle and the boys are taking care of it. They're not going nowhere."

"Good, good. Now, damn it, Liam, you're making me look bad. I hit you and you're supposed to be out cold, not floundering around like a lake trout."

"You're getting old, I guess, Tom," said a woman's voice. There was more laughter at this.

"All right, all right, yeah, I'm getting old, but I've still got it. Watch this."

Tom hit Liam again, and the world went out from under him. He was floating in a void where nothing and nobody existed, not even the void.

Liam woke to pain, and blood and the realization that he was upside down. There was a chalice below him filled halfway with blood. His blood. With a groan, he twisted and saw Atticus to his right, and Ellie to his left. Both seemed sedated or unconscious, with tubes running from their arms to IV bags filled with blood. Unlike him, roped up and dangling, the two baristas were on hospital gurneys.

"Hey," shouted Liam. "Somebody help me! I'm hurt!"

No one answered. He took in the surroundings. Despite the gurneys, they were not in a hospital. The place looked like a government or state office. Plaques shaped like Vermont hung on the walls alongside photos of the mayor of Manchester posing with various people.

Liam dangled from the ceiling near a large mahogany desk, gleaming with a professional finish and covered in official-looking documents. There was an inscription in Latin he could just barely make out in the dim candlelight over the doorway which read *Lux Abscondita*. He didn't know what it meant, only that it was Latin. Liam had taken Latin back in the day but had long forgotten anything he'd learned in that class.

Realizing the futility of struggling, he let himself rest and tried to calm his heart rate as he fought muscle cramps in his arms and legs and the churning of nausea in his stomach. His head was absolutely pounding with pressure, both from being upside down and from where Tom struck him, that sonofabitch.

After a few minutes, the townies piled around the doorway and looked in. Each one held a burning candle. Murmurs rolled through the crowd, and Liam spotted Tom toward the back. Tom met his gaze and fired off a finger gun in his direction. If Liam's hands weren't cuffed, he'd have given Tom the finger. As it was, Liam waited for the game plan.

Liam suspected the townies were trying to scare the living shit out of them, so they'd leave town. Well, Liam had to hand it to them because it worked. He'd never wanted to leave a town so much in his entire life.

"Look, guys," Liam said. "You win, okay? It's just a job. Java Junction is just a job. It's just coffee. We were just trying to support ourselves. But you win, we're going to get the hell out of Manchester. As soon as you guys let us go, I'm going to call my district manager and I'm going to quit."

The townies, and Tom, said nothing. That's when the noon siren went off. It sounded very different up close and personal. Liam must have been hanging close to the pipes inside the wall because he could feel the horn blast through his body and reverberate through his entire being. The townies began chanting in Latin, in low murmuring voices. A wooden panel creaked open in the wall right next to him.

A cold surge of air rushed out of the secret entrance. Footsteps sounded from somewhere in the darkness behind the open panel. As the steps grew faster and heavier, the townies chanted louder and fiercer. Liam struggled anew against his bonds, his wrists raw and his movements helpless. He glanced briefly at Ellie and Atticus, both still sedated and unmoving.

Eventually a figure emerged from the opening in the wood-paneled wall. Its skin was whiter than the marble of the columns supporting the ceiling. Its unnaturally long fingers, bony and porcelain-like, ended in sharp, deadly claws. The figure's eyes, yellow and almost glowing, looked into Liam's eyes and within moments, Liam was dreaming.

Just before Liam drifted off, an unnatural voice whispered in his ear, "I'm sorry, young one. It's only tradition."

In his dream, Liam gazed into the eyes of his wife, whom he'd lost some years prior. A single tear rolled down his cheek.

He had not seen her eyes in years. Once upon a time, they held much love for him.

Happy to be reunited, he sighed and told her of the strange dream he had of living in Vermont. She shushed him and embraced him round the neck. He coughed under the subtle pressure, but she was his wife and he trusted her. Ignoring the discomfort, he gave in to her icy touch until he knew no more.

<u>Motoring Coffee</u>

LOS ANGELES, CALIFORNIA

Motoring Coffee is one of the most unique coffee shops that I have visited for this anthology series. Nestled in West Los Angeles alongside an auto club, the coffee shop is a wide-open space filled with cars and motorcycles. It's not filled with just any cars either. Whether a pristine cherry red Mustang, or grand Prix style racing cars, the lineup changes regularly.

Centering the whole place is a converted truck. The truck bed serves as workstations for people doing business at the coffee shop. The staff are very friendly and know almost everyone by name. Nestled alongside the coffee place is the motor club for members only. Divided from the coffee shop by a waist high wall so anyone can look over are more cars, RVs, trailers, foreign cars. In other words, it is very cool stuff.

If you've been working too long or need to stretch your legs, this place is perfect because you can simply walk around and enjoy the cars. It has a friendly vibe all around.

As I tried to figure out what type of story to write there, my love of found-footage horror movies came to mind. There was also an open call for a found footage anthology. I guess you could say that is what sparked the idea for writing this found footage story. But most of all it was that cherry red Mustang.

DRINK RECOMMENDATION: I do not recommend driving when tired, but if you must, you might as well charge yourself up with a Red Eye.

Down Dark Winding Roads

PAUL CARRO

* Closed Caption is now on. English subtitles. Press ESC to exit full screen. *

CC: *Whir of a camera lens zooming until it focuses on a young TV host standing on a desolate highway.*

"We are here on what some call the *Loneliest Road in America*. Highway 50 in Nevada. But that is not all they call it. *The Road of Death*, known as the home of a restless rider with a fondness for hitchhikers. But make no mistake, if you hitchhike this far out, you are likely already dead. The heat during the day, and cold at night..."

CC: *Multiple curse words while the camera pans away from TV host. The sounds of a camera lens adjusting as it refocuses on the immense desert and distant hills and mountains. Once the cursing stops, the camera spins and reframes the host. Slight wind is audible in the recording.*

"Around the ragged rocks, the ragged rascal ran. Around the ragged rocks, the ragged rascal ran. Blah, blah, blah. Why can't I get through this in one take?" The host asked his camera operator Jill.

"Chill, Tony. Just pick it up from there. Our little show is finally big enough to merit an intern," Jill panned to an eighteen-year-old holding a mic on the end of a broomstick. "You can cut all this together, right, Chuck?

Chuck wore the standard crew outfit of jeans and a sweatshirt. He waved one hand instinctively at the camera which almost caused him to drop the mic. "I can edit on the fly while we're driving between locations. I can even…"

"TMI Chuck." Jill whip-panned away from the intern back to the host who continued his vocal warmups. "Point is Tony, we don't need a single info dump shot. Reveal some here, some there. What you miss, we pick up in the next shot. Rinse, repeat. Chuck will review footage as we go, compare it to our loose as a goose script and feed you anything important you missed. I'm going for a looser look for the show this season."

"Right. What about story order?" Tony asked.

"Again. Intern. And audiences are smart, they think non-linear. But Chuck is ours to use and abuse. During the edit, he will use the entirety of his recently out of puberty energy to make sense of it all."

CC: *A muffled protest relating to puberty from an off-camera voice.*

Tony nodded and primped for the camera. "Legend has it that a local man, one Red Dutton, set out on these very roads in his pristine 67 Mustang. We know this because he stopped at the Silver Dollar Saloon to show off his vehicle before setting out on his ill-fated trip. Highway 50 is not for the faint of heart. Its lengthy highways stretch into oblivion, with no food, gas or lodging for hundreds of miles at a time. Even cellphone service vanishes along most of the highway. Surrounded by brush and desert for miles, the area appears apocalyptic, until one expands their view to take in the majestic hills and mountains in the distance. A bar patron asked to take a picture with Red and his muscle car. It would become the last known image of Red Dutton before his mysterious disappearance."

"Do you want me to shoot the pic of him here, or insert it in editing?" Jill asked from behind the camera. A pro, she kept the shot focused on Tony.

"Now is good. I need a water break. Shoot the pic until I'm back," Tony said and walked out of frame.

Jill spun the camera to Chuck who held up a tablet. "Do you want to shoot as is, or want me to add a frame around it?"

"Give it a frame. Try to make it look like an analog photo. I will be right back," Jill said, lowering the camera to face the ground as she walked away from the jeep.

CC: *Brisk footsteps crunch on dirt. Urination splatter sounds as the camera captures the host with his back to the camera.*

Tony heard footsteps at his rear but was occupied with relieving himself. "Hey, paying the water bill over here."

The TV host gave a one-finger salute over his shoulder, but it threw off his aim causing him to leap as he peed on himself. Thus began the dance of the errant stream before he finally finished and zipped up. Jill captured it in all its glory. She headed back for the vehicle, Tony close behind.

CC: *Cursing combined with laughter. Footsteps fall in line with the camera movement. Everyone stops at a jeep parked nearby. The footsteps cease.*

Jill lifted the camera to capture the intern who showed off the now framed picture of two men and a Mustang taken in front of the Silver Dollar Saloon. Red Dutton, a bull of a man, stood with his arms around the older guy who could have been a prospector from back in the day. Both men displayed thumbs up in celebration of the pristine vehicle. Red wore a straw hat much like a cowboy's as well as a kerchief which was fastened around his neck.

CC: *Whir of a camera zooming in and out while attempting to frame the picture of the men. Indecipherable crosstalk in background.*

"We've shot enough in the road. Let's walk up to that ridge, finish the introduction from up there before it gets dark," Tony said as the camera went black.

CC: *Fumbling clicks as someone turns the camera back on. Multiple footsteps in range of the camera's view. Off-screen laughter from the individuals who hike up a long path. Indecipherable crosstalk.*

Once on the ridge, Tony lined himself up with the camera, but the mic dropped into view. Tony scowled at the intern.

"Come on Chuck. We didn't walk all the way up here to ruin the shot."

"Sorry. I'm tired from the climb," Chuck said.

"Can we get the shot, please? Sun is setting. We need to transition to night mode soon," Jill said from behind the camera.

Tony started. "After showing off his red Mustang, the man named after his car's color set out to test its speed on a highway known for little to no traffic. That was the last time anyone ever saw old Red. The man vanished that day. Theories ranged from a breakdown to an accident. Some suggest he engaged in a street race and crashed. Either way, authorities never found the car or the man. That photo from the Silver Dollar Saloon was the last time anyone saw Red alive. But what about dead? Many who have broken down or stopped for the view on this lonely stretch, have reported being approached by a ghostly red vehicle." Tony stopped and gestured to the valley below. "This is such a great view. Let's shoot the road from up here. I'll voiceover off camera. Just keep our vehicle out of the shot."

"Got it," Jill said and killed the camera.

CC: *Hum of camera turning back on. Crosstalk and footsteps.*

"This looks good," Jill said. She focused on a wide shot of the landscape below. The highway stretched out to infinity, as did the desert.

Tony spoke into the mic just off camera. "Down below on the desolate stretch of road, many people claim to have seen Red. While driving on these very roads, they reported a vintage Mustang riding their bumpers, only for it to vanish without warning. Some claim to have seen the man pull up alongside their stopped vehicles and rev the engine as if ready for a race. Others forced to walk the streets after a breakdown say the car idled alongside them as if seeking a passenger for company. Tonight, we will ride these very roads, searching for the..."

"Guys!" Chuck yelled.

"What the hell, Chuck? I was on a roll."

"You need to see this," Chuck said.

"What?" Jill asked.

"Down there, not even far from our car. That light reflecting."

"No freaking way!" Tony said. "Let's go, now."

CC: *Excited crosstalk with heavy breathing. Dirt crunches as people run down a mountain path. The camera shut off, then turned back on in a different location with more heavy breathing and crosstalk. Whir as the lens focuses on their new location. An abandoned car in the desert.*

"No way! Is that a Mustang?" Chuck asked.

"I can't tell. It's too dark. Dude, where's the light?" Tony asked.

"Working on it. It got dark fast on the way down," Jill said and turned on a camera mounted light over a shot of Chuck and Tony standing near a rusted-out Mustang with deflated tires, and a cracked windshield. Jill gasped.

"How could the police miss this? It's not far from the road. Our jeep is right over there," Tony said.

"We never noticed until higher ground. We could have as easily missed it were it not for the sun reflecting off the side mirror," Jill said.

"This is freaking me out, guys. I think we should go."

"Really, Chuck? You're an intern on a ghost hunting show. We just found a ghost. Let's check the driver's seat," Tony said.

CC: *Multiple footsteps circling an old, abandoned car in the desert. Gasps replace the footsteps as people stop walking and the camera focuses on the driver's seat. Lengthy silence.*

"We need to go. We need to tell the police."

"Yes, Chuck. We do, but not yet," Tony said. "This is him, right? Red?"

The camera shook in time with Jill's nodding. "Straw hat and kerchief. The skeleton looks like a cowboy."

The camera focused on a skeleton sitting upright in the driver's seat, hands on the wheel. Tatters of skin hung off sections of its skeletal frame, but most of the flesh was gone. The clothes had fallen off the corpse except for a straw hat atop its tilted head, and a red bandana that dangled from around the neck in a perfect triangle.

"We need better lighting than the camera's built-in lamp. Let's go get the light kit. We won't have access to all this after we involve the police, so let's get footage now. This will get us all the clicks! This is going to make our show," Tony said.

CC: *Footsteps crunch in time with the feet filling the camera frame. Repetitive clicking from the camera dangling at the cameraperson's side. An engine roars to life. Startled crosstalk offscreen. The engine revs. The sound of gravel spinning under tires. Confused and fearful cursing. Footsteps running now.*

"What the Hell?"

"Run!"

"Is that the car? Its lights are on. What's happening?'

"He's driving right at us!"

"He can't be. Dude is dead."

"Run!"

"Film it. Film it!"

"And get run over?"

The camera dangled upside down as Jill ran for her life with the others. The upside-down shot captured the impossible. The car's headlights came to life and the Mustang roared straight for the crew. Only the desert's soft sand kept the vehicle from immediately reaching the gang. The group raced for the jeep. The oncoming headlights grew so bright the film crew could not track the Mustang's distance. It was close though.

Chuck leaped into the back of the jeep while Tony took the wheel. Jill had only one foot inside when she stopped to film over the top of the vehicle. The Mustang kicked up sand, a whirlwind visible because of the headlights of both vehicles. Chuck gripped the front seat and watched in stunned silence as the car raced closer and closer, its engine revving like a demon from hell. Had they not parked the jeep on the far side of the road, the Mustang would have already made contact.

The Mustang's wheels hit asphalt, the point of no return. Its proximity made the terror more real. The Mustang's glowing interior light remained illuminated the skeleton driving with purpose, gunning for its target.

"Get in. Get in!" Tony screamed.

Jill leaped in and kept filming, aiming toward the Mustang as it made the jump from desert to street. It left the ground and landed on squealing tires, heading right toward them.

"This isn't real, this isn't real," Chuck said, eyes closed, trying to manifest its disappearance.

Jill filmed the pursuing vehicle over Chuck's shoulder. The open top vehicle gave a perfect view of the Mustang which missed their jeep by inches as they sped off. The Mustang rocketed across the road into the turnoff they just drove away from. A larger dust cloud filled the air as the Mustang hit the brakes and turned simultaneously.

The dust cloud enveloped the Mustang while the jeep sped off down the empty road. Tony adjusted the rearview mirror and spotted Chuck rocking and chanting, eyes closed. Jill filmed the errant dust cloud at their rear as it formed a curtain. But not a protective one. The Mustang suddenly burst through, gaining on them fast. The skeleton smiled from the driver's seat.

"Faster. It's gaining on us," Jill said.

"I'm driving as fast as I can. How can a rust-bucket go so fast?"

"I don't know. How can a skeleton drive? Just get us out of here."

The road stretched on as if forever, nothing but black top and night sky. Nowhere to run to. Makeshift roads jutted off in random locations, but they served only as access points for scenic stops. They were vista paths, not thoroughfares. The offshoots were not escape routes but traps. The Mustang's engine roared, and its headlights grew closer.

"This isn't real, this isn't real," Chuck murmured in the back.

Wham! The Mustang struck the back of their vehicle. Tony swerved; the jeep threatened to tip, but he corrected. Any oncoming traffic would have likely ended them. But the roads were empty, save for the pursued and pursuer.

"Stop this. Stop right now! I'm going to sue your company," Chuck said, eyes finally open.

The jeep got back in its lane and the Mustang fell back momentarily. Both vehicles roared at unsafe speeds. Despite the chase, Tony barked at the young man.

"What the Hell are you going on about?" Tony asked over the wind.

"Supernatural is garbage. It's not real. You guys are playing a trick on the poor pathetic intern."

"There is a skeleton driving a Mustang that I am looking at through my eyepiece you twat. And you think we somehow set up a collision?" Jill asked.

"Yes? I don't know. Sure. Why not? You film it and put it on the show and make me look like a fool."

"Hold on!" Tony yelled.

Headlights swept their vehicle again. Wham! Another hit. Harder. The jeep swerved off the road, kicking up sand before returning to the pavement where it now faced the opposite way. The Mustang blew past them, only to vanish in the night. Tony regained control and slowed before coming to a stop. The jeep sat there alone. The world was dark except for their headlights, the camera's light, and the distant moon.

"I'm out," Chuck said and leaped from the jeep.

Chuck walked in the direction they originally came from. He swore, and cursed before finally turning back, though he kept walking backward, eager to put some distance between himself and the others.

"You guys are jerks. Haze the new guy? That wasn't even the same Mustang. The one that hit us had no rust, was pristine. What, did you hide a fake one in the desert, then have another on standby? Is this a prank show instead of a ghost show? It is, and I'm the butt of the joke. Screw you guys!"

The two ghost hunters unfastened their seatbelts, rose in their seats, and searched the road behind them before turning back to the angry intern. Jill leaped out and started toward the assistant, but Chuck kept walking. Jill called out from behind the camera, her comfort zone.

"Chuck, please, come back. We need to get out of here, get somewhere safe, and check the footage. This was real. If there were any pranks, someone played it on all of us. We can talk about it, but we need to move muchacho." Jill yelled back at

Tony. "Start the damn car! We need to get Chuck and get out of here."

Jill headed back toward the jeep which now drove slowly toward her. Before Jill could get in, the roar of an engine cut through the night. Jill took refuge behind the jeep while filming the fast-moving Mustang.

The car's headlights were off this time, leaving only that interior light. Inside, the skeleton gripped the wheel with both hands and leaned forward as if the position gave him more speed. Red was moving fast, too fast.

Despite Chuck's anger and disbelief, he instinctively stepped off the pavement onto the road's shoulder. Jill filmed as the Mustang flew past the jeep and stopped alongside Chuck. Tony and Jill yelled out for their intern, but Chuck threw a double bird at his employers. The Mustang's engine revved, but the agitated intern yelled over the engine and leaned toward the passenger-side window.

Chuck yelled loud enough for the others to hear. "I know what this is. Some dumb prank show. I'm out. I've had enough of you jerks yanking my chain." Still leaning down, Chuck looked toward Tony and Jill. "That is some amazing makeup, though."

Then Chuck was gone! Just like that, Dead Red pulled Chuck through the passenger window. Was the window rolled down? Did Chuck go through the glass? It happened so fast that the pair could not tell. One moment the intern was there, defiant, cursing out the driver, the next he was through the window as if in one yank, legs, and all. Despite the small opening, Chuck vanished through it with speed and efficiency, as clean as teleportation.

The Mustang burned rubber and took off, driving away from the jeep, heading in the direction the crew originated from, specifically toward the spot where they first encountered the rusted Mustang.

"Chuck!" Tony yelled.

Jill leaped in and they both fastened their seatbelts and took off after the Mustang, but it was already gone. They scoured the road ahead, searching for the vehicle. Jill kept filming, but the camera light was useless. Even the headlights picked up nothing. Blacktop and loneliness. Nothing else for hundreds of miles. Neither spoke for a time, they were too shocked. They searched for the Mustang that should not exist.

"Where is it? Where did they go?" Tony finally asked.

"I don't know. I don't know."

"Keep filming. We need to get this to the cops. This isn't about the show anymore."

Headlights burst to life as they drove past the stopped vehicle. It sat just off the road, angled to catch passing traffic in its beam. Tony hit the brakes even as the Mustang rocketed onto the road. Dead Red pulled up alongside them in the opposing traffic lane. The Mustang lined up perfectly with their vehicle, leaving them with a clear view of the passenger's side. There, face pressed against the window, was a terrified Chuck. He pounded on the glass, to no avail. He shouted, but the Mustang's engine drowned out the intern's cries. The driver revved the engine repeatedly, a familiar sight and sound for many young drivers.

"He wants to race. Does he want to race?" Tony asked as the Mustang's engine replied yes. "I can't beat him."

"We need to try. I don't think we're racing for pink slips. I think we're racing for Chuck." Jill, face pressed against the viewfinder, noticed the Mustang's headlights flash. She understood the code. "That's the count. That's two. Next is three. Go, go, go!" Jill yelled.

One more flash of the beams and both vehicles sped off. The jeep kept up with the Mustang as Tony floored it. They raced along the straightaway with no end in sight. Neither driver gave an inch. Tony broke into a sweat despite the cool night air. Jill struggled to film past Tony, doing her best to keep their race in frame.

She glanced ahead. "Where is the finish line? How will we know if we win?"

As if toying with them all along, the Mustang rocketed ahead. Tony pounded the wheel but could go no faster. The jeep's engine whined along with the terrified passengers. The

Mustang's taillights remained in view, two demon eyes staring back at them from a distance. The Mustang suddenly stopped. Awaiting round two?

Tony pulled slowly alongside the stationary Mustang which remained in the opposite lane. Afraid to instigate another race, Tony avoided revving his engine, coming in at a crawl. The Mustang's interior remained lit showcasing Chuck with his face pressed against the glass, crying out for help. But then Red pushed Chuck's face against the glass hard enough to crack it.

Chuck could no longer scream for help with his face mushed against the glass. Drool poured from his mouth. He eyed his friends in the jeep with a look that spoke volumes. *Sorry for flipping the bird, sorry for doubting you. Sorry that I did not believe in the supernatural. I need to pee.* The glass fogged in a tight circle where Chuck breathed through his nose, which was stretched at an odd angle.

"Did we lose already? Or are we racing again?" Tony asked no one.

A hand came into view alongside Chuck's face, a bony hand. Its finger beckoned the ghost crew to come closer. When neither moved, the bony finger tapped on the glass near Chuck's face to draw their attention. The tap was loud in the night. The finger then beckoned once again.

"Oh no, the camera battery is dying. Please let it stay on long enough. No time to change it. Red obviously wants us to get closer. I'm going in," Jill said and leaped from the vehicle.

She circled around the jeep to position herself with a good view of the passenger's window where poor Chuck suffered at the powerful hand of something no longer alive. Chuck's eyes pleaded with Jill, but all she could do was film the scene. A perfect frame of the man struggling to breathe and/or escape. In a daze, Tony stepped from the jeep and joined Jill.

The bony hand that had beckoned them grabbed Chuck by his hair and pulled the man's face away from the window. Chuck took a deep breath. A look of relief overtook his face after experiencing a clear airway again. But the comfort did not last.

Blood and gore exploded against the passenger's window! The bony hand had yanked on the hair in its grip. In one swift motion, Chuck's scalp and face came off, as if the intern wore a mask all along. And maybe it was a mask now. The one piece dangled loosely in the skeleton's grip. Hair and flesh that could have been molded from latex were it not so real.

The gory scene only remained visible through patches of glass not covered in drooling blood. Chuck's now skeletal head hit the glass and bounced away. His dead body settled into a seated position in the passenger's seat. His skull tilted to one side. Red finally had his long-sought passenger. His ride or die. Or ride and die.

As reality sank in, Jill cried out and dropped the camera onto the street. The lens broke, cracking down the middle. The fractured view showed asphalt, tires, and Jill's feet.

CC: *Tires squeal. Intermingled male and female screams. An engine roars before fading in the distance. Screams intensify until those screaming lose their voices. A repetitive beep accompanies a flashing red low-battery warning on a cracked screen. The screams are replaced by low-level sobbing and cursing. Beeping continues while an on-screen graphic announces the camera is about to shut down due to low battery. The beep continues. Beep, beep, beep...*

Woodford General Store
WOODFORD, VERMONT

Woodford General Store, located in Woodford, Vermont is an oasis of civilization in a sea of trees and mountain roads. Owned and run by Ryan Hassett, whom I got to know pretty well while living in Woodford for two years (I just moved to Manchester, Vermont not too long ago).

The General Store harkens back to the days of yore when you could buy a pound of penny candy, local meats and produce, and basics of everyday life all in one place before grocery stores existed. Catering mainly to residents of Woodford, hikers of the Appalachian Trail, and seasonal snowmobilers and skiers, the General Store is where I would get my coffee while working for Headless Hydra Press on many-a-morning, taking in the nearby sights of Prospect Mountain.

It was during these coffee runs, chatting with Ryan, that I noticed the posters for bear activity in the area and what to do if you were approached by one. I asked Ryan how often bears were spotted nearby because I walked back and forth down Route 9 (in the infamous Bennington Triangle, no less) frequently, sometimes bringing my friend's dog Luna with me for company.

I'd even walked from Woodford to Bennington a few times, the trek down the mountain and into downtown Bennington being something like 8-10 miles depending on where you went. He replied that he'd seen the bears often, and so I kept my eyes peeled until one day while walking back down the private road to the house I was living in, a neighbor spotted me while driving back down our road in their truck and told me to be careful. He'd just seen a very large black bear on his security cameras. He drove ahead to make sure the coast was clear, and I cautiously made my way back after he showed me the video of the bear standing on its hind legs and towering over another neighbor's car on the camera footage.

Coffee in shaky hand, I began to imagine what would happen if the neighbor hadn't warned me. Perhaps I'd have run into the bear, and who knows what the bear would have done. Of course, my having horror on the brain and having just watched *Cocaine Bear*, I suddenly had inspiration for this story. I hope you enjoy reading it as much as I enjoyed writing it. Next.

DRINK RECOMMENDATION: For this story, you're going to want a brew that, let's face it, features blueberries. Since blueberries (weirdly) aren't a feature in drinks at many popular coffee chains such as Starbucks or Dunkin' – I tried to think of the next best thing, and for me that's New England Coffee's "Bluberry Cobbler" blend coffee, which you can usually find in many grocery stores that carry the brand. If you care about such things, the beans are 100% Arabica and in your favorite pop culture mug I can promise you that you will have no finer coffee experience to remind you of the wild blueberry barrens of Maine than with this coffee. Bonus if you pair it with a nice slice of blueberry pie for breakfast. Too much blueberry? I don't think so. Also, if pie was a good enough breakfast for Jack Kerouac, it's good enough for me. Enjoy!

Blueberries for Sally

Joseph Carro

Not gonna' lie. When Monika took me aside and sat me down on our smoky, cat-hair-covered couch in our rinky-dink living room, I knew it would not be a pleasant conversation. First, she never had heart-to-heart chats with me like *ever*. Especially not since I became a teenager. Second, she was never home to begin with, always busy with conference calls or at meetings. I learned how to do most things on my own at an early age. Maybe that is why when I turned eleven, I stopped calling her mom and started calling her Monika. I'm not sure why. Maybe because I felt like she wasn't motherly anymore. Plus, it was a way for me to jab her without her being able to get mad. Monika was her first name, after all.

Now Monika sat, looking like she was about to cry or throw up. She grabbed my arm with her bony fingers hard enough that I worried my Doja Cat tee might rip. Monika's face was scrunched up and her eyes were bloodshot. Unsure of what to do, I just stared blankly. Even though I mostly called her Monika, she was still my mom, so I tried not to cringe when she started crying. I just let her do her thing.

She searched my eyes while a tear rolled down her cheek and landed on her tee shirt. It made a tiny dot of moisture on the once white fabric that had turned mostly yellow from her constant smoke breaks. She was up to about three packs of smokes a day, maybe more. She smoked expensive ones called American Spirit. I once told her she should vape instead, but she gave me a lecture about how much worse vapes were for anyone (AKA me) than cigarettes ever were. That was an uncomfortable conversation, but this looming one felt worse. Panic gnawed my guts as it hit me that this was no ordinary talk.

"I'm sorry, baby," Mom said. "I'm sorry."

My face turned beet red in anger and confusion. Like, what was she about to tell me? Did she have *cancer*? Were we about to lose the *house*? I felt like I needed to let her know I was worried rather than my normal state of being—angry. The best way I knew how was to ditch her birth name.

"Mom?"

"Baby, I don't know how to tell you this, but Nana was killed. She's dead. She's gone."

Monika spoke the words as if she were just hearing the news herself for the first time. She crushed my body against hers and started bawling her eyes out. I struggled to fully grasp what she told me. *Nana had been killed? How? Who would do that?* I didn't know what to do, so I just stood there. As mom cried, her tears splashed onto my skin, landing warmly though my heart had gone cold. I wanted to push her away because she sat there crying instead of telling me what she meant. The words were crazy. Nana was KILLED? Like, I couldn't process it!

Nana was the nickname for Monika's mother, my grandmother. I didn't really know how to feel as it sank in because Nana hardly ever visited us. It was difficult to remember how many times I saw her in person. It must have only been a few.

I tried to remember any solid memories I had of Nana and could only think back to my 10th birthday party when she stayed longer than she ever had before. Nana gave me a book for my birthday called *Blueberries for Sal* and brought a homemade blueberry pie to go with it.

Nana said that the blueberries in the pie were special, grown on her own land in Maine, and that I would never taste a blueberry as good as those again. She was right. The blueberry pie absolutely *slapped*. I was, like, *addicted.* How I longed for another, but Nana never brought another one. Such was the relationship. It was the inconsistency for me.

On the book's cover, Nana had glued a piece of paper at the end of "*Sal*" on the book with a handwritten "ly" at the end which turned "*Sal*" into "Sally". It was corny, but that's how boomers were. I pictured her sharing the pic of her little joke with her friends on Facebook where she probably had a bunch of other old people liking and commenting. I still had the book somewhere in my room, but I hadn't looked at it in a few years. Other than that, the only thing I remembered about Nana was that she had two moles under her left eye. I always wanted to pick them off whenever I saw her.

Meanwhile, Monika was still bawling her eyes out and I was just staring off into space thinking about Nana's blueberries and the kid's book and everything and trying to process the trauma, so I stroked Monika's long, brown hair just out of reflex like I used to do when Dad left. I barely realized I was doing it, and just sort of fell back into the habit.

"I'm so sorry, baby," she said, struggling to speak through the crying jag. "I know how much Nana meant to you. They said it was some wild animal, and she was always out in those damned woods. Looks like it was a bear."

"It's okay, Mom," I said back. "Like, a *literal* bear, though? Nana got killed by a *bear*?! Like how?!"

She bawled harder, refusing or unable to elaborate any further. I went numb on the inside, and I cried a bit later—but right then and there, I just dissociated.

Monika crushed me in her bony arms, and I could smell the cigarettes on her breath when she kissed me on the forehead. "I love you, baby," she said repeatedly, rocking me back and forth. I just sat there awkwardly and let her do it for as long as she needed while I counted the orange cat hairs on the couch and felt my iPhone buzzing out notifications in my jeans pocket. One of my posts was finally blowing up.

Before Nana, I'd never been to a funeral. It wasn't what I expected. It wasn't fair that, like, I couldn't try to process my trauma by posting about it on TikTok or at least my Snaps without coming across as some sort of psycho. Like, everyone handles death differently, but everyone thinks it's such a huge issue for me to speak my truth and deal with Nana's death in my preferred way.

Nana was a boomer and didn't understand social media, but if she did, I'd bet she'd *want* me to do it. It's not like it was an open casket or whatever, because of the bear attack. I didn't even glam up or anything. My dress was subdued and black, just like my shoes, and I didn't even wear any makeup. Any time I brought out my phone, even just to check the time, Monika looked me in the eye and shook her head no. Then I'd roll my eyes and shove my phone back into my purse.

The buzz of notifications was blowing up my phone, though, and it was high key giving me anxiety. One of my BTS

TikToks was going viral from a few days before. So many people were commenting, because the Korean pop group was one of the most famous bands in the world. It was the first TikTok I ever had go viral, and it felt good, like it was something I was supposed to do. Maybe this could lead to a partnership with Shein if I kept getting bigger, or maybe I could meet BTS. Last time I'd looked, the TikTok was at over 600k views and growing. Nana might have been killed, but that didn't mean my life stopped. But in a way, it had. At least for a few days, so I guess I just had to deal with it. BTS was forever.

Nana's funeral took place in Bridgton, Maine, on a hill that looked out over a forest near a ski lodge. The lodge was closed, as it only opened in winter. I felt like I couldn't even take a pic for my Insta, but I snuck a couple that I would post a day or two later once I was past the funeral moratorium. (God forbid, I post live.) I was surrounded by random family NPC's I'd never even met before. At one point, Uncle Andy asked who in the family wanted to be a pallbearer. Monika raised her hand and then looked at me so hard I had to say yes, too, or it would make her mad.

I raised my hand, unsure. "I will, I guess."

Uncle Andy had bushy eyebrows that seriously needed a trim. I mean, have some self-awareness. (*Men, I swear.*) Andy raised both brows in surprise at the notion of me volunteering, as if I couldn't be a pallbearer at my own nana's funeral.

"I will," I said again, a lot louder and meaning it even more.

I stood up and moved next to Monika, who rubbed my back in support. I offered a weak smile, but the back rubbing was embarrassing, so I pretended to tie my shoe even though I had no laces. Uncle Andy shrugged, then motioned for us to get to our spots near the back of the hearse. I took the middle spot on the right and Monika the middle on the left. She looked at me all weird through eyes glossing over with tears. I guess she was proud of me or something.

Uncle Andy stood behind me wearing a cheap-looking suit that didn't fit him well. Andy's son, Lester, stood behind Monika. Lester was around my age. He had shaggy hair and wore a blazer and jeans. Ahead of me on the left was Uncle Frank, who looked like a guy from some 1950s meme. A guy from Nana's work named Tony took the front right. Tony looked pretty rough, not gonna' lie. His glasses, taped in the middle, sat crooked over his nose. His hair was a mess, and he had gray stubble. The man gave off serious divorced dad vibes. In comparison, Uncle Frank looked clean cut, smooth-shaven, and wore a sharp suit.

When the funeral director motioned for Uncle Frank and Tony to grab the handrails on the casket, all I could think about was Nana laying inside that box, not getting any air. I choked up as I felt my own lungs strain while I fought to breathe for her because she couldn't. Tony nodded to me as he pulled the front of the casket out and motioned with his head for me to get behind him and grab the handrail. I did after stumbling and realized I was crying. I pulled on the handrail as hard as I could, trying not to drop it and embarrass myself, but Uncle Andy grabbed the handrail and grunted under the weight, taking some of the burden off me.

I was barely supporting it because I was in such a daze. While carrying Nana's casket, I thought I heard her rolling around, which made me queasy. We neared the waiting hole. I couldn't believe that we were putting *Nana*, like, into the *actual ground*. We set the casket into the moorings and then stepped aside, where I pretty much dissociated from everything.

It was difficult to focus, which meant I didn't remember a thing that anyone said or did during the service. I only knew it was over when Uncle Andy put his hand on my shoulder and said, "Nice job, kiddo," and then Monika led me away to a group of family. It took me a few minutes, honestly, to wake up from whatever dissociative daydream I was going through.

I stayed back against a tree to collect myself and watched the rest of them mingle like weirdos because who could mingle *at a time like this?* I fought to make sense of reality. Funerals were so weird. Monika was crying and hugging Uncle Andy and Uncle Frank. Uncle Andy said his goodbyes, then waved at me. I gave a little wave back.

Then, Monika and Uncle Frank became very animated. Bits and pieces of their angry-sounding voices carried on the fall breeze, but I couldn't hear what they were saying. I immediately wanted the tea. Placing my sunglasses on my face, I went into stealth mode and side-eyed the fight between Monika and Uncle Frank. I totally felt like Wednesday Addams because my family was just as weird.

Soon, they parted ways angrily. Monika stomped toward me, both her arms crossed in front of her, looking mad as hell. Uncle Frank threw his hands in the air and looked like he was trying to wave a bunch of black flies away from his body and head.

Mom grabbed my arm and said, "Let's go."

I replied "Hey!" and tried to pull my arm away because it hurt.

Mom apologized, straightened out her dress, and said, "I'm proud of you, baby."

I rubbed my arm and tried to offer a smile. Even if she was mad at Uncle Frank, she didn't have to take it out on me. Still desiring the tea, I followed her toward the car and asked, "What were you fighting about with Uncle Frank?"

"Nothing, really. He's just being weird about the cabin stuff."

The cabin was where Nana lived during the last twenty-five years of her life, at least from what I'd heard during the talk around the funeral. She was a biologist and an immunologist and had been doing some work for the actual government. Turns out, Nana was sort of a baddie in her day. "Like, he was being weird about who the cabin is going to belong to?"

"Yeah," she said, getting into the car with a sigh. I sat down in the passenger seat and stared at her expectantly as she started up and began driving the car toward Nana's cabin where we'd be staying. "Uncle Frank is acting really weird. But we didn't drive all the way here just to stay in an Airbnb. It's not like he can't stay at the cabin with us, too. I just want to sort through Nana's things."

"So, he's mad we're staying there?"

"Yeah, he keeps saying it won't be safe because of the work Nana was doing and because of the bears out there."

"I thought they killed the bear after?"

"They did, but there's not just one bear, honey. This is Maine. They're all over the woods."

"Well, what kind of work was Nana doing that's not safe? Wasn't it just plant stuff?"

"Yeah, but it's not like she was concocting plant poisons or anything. She was basically a glorified biology teacher."

I tried to imagine Nana teaching a bunch of kids my age or even older, using corny puns like the one on the cover of the book she gave me. Monika sparked up a cigarette without noticing my open display of cringe. A strange flash of Nana getting mauled by a bear hit me, which made me want to cry, so I cleared my throat and moved out to the porch. There I sat and watched the trees blowing around in the wind.

I had two weeks off from school. I felt guilty for being excited about it at first, and even more guilty about wanting to talk about it on my TikTok live. Part of me wanted to go to school so I could hang out with Kiki and make TikToks in the gym during lunch, but I guess it was nice to, like, deal with my trauma or whatever once I thought about it, and then I didn't feel as guilty anymore.

When I helped carry Nana's casket as a pallbearer, it had hit me how sad it was that she was gone. She was *really* gone, like as in *never coming back*. But the book she left me still had her handwriting, which was mad weird because like how could she be gone forever but her handwriting looks just as new as when she first gave me the book? It was just sitting back home somewhere on my bookshelf, probably next to my Rupi Kaur poetry and I could still, like, look at her handwriting any time I wanted.

Then, I thought about how I would feel if Monika died and, like, how I would deal with it. Nana was old, but she'd been *killed*. I couldn't even imagine how scary it must have been for her. I wondered if we were in any danger at the cabin. But Uncle Andy had said that they shot the bear that killed Nana and that bear attacks were rare. Just bad luck.

Mom and I had been sorting through Nana's things for a couple of days already because she had to decide what to keep and what to sell or give to other families or Goodwill. I'd seen no bears at all, and not even that many other animals. We had to stay there for a few more days. There was going to be a meeting for everyone with Nana's lawyer to figure out what Nana left them. Monika stopped asking me if I wanted any of Nana's clothes after I laughed at the massive shoulder pads stitched into one top. I would have looked like Travis Kelce in it.

Yesterday, Uncle Frank showed up, and Mom excused herself so they could talk in the backyard. I heard their voices raise before Uncle Frank came inside looking mad. He still said hi to me, but then he said, "Excuse me, Sally" before rummaging around in a bedroom by the back of the cabin. Things crashed around. When Mom came back inside, she rolled her eyes hard. Twenty minutes later, Mom and I were sitting on the couch when Uncle Frank reemerged, red faced. He left in a hurry.

"What's his deal?" I asked.

"Uncle Frank can be a weirdo sometimes. He was always a weird kid, too."

"Yeah, he seems like the quiet kid, nice guy type."

"Well, he was very close to Nana in his own way. He means well, but he's just being shady and thinks she must have money or something else of value stashed somewhere."

"Does she?" I asked, sitting up, suddenly invested.

"I already looked," Mom said. The way my jaw immediately dropped.

"MOM!" I said and play slapped her arm. We both laughed until she started crying again and excused herself.

Mom occasionally mentioned that she regretted how I didn't have an extended family in my life like she did while growing up. So far, though, from what I'd seen, I was sort of low-key glad that I had no more Uncle Franks or Cousin Lesters. I mean, yeah, they were "family", but I never really saw them or interacted with them.

I had a stronger connection with my TikTok and Instagram followers. Same with my friends on Snapchat I had Snap Streaks with for almost a year now. On TikTok, people liked my fits, commenting that I was pretty. A queen. I could talk about Addison Rae or Charli D'Amelio, and I could film makeup tutorials. What did Cousin Lester or Uncle Frank ever do for me besides act awkward AF at funerals, weddings, and the occasional Christmas get together or summer BBQ?

It was hard not being on social media while in Maine. There was no Wi-Fi, so I was experiencing withdrawals. Like,

I hadn't been able to post about what I was going through. At least when I walked outside to the top of a nearby hill, I could get reception when I held my iPhone just right and I'd had a few texts from Kiki, but some of my response texts didn't go through so I gave up trying.

The last morning, I tried to connect to my TikTok account, which was our fourth day there, I had an idea strike out of nowhere. I was trying to see how many likes my BTS TikTok video had accumulated, so I went to the top of the hill and waited for the phone to get a signal, but it froze on a baking TikTok.

At first, it annoyed me, but as it buffered, I noticed this completely gorgeous woman just baking a pie, living her best life, received so many views and likes. She was making blueberry pie. I thought of Nana's blueberry pie when it hit me. I could do soooooo many aesthetic things to make my TikToks pop. Everyone loved grandmothers, so I could totally talk about Nana and her pie and what it meant to me. I could make her pie and then start a baking TikTok glow up.

This was my plan to go viral.

Back at the cabin, which Mom referred to as the "cozy lit-tle A-Frame" to anyone she mentioned it to, I rummaged through Nana's old things. Starting in the kitchen, I hoped to find her cookbook, but after a couple of dead ends, I moved to the room Uncle Frank had torn apart a few days back. I combed through Nana's belongings while Mom ran a few errands. That left me the whole place to myself.

With each item I handled, I felt like I got to know Nana as a woman beyond her title of "Nana." For one, she appar-ently loved to read because stacks of books filled the room. She liked F. Scott Fitzgerald a lot based on how many of his books she owned. She also had multiple copies of *The Great Gatsby* in different editions nestled alongside Hemmingway and Toni Morrison. While her literary tastes were eye-open-ing, the balance of the books stood out to me as strange.

There were shelves and shelves of science books and journals written by people I'd never heard of before (all of whom I assumed were wicked smart.) After opening a few and trying to understand the contents, I gave up. Many appeared to revolve around Nana's interests. She worked with plants.

A soft scratch at the door caused me to stop rifling through things. I listened to see if Monika was back. "Mom?" I asked out loud after a few moments of silence.

There was no response, so I went back to sifting through the old stuff. There were multiple tops with ever bigger shoulder pads, and a whole drawer of eyeglasses (one with cool pink frames I planned to ask mom if I could keep).

I found more books, including a small, stamped copy of *Little Women* she apparently bought at the Orchard House in Concord, Massachusetts. That was where Louisa May Alcott wrote *Little Women*. But still no cookbook. Sighing in frustration, I plopped down on a pile of clothes in the middle of the floor. Before I knew it, I was asleep.

When I woke, I was unsure how much time had passed. It wasn't dark out, but the sun was low in the sky. I rolled over, which is when I spotted it. Under the bed, hugging tight to the shadows, sat a small metal box. Next to the box was a leather book the binding of which read "RECIPES." I grabbed the book and opened it. The pages had turned yellow with time, but the handwriting remained legible.

Inside there were recipes of all sorts. Weirdly, blueberries were the key ingredient in most of them. Blueberry whoopie pies, blueberry cobbler, lemon-blueberry cake, blueberry-pecan pancake bread pudding, blueberry pie bars, lemon poppyseed crepes with blueberry cream cheese filling, and finally—a blueberry pie labeled *Blueberries for Sally*. Jackpot!

I could see it now, me, wearing a cute blue dress, making pies and pastries and cakes on TikTok. But what would my username be? My PFP would be easy. I'd have my friend Millie draw me in front of a blueberry-colored background. The username was trickier. *BlueberryBakesBySally*? Too long. *BerrySweetASMR*? Corny. Obvious. *BlueberriesForSally*? Still long, but it might work.

While daydreaming, I flipped through the rest of the book, thinking of various trends I could push. That's when a tiny key fell from the book into my lap. I immediately remembered the metal box from under the bed. I set the cookbook aside and grabbed the box. It felt light for being made of metal. Setting it in my lap, I inserted the key and opened the lid.

Inside the box were notes, disorganized and handwritten in Nana's immaculate way. I couldn't make sense of most of them because they looked like scientific formulas. There were also some photographs of blueberry bushes and blueberries. The pics reminded me of my friend Kiki's pics, that she takes on an Instax polaroid camera. Blueberries in the photos appeared in different growth stages. Someone had labelled the pics of plants.

The no-longer-a-mystery box also contained vials of blue liquid. It looked like blueberry juice. There was also a map of the cabin with a diagram explaining where Nana's special blueberries grew. Finally, there were pictures of a bear in the blueberry field.

I froze. Was that the same bear that had gotten Nana? Had she been feeding the bear the special blueberries? Were they safe to eat? I ate them before, and nothing happened to me. The berries must be okay for humans to eat. Maybe not the bears, though?

My heart pounded in my chest as I considered all the new tea I'd have to share with mom. Was this what Uncle Frank was looking for? Should I hide it? Should I even tell Mom I found it in the first place? First thing first, I wanted to see the blueberry patch for myself. If it was even there anymore. And if it was, I planned to get the blueberries before Uncle Frank. I think Nana would want me to have them if she knew about my possible Shein sponsorship. Maybe I could even get Temu. But first, the blueberries. I hid the box in a cabinet over the fridge and left the cabin.

Finding the blueberry patch was easier than I thought, considering the complicated map. After a twenty-minute convoluted walk, I discovered the patch. The spot overflowed with blueberries. Some of the outer bushes appeared as picked clean, but those in the middle had the most plump, juicy-looking berries I'd ever seen in my life. Nana was a genius.

I picked a berry that felt heavy for its size and bit into it. The flavor hit differently from any other blueberry I'd had, even better than those in the pie years ago. Before realizing it, I picked berry after berry, shoving them into my mouth. Soon I'd picked clean almost an entire bush on my own. I slowed down, allowing more time to savor the flavor and juicy tang of the berries.

"Hey, kiddo. I've been looking for this patch for a while now."

Startled, I tried to scream, but with a mouthful of blueberries I gargled instead as blueberry juice rolled down my chin. My heart shot into my throat. Uncle Frank noticed me choking.

"Oh my god," Uncle Frank said, rushing over to me. "Are you okay?" I pointed to my throat, making it clear I couldn't breathe. "Jesus, Sally, hang on."

Uncle Frank gave me the Heimlich maneuver. Clotted and clumped blueberry skins shot from my esophagus onto the ground. He let go, and I dropped to my hands and knees, taking in huge gasps of air. Uncle Frank patted my back.

"Sally, are you okay? You scared me there."

"Yeah," I managed, between gasps. "I'm sorry. You scared the crap out of me."

"I'm sorry. I watched you walk from the cabin toward the middle of nowhere. With Nana's bear incident in the rearview, I couldn't let you go alone."

"But they shot the bear, didn't they?" I rolled over to sit down against a large rock. Uncle Frank stayed kneeling next to me with hands clasped over his knees. I let the air flow back into my lungs. My vision darkened around the edges before Uncle Frank saved me. "Thank you, by the way," I said.

"Yes, they shot it, but the bear's body went missing, so we don't know if it is actually dead. The game warden told us to be careful and keep an eye out, as it might come back to its old hunting ground if it's still alive." Uncle Frank motioned to his chin. "You've got some juice on your chin there."

I wiped my chin with a nearby leaf and it came away streaked with a purple-blue color.

"Speaking of," he continued, "You do realize these are berries that Nana was tinkering with, right? That is why I've urged your mother not to stay here. It's dangerous and you don't even know if those are safe to eat. Did you find my mom's notes? Is that how you found this place?"

"What's in the notes?" I asked, trying to play dumb before realizing I didn't understand the notes anyway, so I didn't really have to lie to Uncle Frank.

"I don't know. But some feds came and asked to buy her research papers. I didn't know where they were. They said it was important it didn't fall into the wrong hands, and that if I found it, I should call them."

"That's why you and Mom have been arguing."

"Yeah, your mother is just as stubborn as mine was. I think it comes from the Irish side of our family. Anyway, you didn't answer my question. Did you find Nana's research notes?"

"How much money were they going to give us?" I asked.

"It was a lot. Enough to set us up as a family for life, honestly. But only if it's the research notes they were looking for. She's supposed to have some special serum in some vials and some formulas for genetically altering the DNA of blueberries. Your Nana was working with other scientists, trying to cultivate a special strain of blueberry filled with major health benefits."

"Does Mom know?"

"Your Mom just doesn't understand your Nana's work. She's never understood it. You've probably heard her say this, but she's convinced Nana's work wasn't science based."

"Well, if I found it, how much money would I get? I'm trying to start up a TikTok brand and I need money to buy everything I'm going to need for the videos."

"You found it, then? Tell me where it is. Do you have it with you now?"

He grabbed my arm a little too roughly. I backed up and reflexively ripped my arm from his grasp. I backed away.

"I'm sorry, Sally, I'm just kind of frustrated. It's a lot of money, and none of us knows what to do with her research, anyway. I didn't mean to grab your arm so hard. It's just that they think these berries might be dangerous. They kept asking if I'd noticed Nana moving after she died. Such a thought angered me while I was dealing with her death. I told them to fuck off, but they left me with a business card."

I seriously considered telling Frank where the pages were, but I didn't want to miss out on any money. It also felt wrong telling him without talking to Mom first. I backed up and Uncle Frank took a step forward. That's when the bear behind him stood on its hind legs, casting a shadow over both of us.

"Holy sh…" was all Uncle Frank could get out before the bear pounced.

Its claws were massive and went through Frank's chest as if it were paper. Frank screamed as the bear chewed on his face. The beast stretched Frank's bottom lip until it tore away. Frank screamed the entire time while the bear tore skin from chin and cheek as well.

One side of the bear's head was visible to me. The fur looked like it was singed, and its skull lined with cracks. There were pocks on its face, maybe the result of a shotgun blast. A horrid ripping sound brought me back to what I tried to block out. The bear tore off a huge chunk of Uncle Frank's face from his chin up to the area right under one eye. Uncle Frank's jaw and mandibles were in full view.

I retched into the grass, then ran for the cabin. As I rushed past the distracted bear, I heard Uncle Frank's screaming cease when the bear crushed my uncle's throat. The cries turned to gurgles and then nothing.

I ran as fast as I could toward the direction I'd come from. Panic set in as I wondered if I was going the right way. I didn't want to go deeper into the woods with that thing out in the wild. So many thoughts ran through my head that I couldn't really deal with or process. Uncle Frank was unalived by that massive bear. But how could the bear attack with half its face blown off?

Somewhere along the way, I realized I'd been crying. The tears made it hard to see, and I stumbled over branches and rocks with no time to stop and collect myself. Looking over my shoulder, I glimpsed the bear jogging toward me. It had finished with Uncle Frank and now came for me. Blood soaked its face, front legs, and chest.

Fear filled my guts, and I wiped my eyes with my arms and pumped my legs as hard as I could. Nobody told me how fast bears can run even with a limp (its front left leg looked to be damaged). It was gaining fast. I was out of breath but had to keep moving or I was cooked. My breaths came in gasps, like when I choked on the blueberries. I didn't dare to look behind me. I could hear the bear's body bounding behind me, breaking branches and rustling leaves in its path of murder.

Soon, the cabin came into view, but I feared I wouldn't make it. One minor slip meant getting torn apart, like Uncle Frank and Nana. I screamed for Mom, thinking how if I got out of this, I would never call her Monika again. She was my mother, and I loved her.

That's when the bear bit my shirt all the way through to part of the skin on my back. Luckily it hadn't grabbed hold fully, but I felt the gash as my shirt tore off at the hem, exposing my lower back to the chill fall air. The bear, maybe thinking it had grabbed more than just part of my clothes, stopped momentarily to maul the piece of shirt in its maw. It shook its head violently. I focused on getting to the front door of the cabin, which was already open.

When I ran inside, I screamed for mom and slammed the door behind me, locking it and pushing a chair against it. Shaking, I backed away from the door as the bear caught up and slammed its body against the door. It roared, which sent chills down my spine. I moved a hand to my back and when I looked at my palm, it had streaks of blood on it.

"Mom," I shouted again.

Something gurgled behind me. I turned, confused. Mom stood there, embraced by what looked like Nana. Except Nana looked as though she had ridden through a woodchipper, or, of course, mauled by a bear. Mom's eyes were lifeless. Nana held my mother upright while tearing large chunks of flesh out of Mom's neck.

Calling for my mother drew Nana's attention. Nana turned to me and dropped my mother to the ground. Jagged claw marks covered much of Nana's mutilated face where the bear had mauled her. Seeing her torn flesh up close reminded me why the funeral was a closed casket. Then I wondered who would carry my casket.

"Nana," I said, unable to move.

And then she hugged me, too.

The Spot

CULVER CITY, CALIFORNIA

Warning: Before I get into describing the coffee shop that inspired this story, I ask you to proceed with caution. I don't generally write extreme horror or splatterpunk even though Kirkus said of Abject Fear, "the horror sequences are delightfully grotesque..." While we have had plenty of gore in all volumes of Coffeeshop so far, this one might be the closest to splatterpunk. I only warn based on a history of other stories in the series being less violent. If you're cool with that, strap in and let's go.

The Spot is a cool, unique, well, spot in a quiet part of Culver City California. While businesses around this place have come and gone, The Spot has remained for as long as I can remember. It may have been a different coffee shop years prior, but it has been there as long as I can remember.

What is unique about the place is how tight the space is, and that is not a drawback. Past the parking in the rear is a screen door. As soon as one enters the bathrooms are on the left and after that it is one tight squeeze of a corridor lined with tables designed for four. Cool artwork hangs on the walls. I mislabel it as tight. It is intimate.

Once past the intimate area, the place opens into a larger room at the front, but the counter takes up most of that space and there is some more seating as well outside next to the street. Unlike many of the coffee shops I have visited over the years for these anthologies, this one is known for its boba.

The clientele is mostly youthful, a blend of local school kids when the nearby high school lets out, but soon after that it becomes a spot for college kids to study, work, and socialize. While writing there I overheard students talking about high rents and how they were forced to live with multiple room-mates.

Those conversations combined with the narrow hallway (which turned into a staircase in my story) inspired this grue-some tale.

DRINK RECOMMENDATION: For this one, I recom-mend a green tea boba.

When One Door Opens

PAUL CARRO

"**D**on't die Bessie, please!"

Bessie was my bestest girl, but I could tell she wasn't long for this world. I worked since age sixteen to purchase Bessie back in my senior year of high school. Now she was the only reason I remained in college. Because I am not the living large type, my jobs are paying my tuition. My car, Bessie, was essential to my employment as a pizza delivery driver. The other more famous food delivery companies deemed Bessie unreliable, so I had to find work where I could get it. Joe's Pizza it was.

But now, in the middle of nowhere, my car shuddered as if begging to stop on its way to that great rust bucket retreat in the sky. *Tik-tik-tik. Tik-tik-tik.* That shrill noise always signaled engine failure. The last time I stalled it cost me four hundred I didn't have, that I never have. But maybe I would have the cash if people treated delivery drivers better.

There are two types of people in this world. Those who tip and assholes. I wasn't sure which type (let me check the order again) Tina Ono was going to be. I would soon find out whether she, he, or they were going to be cool or not. Cellphones did not work in "the outer reaches" as those of us at the pizza shop called the countryside. With no internet, Tina had ordered eight large pizzas from a landline. Without the app, there was no way to tip in advance. The revelation of her character would come during a face-to-face showdown.

City planners built the college campus in farm country. Back downtown, where the school is located, apartments are everywhere and then the town gives way to mini mansions that house overpaid professors. Beyond all that, the town turns into dense forest and farmland. While plenty of local farmers ate pizza, they were all in bed by eight o'clock.

Since I was on a midnight delivery, it meant college kids had ordered. It was my last run of the night if I could make it. *Tik-tik-tik. Tik-tik-tik.* Hang on Bessie! As a sophomore, I still lived in the dorms with freshmen because of my financial situation (financial aid paid for my dorm room). Other upper classmen moved out of dorms as soon as possible.

Where they sometimes moved to were old farmhouses. The enormous properties made perfect rentals because of their size. It was not uncommon to cram as many coeds as they could into the one house to defray rent costs.

The farmhouses doubled as informal frats and sororities. Parties at the farmhouses were legendary. Not that I would know firsthand because I held three jobs just to stay in school. (Besides pizza delivery, I am a tutor, and social media guru.) Most students I met were on the mommy and daddy financial plan. Not me. I delivered food to parties, rather than attended them.

Bessie spit and sputtered and shook like a TikTok dancer as I drove up a steep driveway once I finally found the place. Remote as hell. No wonder there was no cell service. *Tik-tik-tik. Tik-tik-tik.* Hang on, girl. I was reluctant to turn off the engine for fear it would not restart when I returned, but maybe Bessie needed a rest was all.

Looking through my car's cracked windshield, I examined the front yard. There were plenty of vehicles in the driveway (all fancier than mine), but the place looked kind of dead. The farmhouse stood three stories high, with a bonus attic based on the tiny windows crammed in just below the eaves. A few lights were on inside, but not enough to scream kegger. Maybe the action was in the back of the house.

Only one way to find out. I grabbed the pizzas out of the thermal bags, stacked them on the roof of my car before scooping the pile into my arms. If I didn't smell like pizza from working in the shop all day, I did now. But I was not trying to impress anyone beyond eking out a substantial tip from college kids that were better off than me.

The leaning tower of pizza was heavy, so I rushed to the door. I was not a gym guy, and ate mostly cheap frozen dinners, so I rated high on the beanpole scale. Five or more pizzas were a struggle, especially while climbing such a long driveway. The place had a wraparound porch. I climbed those steps, walked to the door, knocked, and it creaked open.

Honest to goodness creaked. Not good. A crowd waiting for pizzas should have drowned out the creepy squeal of old hinges. That meant the party was likely on the property out back which meant more walking for me. Still, I had to check. I leaned my head in and yelled hello.

A whiff of something other than pepperoni hit my nose. I scrunched my face. Something smelled yuck. Probably manure, or twelve guys crammed into one home. Either way, the dank pizza odor covered the smell a bit.

I stepped into an enormous foyer. A staircase rose above me alongside a hallway that ran straight to the back of the house. The stairs were creepy AF. Lights glowed from somewhere on the various floors, but it was mostly dark and hard to see. The steps ran straight to the highest level of the house with corridor outlets branching off on every level. The higher steps vanished into shadows.

A swing door stood off to my left. I pushed that open and yelled another hello. The smell grew stronger, so I stepped away. It was a dimly lit kitchen. There was no one there, which made sense. Why cook when pizza was on the way? The door continued swinging as I stepped back into the foyer. Sucker was on very loose hinges. I would have stopped it were my hands not occupied with increasingly heavy boxes.

Light spilled from an open arched doorway to my right, so I walked through it. "Pizza delivery!" I said loud enough not to sneak up on someone and scare them. No one answered. I was in an enormous living room.

Not cool! The room freaked me out. For starters, burning candles took up every corner of the room. My bowels clenched like I needed to take a dump, but I didn't know why. Then suddenly I got a hint. My brain finally caught up to what I was subconsciously staring at.

A freaking Ouija board sat in the middle of the living room on a glass coffee table. It looked different and older than the one I played with as a kid at a friend's house. Everyone knew someone who had a Ouija board. My friend who owned one was Frankie. Frankie was a weird kid.

I looked down at the Ouija board and noticed the heart-shaped thing with a magnifying piece of glass in the center was cracked. (And wet?) It looked like someone spilled a drink. Which reminded me I needed to locate the party. Except it was way too quiet. Another open arch doorway across the living room opened into deeper parts of the house.

Moving in that direction and feeling every calory in the pizzas, I spotted a vast, dark section of the house with twin corridors leading to who knows where. An outdoor porch light in the way back shined through a backdoor window. As my eyes adjusted to the gloom, a light turned on in a distant bedroom with an open door.

Even from a distance, it appeared to be a female student's room. I could be wrong, but who cares? Lots of pink, whoever it belonged to. A woman exited the room, only to vanish into the darkness of a distant corridor.

The brief glimpse revealed a woman with a skin tone whose nationality escaped me from such a distance. I think she was Asian, but I could not tell for certain, not that it mattered. She was hot whoever she was.

Long black hair cascaded over her back and shoulders like a furry waterfall. I couldn't see her face because her head was turned, but her tall, athletic body was Only Fans material. The toned woman stood about five-seven.

What struck me the most were her boobs. The woman wore nothing but a white bra and panties. Not the white that hangs loose kind of bra, or even the Vickie's Secret sexy style, but pure functional support for a well-endowed woman. Like the Seinfeld episode, I couldn't look away, but she simply walked into darkness and was gone. There was something off about the way she moved, but then she moved too fast, and I was focused on the tits.

I am not proud of my reaction, but it is what it is. It's a college town and there are lots of hot students. It is not every day I get to see any in their underwear. Still, I don't enjoy sneaking up on women or leering. Besides, from what I saw, she could probably kick my ass. I should have called out, but my bowel clenching grew worse. I didn't know why.

Because the place was so quiet, (where was everybody?) I was able to overhear footsteps walking up the stairs back in the foyer. Heavy and lazy footsteps climbed. It had to be the woman I just saw. Obviously, the corridor ahead led back to the stairwell, but I didn't know for sure, so I returned the way I came.

By the time I reached the foyer, I saw the woman near the third floor, climbing up the steps. Her ass, which I had failed to notice before, was spectacular. Still, I could not see her face, just the long hair and super tight butt. She vanished into shadows before I could even gather myself.

I was at a loss. With no cellphone reception, I couldn't call Tina or the pizza shop to see if anyone called with updated instructions. There was no way the nearly naked student was Tina. Pizza boy fantasies were just that. No woman dressed like the woman on the stairs and ordered pizza. They used ring cameras and told people to leave it on the stoop in most cases.

Not only did we not get banged on the job, but most people labeled us losers. (Yet those same people couldn't get by without us.) No, the woman above was likely a drunk or stoned roomie. I was not against taking my tip in weed, but first I had to find somebody who knew about the order.

They had to be out back. I looked back to the front door and figured it was best to exit, circle around the house, and find Tina and the big party. As I turned back toward the front door, the strangest thing sounded behind me. Something dropped onto the stairs from high above. It sounded like a ball bouncing down the stairs, thumping on various steps but without the normal buoyancy of a basketball. No pok-pok-pok, just a thump as the ball hit random steps.

The thumping got louder as it grew closer. It picked up speed as it neared me. By the time I turned, it was already on the last steps. The 'ball' rolled to my feet and stopped.

It was a fucking head! A decapitated noggin of a dude about my age. The dead dude looked as surprised as me. The pizzas flew from my hands and splattered across the hallway. Feet shuffled upstairs, reacting to my yelp.

I was scared so shitless I couldn't even reach for the exit. My hands waved about instinctively, trying to catch the pizzas, but they were already gone. I yanked my foot away from the gory decapitated head, stumbled back, and saw the freakiest thing I ever witnessed in my life.

Thump-thump, thump-thump. The ominous sound originated in the shadows. It was rhythmic enough to dance to. *Thump-thump, thump-thump.* Then the sound's source revealed itself. White bra girl, except she wasn't walking down the stairs, she was walking down the freaking banister!

Thump-thump, thump-thump! Right foot left foot. She didn't even stretch her arms out for balance. The angled handrail was thinner than a balance beam. Not even a gymnast should have been able to navigate it so confidently. Something remained off about her head. Not that I cared because I wanted out the moment that she picked up the pace.

Thump-thump,   thump-thump,   thump-thump, thump-thump! She ran down the banister never missing a step. But I did. I turned to the open front door, and it slammed violently shut on its own. There was no breeze, just the whoosh of the door before it slammed closed. My foot landed on one of the fallen pizzas.

I might as well have been wearing skates on an ice pond at that point. I slid across the floor and hit the kitchen swing door. The door offered no resistance, so I flew through and landed on linoleum. Like earlier, the door swung wildly open and closed. Each time the door opened I glimpsed her feet moving closer to the end of the banister.

The smell from earlier had grown worse, or I had landed closer to the source. The scent was not cow manure. I knew that odor from driving around the countryside. No, the stench resembled spoiled meat, an odor I knew from the pizza shop. Glancing over my shoulder, I spotted the refrigerator door open. It was the only source of light in the kitchen.

Thumping ceased. I looked at the door and understood why. She had reached the end of the railing. Through three successive swings of the door, I saw the woman leap off the end of the banister and land in a full-blown comic book movie three-point stance.

I rose and started to close the refrigerator door, with the hopes of plunging the room into darkness to buy myself time. But moving the door revealed something horrible behind it. An arm fell on my foot.

A body sat slumped against the wall on the floor, previously hidden behind the open refrigerator door. It was a guy, in sweats, sort of. Once upon a time gray, the sweatpants were mostly red. Our college logo lined the leg of his sweats, but every second letter dripped with blood.

I had to focus on the college logo, otherwise I would have focused on the horrible image of a student missing both heads! There was nothing sitting above the torn flesh of his neck. And somehow worse, (so much worse) a tear in the fabric near his groin revealed a fleshy hole where a penis used to be. I wanted to throw up, but the swinging door stopped mid-swing, held firm by the hand of the woman in the bra.

"*Tik-tik-tik-tik,*" she said, which made no sense.

White bra lady stood sideways in the doorway, not facing me directly. I was so frightened that I could not focus on her physique anymore, even though such a profile view would normally have been my weak spot. Except I had no time for that. The same thing that made my bowels clench earlier told me if I did not run, everything would be over. I closed the refrigerator door completely, which engulfed the kitchen in darkness. I hoped it would buy me time.

I scrambled for a nearby door at the back of the kitchen. It took me into a hallway with no good options. Doors lined the corridor, which split off further down the hall, but I could not spot a rear entrance from where I was. A window would do. I entered the third room I came to and closed the door behind me. There was no lock. The room had pictures of women on a desk and walls. Everything was soft blue and smelled nice, especially after the rotting meat in the kitchen.

A window took up part of a wall near the foot of the bed. I rushed to it, lifted the sash, hoping I could fit, when something grabbed my ankle. It frightened me so much I kicked out instinctively, even as I fell. I struck something soft and heard someone cry out in pain. Footsteps thudded down the hall outside.

I fell on my ass and spotted a woman under the bed. She placed a finger over her bleeding lips and waved for me to join her. I scrambled underneath as the door burst open with tremendous force. White bra girl's feet came into view, and I finally understood why she seemed "off." The woman walked sideways rather than straight.

"Tik-tik-tik-tiiiiikkkk!"

There was anger in the woman's nonsensical vocal cord glitching, which reminded me of my car protesting before it died. I wished I could be in Bessie right then, driving away with my tip, but no, I was under a bed with a woman (instead of on top of a bed with one) while another woman stalked the both of us.

White bra lady's voice was deep and guttural as it spoke in ticks rather than words. It took everything in me not to scream when the window I had opened slammed shut with a tremendous bang. Then it opened and closed, over and over. That made no sense because the woman remained standing in the doorway. The window somehow moved on its own. After slamming multiple times, the glass shattered and rained down. Shards lined the floor near where I hid under the bed with an unknown female. She gripped my hand, and I gripped back.

At the door, bra lady leaped out of my view, straight up. I heard scrambling, like fingernails and feet racing across a floor on all fours. Except she was not on the floor as far as I could tell. I finally isolated the sound. It came from the ceiling as she somehow crawled across it! Then a loud crash sounded, and the last remnants of glass tinkled to the floor. The awful tik-tik of her odd, deep voice had ceased, and all went quiet. It was hard to know for certain, but it appeared as if bra lady had left the building. The woman under the bed scrambled out into the open.

"Hurry, we need to go," she said.

"You're bleeding," is all I could say as I crawled out and stood before her.

"Thanks to you. You kicked my face."

"I am so sorry," I said.

"Seriously? We don't have time for this."

She rushed to the door. I was not so quick to follow. Bloody handprints ran in a straight line across the ceiling, vanishing near the broken window. White bra had indeed crawled across the ceiling.

"What the f..." I started, but the woman grabbed me and yanked me out into the hall. I pointed back. "Crawled. She crawled across the ceiling."

"That was a novelty about thirty minutes ago. We need to get to a phone," she said.

"We need to get to my car and get out of here," I said.

She grabbed my hand and pulled me toward the stairs. "He is outside, so we don't have long. We have two phones. One is in the kitchen but I'm not going where... Justin is. The other is on the third floor."

For the first time since I kicked her in the face, the woman on the stairs seemed vulnerable. She obviously knew the headless corpse. We ran up the stairs and I finally noticed what my under the bed friend looked like. The woman wore fleece shorts that said Juicy on the ass. She also wore a tank top in a matching color.

"You said he's outside," I said, out of breath as we raced up the stairs.

We neared the second-floor landing, and she spoke over her shoulder. "It was Tina, but now it's Hairy."

"Harry?"

"Not a guy's name like that. Hairy, like..." she pulled at her blonde hair.

"Tina is now Hairy?" I asked, confused.

"Mmmmff," someone whimpered in the distance.

Juicy raced down the hall. I eyed the third floor where Juicy mentioned the phone was, but I didn't know my way around, so I followed her. Juicy stepped into a dark room and opened the closet. Inside sat a woman pressed against clothes and other crap. The woman's navy quarter-zip top dripped blood. Someone had torn the fabric across her chest, exposing a breast. The rip was large enough to reveal both tits, but I only spotted the one. Then I saw the second boob dangling down toward her belly, barely hanging on by a thread of skin.

"Steph," Juicy whispered. "Can you walk?"

"My boob, she nearly tore it off," Steph whimpered.

"I know, hon, but we need to run," Juicy said.

Steph nodded and cradled the dangling body part as Juicy helped her to her feet. Juicy leaned Steph against me and rushed to the bed where she yanked a sheet free and returned to her friend.

Juicy started from below the boob and quickly wrapped the sheet around Steph in a way that lifted the damaged tit slightly, pushing it roughly back in place. Steph winced throughout the triage but steadied as the wrap firmed up. Never once did Steph ask who I was. That was why I knew whatever was happening was bad.

"Where is she?" Steph asked.

"It is not she. Not Tina anymore. It is Hairy," Juicy said. "Hairy is outside, but not for long. He knows how many of us are alive. Let's go."

Steph nodded in agreement. They were speaking a foreign language, but I followed them as they ran upstairs and rushed down the hallway. We stopped and someone cursed.

"The phone is freaking gone!" Juicy cried out.

A literal hole took up part of the wall that Juicy pointed at. I assumed the hole used to hold a community phone. Prison style, for all to share. *Maybe not prison, more like asylum*, I thought. I felt I was going crazy. Juicy ran her hands through her hair and paced in a circle, murmuring.

"Hairy? Help me understand," I said.

"For weeks we have been using a Ouija board. It was fun at first, but Tina became obsessed, making us use it all the time. Most of us understood they don't work, someone is always guiding the planchette," Steph said.

"Planchette," my dumb ass asked, like I never used one before. I just didn't know the term.

"The heart-shaped thing. We were usually drunk, so it was goofy fun until we connected with someone. When we asked him to spell his name. He spelled it Hairy. We tried to correct him and tell him the spelling was like Prince Harry. Hairy moved the planchette and assured us the spelling was correct. That night Tina had a dream and drew a picture. She said this was Hairy." Steph pulled out her cellphone, doubled checked for bars and swore when there were none. Then she pulled up a pic and showed it to me.

Nope. Nope. Nope. No sir, not even. Not interested. My mind tried to justify what it was seeing on the cellphone. The drawing was pen and ink, which somehow made it worse. It showed a tall, slender figure covered head to toe in black hair. There was no mouth or nose visible, nothing but a body covered in a sea of black hair as thick as porcupine quills and a set of eyes where a face should be.

The face had something approximating a lion's mane, but darker and covering the entire face, not just its perimeter. Its arms spread out at its side like a T-Rex's arms, but rather than being useless and short, they were oversized. The freaking thing's elbows landed near its knees before the forearms spread out on either side. The legs were obscenely long as well and bent the wrong way at the knee.

"I just deliver pizzas. I need to go," I said.

I hitched up my pants (something I had never done before) and prepared to march right on back down the stairs and out the front door. Until something landed on the roof. Could have been a cougar, could have been an elephant. Heavy or light, it landed with enough force for us all to scream at once. I think my cry reached a higher pitch than the girls.

"We need to find the others," Juicy said.

"Hello?" a voice called out from a dark down the hall.

"Leeanne?" Juicy called out.

Before the woman could answer, glass and wood exploded within the same room the voice came from. Leeanne screamed and raced across the hall from the dark room to the lit one. Hairy was inches behind the poor woman.

We could not see what was happening but there were sounds of a struggle and the light inside the room shifted, moving low to the ground, likely an overturned lamp. Me and the other two girls sat frozen, terrified, trying to figure out what to do.

I didn't know what Hairy was, but clearly, he was the conductor of the train known as Tina. The image of the porcupine face with eyes that appeared soulless and cruel filled my mind. Hairy was wearing the skin of a beautiful woman, but if the drawn picture was the real deal, there was no doubt it meant harm to others.

Shnick! A horrible stabbing sound erupted at the end of the hall followed by something ripping like Velcro. A violent snap followed and Leeanne's scream, which had gone wet with a gargle, fell silent. It sounded final.

But it wasn't. Leeanne stepped out into the hall. The student walked toward us, bathed mostly in shadow. She appeared drunk, staggering on feet as if they were new and she was giving them a test run. Her footfalls were awkward.

She was alive, though. What were those sounds from the room though? Had she defeated Hairy? Was it possible? Leeanne was speaking, and it took a moment for me to understand the words. As she neared us, I heard her clearly, but the words made no sense.

"Ha, ha. Chocolate. Ha, ha. Chocolate," Leanne said, repeating the words after every footfall.

"Leanne?" Steph called out.

The shadow figure jerked her head as if attempting to nod, but it didn't work. None of us were laughing, except Leeanne, who apparently now found an ice cream flavor funny. It made no sense.

Until she stepped into the light.

Juicy buried her face into my back and screamed, muffling the cry into my clothing. I clasped my hands over my mouth and fought not to gag. Steph whimpered.

"Ha, ha. Chocolate," Leeanne said again, and we finally understood.

A bone jutted from her eye socket. The eye was gone, encircled by gore where Hairy stabbed it. The woman wore a simple nightgown that stopped midway down her ass and was covered in blood. Leeanne walked with a limp.

"Ha, ha. Chocolate. Ha, ha. Chocolate."

Leeanne walked past us as if we weren't there, heading for the stairs. When she passed, I turned and saw the most horrific thing. Her panties were gone, exposing everything below her waist. One ass cheek was missing, the flesh torn from buttock to the back of her heel.

Exposed bones gleamed white within the bloody sinew. Meat flaps dangled the length of the ruptured leg where one bone was missing. I did not know the anatomical name of the bones, never paid attention in biology, but I knew there were normally two in the lower leg, and one was missing. The break was visible. The missing one was sticking out from her eye where Hairy had lobotomized the poor student.

How Leanne still walked made no sense, but then, maybe she was not there anymore. Maybe pain became an afterthought. Maybe Leanne could no longer think. The victim neared the stairs.

"Ha, ha. Chocolate."

Leanne navigated the first stair, but the second footstep didn't take. Her broken leg finally collapsed, and she flopped like a wet sack while tumbling down the stairs. The whole time Leeanne tumbled down the steps, the woman kept laughing about chocolate.

I was so lost in watching Leeanne that I failed to see that which the girls did. They grew fixated on something at the end of the hall. Like me, they were out of screams but fear itself was endless. There, sitting cross-legged on the floor, was Tina, or Hairy. She sat in profile, her body facing the lit room, but her head faced us. She giggled, her fingers curled around her bottom lip like a child caught doing something bad.

Her giggle sounded baritone, deeper than any voice I ever heard. The *tik-tik* had ceased. Apparently, Hairy was learning how to use the vocal cords. Hairy seemed to look straight at me like I was some prize to be had.

"Brew Crew!" Juicy yelled and the women ran toward the stairs.

As usual, in the short time I had been in the house, the women said something that made little sense to me. I looked toward them, then back to Hairy and cried out in surprise. Hairy sat in the same position except on the ceiling, upside down.

"Oh, hell no!" I yelled.

When I caught up to the women they ran upstairs. That was the attic based on what I noticed from outside earlier. I had only scoped the place out because I was trying to locate signs of a party. Why would the women go up and what did brew crew mean?

I decided I did not care. I was going for my car. Down it was. That was the best option. Because I was so scared, I battled to stay on my feet as I hauled ass down the stairs. Once I hit the ground floor I grabbed the front door, turned the knob and yanked. Nothing. It would not budge!

"Shit!"

It was an old school knob. There didn't seem to be a lock of any kind, but the door would not budge. Not even an inch. In all the craziness, I had forgotten how it slammed on its own earlier. Was it too much force? Did it jam the damn thing, or was this something to do with Hairy?

As I stepped away from the door, I felt the hair rise on the back of my neck. It was quiet, too quiet. I needed to get out but was suddenly afraid to move. Turning around, I looked up those damn stairs. It was the feet I noticed first. Hairy, or Tina, or whoever, floated down the staircase, feet about one foot off the ground. She moved silently, quietly, slowly. Her body faced forward; her arms dangled at her side. She could have been a corpse the way she stood so still and loose while descending the stairs on some invisible air current.

Any other time I would have marveled at her body, but I was way past all that. It seemed impossible that the scantily clad woman posed such a threat, but then I found her face as it emerged from a shadow as she moved closer. The woman's head remained sideways, though her body remained straight. Hair covered half the woman's face. The right eye (the only one visible because of the angle of her head.) showed through the strands of hair and was white as if rolled up in her skull. Her white orb moved about like someone in REM sleep, but it remained locked on me.

I was out of there. With no interest in seeing the headless dude in the kitchen again, I ran through the living room. Blood, the liquid on and around the Ouija board, was blood. I don't know why my brain could not make the connection earlier. But then again, I once lived in a time when spilled red wine was a possibility. My mind raced as fast as my feet. I struggled to keep up with both.

Unaware where I was going, I ran through the living room toward where I first spotted Tina walking half-nude. I passed a laundry space crammed in an alcove off the corridor. A floating shadow appeared at my rear with its feet hovering above the ground. I was not sure why Hairy had gone silent. Maybe he was taking inventory. There were only so many heads of both types to rip off people's bodies left.

Turning a corner revealed a fresh row of rooms and a corridor that looked like it led back toward the foyer. The shadow following me turned the corner before the body did, and the silhouette revealed the head turned at the same forty-five-degree angle.

I think Hairy broke her neck and Tina was long gone. I wondered what happens to a possessed person if something happened to the host. How long does the new host get the car keys? I decided I would only call my pursuer Hairy now. Sadly, the young college woman was no more. I hoped she had not suffered like many of her friends had and I felt bad for leering at her when I first arrived.

Hairy's silence frightened me as much as anything else. Why had he gone quiet? My footsteps made it sound like a moose was loose in the house. I slowed my steps and tried to find the nearest exit. Then I saw the head and almost screamed.

The female head rested just outside a doorway, but on the floor. Unlike the head at the foot of the stairs earlier, this one blinked. The head shushed me and vanished back into the room. What had looked like a TikTok prank where people rested their heads at floor level to scare the Twinkies out of loved ones almost caused me to reveal my position to Hairy.

I entered the room and the woman, whose head remained connected to her shoulders, yanked me against the wall just inside the door. We stood inches from the opening. She saw in my eyes the desire to close the door. She shook her head and whispered.

"He knows which doors were open. He has been passing by for some time. I've been too afraid to move."

Never did she ask who I was, but then again, my name tag gave it away. I should have asked her name, but I had another question. "What does Brew Crew mean?"

She lit up and whispered. "Where did you hear that from?"

"Steph and some girl with Juicy written on her ass."

The woman breathed in, as if surprised anyone besides her still breathed. "We need to get to the attic. I'm Selina."

"Mike," I said, like it mattered.

Selina's hair stuck across half her face like Tina's, so I was a little nervous about whether she was legit. But she was the only lifeline I had in this house of blood. I waited for her to tell me the plan, because mine went for shit the moment the front door failed to open.

The oppressive silence made my skin crawl. There was a strange sound that accompanied someone floating rather than walking, an electricity of sorts. It was not natural and kicked in some ancestral DNA in my core. (Not the fight kind, the flight kind.) I wanted to run, but I had a companion to think about. My new best friend, perhaps the last one I would ever meet.

From where I stood against the wall, I had a limited view, but I watched Hairy's shadow cross the hallway wall. The shadow's feet remained off the ground, floating silently. A wraith on the move. Soon Hairy was gone. The danger had temporarily passed, but my fear continued to build. There was something in the way the shadow moved at the end that bothered me. My lizard brain tried to warn me of something.

Selina did not pick up what my internal vibe was throwing down. Maybe the multiple sweeps by the floating dick-ripper had turned routine for her. I don't know her life. But when she headed toward the hallway, the intangible danger took shape. A black cloud dangled from the ceiling just outside the door. No, not a cloud.

Hair!

Too late. I cried out to Selina, but she was already screaming. Hairy's hair dangled from above, where he levitated against the hallway ceiling. Selina noticed a strand brush against her face as she exited the room but by then it was too late.

Hairy grabbed Selina's hair and lifted her off the ground. Selina kicked and wailed while being dragged toward the ceiling. Hairy laughed so deeply I felt it in my chest. I reached out for Selina. She grabbed my hand, and her cries ceased when the unthinkable happened. Hairy had waited for me to act as an anchor and then he yanked with that meth-head strength.

The ripping sound was sickening. Selina and I looked at one another as we fought to understand the source of the sound. When blood splashed my face, I had a good idea. Selina's forehead skin had torn away along with the balance of her scalp. She dropped to the floor in a heap.

Selina landed, bounced after hitting the floor, and fell against the nearest wall at a weird angle because I still held one of her hands. Her head pulsed with blood in a way that looked like ants were marching across her skull, but it was merely rivulets searching for an out. She was confused.

"What happened? What happened Mike?"

I tried to tell her, but my mouth threatened to fill with vomit, so I kept it shut. Before I could puke, she was on her feet. A wet splotch hit my shoulder. It felt substantial, like a rat. I screamed and brushed it away. Her scalp fell to the floor with a sick squish. Hairy had dropped it on me. He cackled with glee even as he descended in a float back toward the floor.

We didn't wait for him to land. Selina, in warrior mode, led us back to the stairs. She rambled about the other housemates and the brew crew. I followed her despite believing it was a bad idea to go up. Lights flickered all around us. Lights in various rooms turned on and off.

We arrived on the second floor when it hit her. Selina screamed and fell to her knees on the steps, almost tumbling back down, but I was there to stop her.

"It hurts, oh it hurts! What happened Mike? What happened?"

Blood had already poured down the back and sides of her head while we ran, but leaned forward as she was, the blood poured down her face. She wiped at it, then looked at her crimson hand.

"What? What? Oh, please, it hurts. My hair? Is it..."

Laughter from the bottom of the stairs. Hairy had discovered his feet again. His feet hit the floor with every step, smacking harder than normal footsteps, like someone still learning to walk and thinking stomping feet was the norm.

"We have to go," I said.

"I can't. My hair, oh my head, oh please make it stop."

She started crying, but I grabbed her under her arms and lifted her to her feet, taking her along for the ride. She knew something I didn't about the attic. We needed to get there sooner rather than later, because Hairy leaped onto the banister again and climbed at that crazy speed. Thankfully, climbing up a banister took more effort, so Hairy moved slightly slower. I carried Selina.

Selina wailed in pain the entire time and who could blame her? She was going white, and I worried if we did not hurry,

I'd end up carrying nothing but a corpse. The splotches of her hair that remained on her head soaked up some of the blood which had already begun clotting.

We reached the last mini set of steps that led to a half-door. I pounded and yelled for them to let us in.

"Who are you?" Someone on the other side yelled.

"Mike," I said, looking back. Hairy was gaining.

"Who?"

"Pizza guy. The pizza guy."

"Guys, it's me," my half-corpse partner said.

"Selina?" a voice inside asked.

The door opened. Juicy and Steph held metal baseball bats. They looked past the two of us and screamed. Hairy was in view. They screamed for us to hurry. I ducked and entered, but Selina did not get the memo. Her head hit the low door frame. A splotch splashed a dash of gore on the frame and onto me. She did not scream, simply uttered an odd "ugh" before her body dropped to the floor and she went into a seizure.

Problem was, she blocked the door. The women dropped their bats, and each grabbed an arm, yanking Selina inside. I slammed the door closed even as Hairy hit the other side. He struck the door so hard I bounced away but fell right back into it. I locked it but figured it would not hold for long.

But immediately, the pounding stopped. The women were pulling Selina clear and panicking over her condition. Then they looked at me and screamed. Unable to see what spooked them, I assumed it was all the blood on my shirt. I stepped toward them, waving at the shirt.

"It's not mine, it's hers, he scalped her, he…"

The laughter shook the floor, a mini quake. I looked back at the door, which had a small gap underneath. There, one eye surrounded by strands of hair looked in at us. Hairy was impossibly bent or floating upside down, as he did not appear crouched. Either way, he had one eye from that weird turned head looking our way.

Storage boxes of clothes sat next to a bag filled with aluminum bats. I grabbed the boxes and stacked them against the bottom of the door. That move prompted an angry whap on the door, but at least Hairy was temporarily blind.

Selina had stopped seizing but lay still, moaning. Juicy rushed over to the boxes and grabbed some shirts from one. The tees were team shirts with the name Brew Crew on them, along with a red Solo cup.

"Our softball gear. We used to be on an intramural team," Steph said, as if reading my mind.

They acted as a team. Juicy arrived with the tee shirts. Steph cradled Selina in her lap. Neither woman asked what happened, or how. The women went to work and tried to soothe their friend.

"Honey, this is going to hurt like a bitch, but we have to stop the bleeding, okay?" Steph said.

Selina just moaned. Then the women wrapped tees around Selina's head. The cloth blotted with blood. Selina's eyes went wide, then she thrashed about, kicking her heels against the floorboards, fighting her rescuers.

"Help us!" Juicy yelled at me.

I dropped to the floor, pressed my hands against Selina's tits, and pushed her hard onto the floor. She eyed me and growled, frothing at the mouth and cursing while the women tied off the shirts. I couldn't even dig up a primal sexual urge for the contact I had with Selina. We were just four flesh bags fighting to survive. Nothing else mattered.

Wham! The window opened and closed. Though not full-sized, the attic windows still had upper and lower sashes. The window rose and fell like a blinking eye.

I thought we'd have more time. The single bulb in the room flickered. The door shuddered like a hurricane trying to blow it open. With a loud crack, the lock snapped, and the door blew open. Deep, grotesque laughter filled the room.

Selina was moaning and useless on the floor, and Steph still cradled the woman's body. It was Juicy who went for it. She grabbed her bat from the floor, ran past me, and waited for Hairy to enter the room. Hairy bent through the doorway and entered. Before Hairy could stand to full height, Juicy swung.

Whack! Crack!

Juicy gave it her all and the strike appeared to break (re-break?) Hairy's neck. The problem was Hairy never slowed, simply took in the view from his repositioned head. It was back in a forward-facing position. Hairy laughed and my blood went cold. We were in relatively tight confines. Only the ceiling was very high, as it rose to match the pitch of the roof.

With unnatural speed, Hairy lashed out and struck Juicy. She cried out and went sprawling. It was merely a glancing blow, but powerful enough to knock her off her feet. Her bat skidded across the floor. I raced for the bag of aluminum bats even as Steph rose and raised hers.

She swung and struck Hairy on the shoulder which caused him to stumble back, but he came back laughing. Steph swung again, but Hairy caught the bat. I struggled to free a bat from the bag as I watched the scene play out.

Before Steph could let go of the bat, Hairy yanked it, drawing her close. He grabbed the arm holding the weapon and snapped it. Steph screamed and fell to her knees. Hairy was not done. He grabbed the back of Steph's head and shoved it into his crotch.

"Eat it!" Hairy demanded as he pushed the woman's face against his groin. (Or Tina's. It was difficult rectifying her body with the new persona driving it.) "Eat it," Hairy said again and pushed harder.

Steph struggled, and her muffled cries suggested she could not breathe. She fought with her one good arm to free herself. I finally grabbed a bat and Juicy finally reached her fallen one. We were both too late.

Hairy shoved Steph's face deeper until his legs gripped both sides of her head. With a sickening crunch, he twisted his legs, and Steph's neck snapped. Her body fell immediately limp, even though her head remained trapped between Hairy's legs. Hairy twisted the legs again and with a pop, the head came free, Steph's body fell flat to the floor, spewing at the neck.

Juicy screamed as much with anger as fright and struck Hairy on the back. It loosened the head between his legs and Steph's head rolled toward me. I swung and hit Hairy's shoulder. He twisted toward Juicy, who struck again. The combined strikes appeared to throw Hairy off. He could not seem to focus on one of us.

We circled Hairy, both striking. The entire time, Hairy laughed. Juicy and I circled and struck over and over. The sounds were horrible, but we could not stop. It was life or death. Yet Hairy still stood. I grew tired and assumed Juicy was as well. It was time to change my strategy. I went for a knee. It popped so loud in the tight attic, echoing off the wood panel walls. Hairy's leg dropped out from underneath him. The broken knee rested on the floor while the other leg remained planted. An awkward and hopefully painful position.

Hairy eyed his lower half as if understanding the body's weakness. Hairy caught my next swing and tugged at the bat. I could not give it up, could not give him a weapon, but also did not wish to be drawn in like poor Steph. He had other plans. He swung the end of the bat and sent me sprawling. I crashed into the stored crap off to one side of the room. Boxes tumbled over me.

I didn't see what happened to Juicy but heard her cry out and crash elsewhere in the room. Looking back to the middle of the room, Selina had risen and raised a bat above her head. She ran and cracked Hairy right in the skull. This time, Hairy cried out in surprise and growled at the woman. She had gotten too close. Hairy grabbed Selina and forced her to her knees.

With tragic speed, he pressed his open hand against the top of her bloody skull. He pressed his fingers down, pushing the fabric deep into Selina's head. She cried out initially, then only gurgled and shook as Hairy dug his fingers through her skull and into her brain.

Selina's limbs danced and shook in all different directions. Hairy was now a puppet master, and he was moving strings around in her think box. The pinky finger against the brain? Selina's right foot twitched. A thumb against the frontal lobe? Selina's hips shimmied to a beat that only she could hear. It was horrible to watch the brave woman twitch herself into spasms of uncontrollable movement, all while gurgling incoherent words.

Hairy raised his head and looked at me, as if enjoying the terror on my face. The *tik-tik-tik* of learning how to use Tina's vocal cords had vanished. He was in control now and enjoyed the violent play. When Selina stopped squirming and dancing, he let her fall to the floor. Suction sounds accompanied his fingers, breaking free of her brain.

"Next," Hairy said.

From the ground I looked toward Juicy. We nodded at one another. Simultaneously, we rose, grabbed our bats and swung at the wraith. Hairy's movements were awkward because of the broken knee. It appeared there was only so much he could do with a broken body. I earlier wondered what happened when a possessed body perished. It looked like we were about to find out.

As if seeking vengeance on Hairy's obsession with sexual parts, I swung at her/his boob with all my might. Juicy hit him in the back. I struck the head once again while she got his shoulder. Now Hairy was our puppet. He danced in place as we went to work with the aluminum bats.

Unable to stand any longer, Hairy levitated off the floor. Despite seeing it earlier, it gave me pause. The broken leg dangled in the air as Hairy levitated a foot off the ground. I eyed the high ceiling.

"Now. We must strike before he gets to the ceiling. We can't reach him there."

I struck the other knee and with a crack, that leg fell into a dangle. Juicy hit the tailbone. Bones cracked, flesh squished, it was sickening. In any other circumstance, it would have been a brutal murder. Hairy continued to levitate toward the ceiling, but each strike caused the motion to pause. We were getting somewhere.

Hairy went from vertical to horizontal, like sleeping on his back except the broken legs dangled toward the floor instead of remaining rigid like the rest of the body. The move was a mistake. It gave us better angles from which to strike. Hairy reached for our bats, but he was no longer fast enough. We swung again and again. Juicy worked the stomach while I raised my bat above my head and aimed for his face. Except it was not his face. It was Tina, a beautiful student. How could I hit her? I knew such a hit would be lethal. Then Hairy laughed at my raised bat. That was enough.

Whock!

Hairy's head snapped at the neck and the body finally dropped to the floor with a thud. The figure's eyes teared up. Was he crying? No. she was. Somehow Tina was back.

"Mike, why?" she asked before blood poured from her mouth. She choked on the flood of red, spewed it into the air and then fell still.

Juicy dropped to her knees, grabbed her fallen friend's hand, and sobbed. I could not take it anymore and turned away to puke my guts out finally. I didn't care what I hit. The whole place was a sea of blood, anyway. Tina smelled bad, like a rotted corpse already.

When I looked back, Juicy just sat there staring at her friend. She had stopped crying and appeared in a state of shock. I reached out to help her up, but she didn't even look at me. She was staring into the eyes of her dead roomie. Thinking it best to get her out before she focused on the other dead friends, I stood behind her, placed my hands under her armpits, and lifted like I had Selina earlier.

"No phone here. We need to get on the road, get the police," I said.

Juicy didn't respond, simply allowed me to lead her down the stairs. She almost fell, and I had to catch her. I considered a piggyback, but I was too sore and worried we would both tumble to our deaths.

Once at the bottom of the stairs, I worried the door would still be locked, but it opened. It seemed a lifetime ago I arrived with pizza. The slices lay scattered throughout the foyer. Juicy was in shock and non-responsive.

I wanted to ask if she had the keys to her vehicle, but I could tell by her flimsy clothes that she had no keys with her. After everything, I needed to rely on Bessie starting up. Leaving Juicy by the passenger side, I rushed to my side and leaped into the front seat. It felt good, comfortable. Mere minutes earlier, I thought I would never see Bessie or anyone else ever again.

Looking over, I found myself alone. Dang! While escaping a being from somewhere beyond our realm, I had talked to women other than ones I worked with for the first time in so long. Whether she was too in shock or waiting for me to be a gentleman, Juicy never opened the car door. I rushed back out, opened it for her, and helped her sit. Based on the look on her face, I needed to take her to a hospital.

Bessie spit and sputtered when I turned the key, but she started up. She really was my bestest gal. If ever I needed her to make the trip, it was now. I pulled out of the driveway and onto the long winding road, eager to put some distance between myself and a house full of corpses.

Unaccustomed to having women in my car, I stared straight ahead and kept my hands on ten and two. It was best to wait for her to say something. It was her friends. I could not imagine what she went through. I was simply glad to be alive and happy Bessie was as well.

After such craziness, I found peace on the back roads. It would be a few miles before I arrived on the downtown strip. I still wondered what became of Hairy after we bashed his host.

Poor Tina never had a chance. Her life was over the second the wraith named Hairy showed up.

It was then I remembered the blood. I looked down at myself. Something bothered me beyond simply the blood. The same neanderthal part of my brain that made me chase women and fear danger tingled at the back of my skull. Finally, I noticed how my name tag was totally covered in blood.

The name tag was unreadable, but in Tina's last moment, she called my name. She asked why I hurt her or something like that. How did she know my name? It meant she was still Hairy at the end. It also meant Hairy could get into people's heads if he knew my name. I was relieved he did not get in it the way he had with Tina.

A dreaded sound reached my ears. *Tik-tik-tik*. Oh no, my car was going to die. If the *tik-tik-tik* continued, we would be dead on the road. *Tik-tik-tik*. It kept going. I leaned toward the dash, listening.

Tik-tik-tik. Then it hit me. The sound was not coming from the engine. It was coming from the passenger seat where someone was learning how to use new vocal cords.

"Tik-tik-tik."

Rose Park Roasters
Long Beach, California

Rose Park holds a special place in my heart because it was down the street from one of my first book signing events, Midsummer Scream. The event was a blast and drew about 60,000 people. However, that came later. I had already visited here and conceived this story earlier in the year. I went for a weekend getaway and my hotel was nearby.

This was close by, and it was a great place to get some writing done. It has a bright interior that has no frills, but still has outlets which is rare today. Even better is the outdoor patio. Sitting outside, one can catch the ocean breeze and enjoy coffee in a spot with a fantastic view.

Music blasts quite loud and baristas argue over the music choices but that makes the place unique and fun. It was while sitting here and enjoying the quiet that an idea hit. Someone was having a tough mental health day and was being quite loud across the street. They made their way inside the coffee shop and passed through in a manner that frightened people.

What struck me was how normal it appeared to everyone. After a bout of initial surprise, everyone went back to their conversations as if there was not a lost soul dancing through the premises. To see people unfazed by someone in such a state prompted this story. Also, we are so divided in this country. I sometimes wonder what would it take for people to reconnect again?

Finally, it was Joe that inspired this story as well. He was working on another project and mentioned he was writing an epistolary story. That gave me the idea to use that format for this story with a twist. Instead of journal entries, I went a little more modern. The event that day combined with Joe mentioning epistolary stories led me here.

DRINK RECOMMENDATION: They have an amazing caramel miso latte. If you can't get it with that miso bounce, then settle for a caramel latte.

Next Caller

PAUL CARRO

"My name is Judy Pringle. Like the chips. I am salty after all. Sorry, I make stupid jokes when I'm nervous. Can't believe I'm talking to Rockit Rick. *On the radio, from the stars to your ears*! I don't sell it like you do. Oh gosh, I think I'm going to cry. Why should I cry? How embarrassing. I love your show."

Judy sobs in a quick burst. She sniffles and blows her nose. Finally, she coughs and starts up again.

"I work from home while my husband works at a factory. We never go out. Can't remember the last date night that didn't involve horror movies and blowjobs. Not sure I can say that on the radio, but does it really matter now? Brad's always been hot tempered and cranky, especially after work. After my day job, I had a second job. Calming him down. But one day he was late coming home. He was never late. Get home, crack a beer, turn on a movie, unzip his pants. But now he was late. At starting-to-worry-o'clock my cellphone rang. It was Brad, cussing up a storm. That was unusual. Normally, he yelled at me in person. That was how I knew something was wrong."

Another crying jag, slightly longer. More sniffing and nose wiping.

"I'm sorry. Just how did I put up with it for so long? Everything was shit during and after Covid, and then, well, that was just the warmup, huh? Anyway, he's yelling how he got in a fight, and hadn't I been watching the news? He knew I can't stand politics, so nothing but reality TV for me, and his movies. Before I could figure out why his fighting someone was my fault, he said he was on the way and to have bandages ready. Christ, the way he burst through the door I thought he was ready to kill me, screaming, and yelling. Only then did I notice most of his right arm was dang near gone."

I'm an approaching hurricane. Will you be ready? Do you have the insurance you need?

"Sorry, for those just tuning in, our commercial beds are on timers. I have to shut them off manually after they start. Can't anger corporate. They designed it this way to make sure DJs never miss a commercial break. We have Judy's call going. Let's get back to it," Rick says from the DJ booth and hits play.

"Brad was bare-chested and all I could think of was how much his beer gut had grown. Silly, huh? Him bleeding all over our carpet and I'm thinking, when did my man let himself go? He was half-naked because he used the shirt to wrap the arm.

I had prepped little bandages after his call, not thinking things were so severe. I ran to the bathroom to get the proper stuff while he screamed and thrashed about, getting angrier by the minute. Took me time to gather everything. When I returned to the living room, I didn't see him. Then I felt the cool air. He was out on the balcony. We live on the eighth floor, with a marvelous view. I stepped out on the balcony, and it wasn't good. He looked at me out there. I mean really looked at me, not through me like normal. Then he said things I never heard from him before."

Judy speaks in a bad variation of a male's voice.

"I was a shit to you, weren't I? You deserved better. You always did. The thing is, I knew I mistreated you as much as I knew I would never stop doing so. We were too weak to leave each other. But I'm leaving you now, ladybug. For once, I can say I did the right thing by you."

Judy pauses, fights a sob before continuing the call.

"He used to call me ladybug when things were new, when they were fresh, when he was a good man. Then I noticed he was crying, and dang if the tears weren't of blood. He growled and spit at me, and I feared he changed his mind about leaving, but then he turned and leaped off our balcony!"

As if forgetting she is on the radio, Judy falls silent for an uncomfortable amount of time.

"I heard screams below but only then realized there were screams the whole time, and sirens, and helicopters. The world was so loud, and I had not heard a thing until then. My heart initially beat so hard at hearing how he planned to leave that nothing else mattered. I did not realize how happy that thought made me. I still did not know what was going on until I looked over the balcony and saw Brad pancaked down below. As I watched, he stood right back up and intercepted some poor kid on one of those electric scooters. Brad ripped up the kid good and a bunch of others came and joined the party. There, many floors below, on the city streets, people celebrated in a feast. I didn't turn on the TV for information; I turned on your show. And I plan to listen as long as you broadcast. I LOVE YOUR SHOW! Bye."

"Thank you, Judy, for the voicemail. Listeners, you know by now there are no phone lines anymore, but I still receive your emails. I have a backlog of voicemails and will play them all, I promise. But for now, I have an email from hickorysmoke425. It reads: Dear Rick, thank you for your show. I wanted to write about my wife. She is an angel, Rick. Kind. Too kind. When things started, you know at the outset, it all happened fast. I drive a forklift where I work at the lumberyard. Anyway, a single customer led to a series of events that took down almost all my coworkers. I escaped by driving the forklift to my car. Once inside, I called my wife, told her to stay in, to not open the door for anyone. But my wife helps people. She would answer any knock on the door. She thinks the best of everyone. I called her, Rick, I begged..."

*Anxiety got you down? New Oxyphallowhyphedria can relieve symptoms up to four times longer than the competitor does. *Side effects may include rectal bleeding, jaundice, stomach cramps, abnormal heart arrythmia, acne, liver problems, and blood clots that could lead to death. Consult your doctor if you have ever been or ever plan to be pregnant.*

"Sorry folks, even DJs need bathroom breaks. Now where did I leave off with hickory? His wife was kind, blah, blah, blah. Oh, yeah, this is where it gets real. He writes: the door was open when I got home, Rick. That was all I needed to know. I heard her wandering through the first floor. Blood smears were everywhere. The blood trail originated from the front porch. Someone probably knocked, looking for help, then turned on her. Her back was toward me when I found her in the hallway. She swayed in place while deciding which way to go. Seeing her sway, I thought of our wedding, Rick, and our first dance as a married couple. Because I have two left feet, my wife kept it simple. We rocked in place together, dancing to Journey's *Open Arms*. I want that back, Rick. I want to dance to Journey and hold her forever, Rick. That's all I want. That's all I wanted, I should say. Instead, I let her chase me to the kitchen, and I stabbed her in the eye with the knife-set gifted to us at our wedding. It's not fair, Rick. None of this is fair."

Silence goes out over the airwaves. "I hear you. This is for you if you're still listening hickory." *Open Arms* by Journey plays.

"That was *Open Arms*. Now, if you're new here, welcome. I know all TV and cable are dead, so the radio is where it is at. You can get some videos on the internet but it's mostly down. Bandwidth is for shit. Keep the emails coming though, they sometimes get through. Now, out of the hundreds of voicemails I got, some are very short. I promised I would play them all, so here are some of the shorter clips, listener discretion is advised."

"They're at the door, Rick. Can you call the police for me? There are too many. It's breaking, they're, oh!" Sounds of wood breaking and loud snarling, then a scream. "No, please, ah, help, no, ahhhh...."

"Yee-hah, Rockit Rick! Just last month, the police did a welfare check. Someone at the gun range reported me to the authorities for my ammunition purchases. Who's laughing now, Rick, huh?" Gunshots threaten to blow the speakers. Wet splotches sound in the near distance after every shot. Shot after shot sounds. The man yells to be heard above it all. "Best target practice ever from my roof, I tell ya', wait, whoa, what?"

The shooting stops as the phone thuds on the rooftop and rumbles during a slide down the pitched roof.

"Dang, my phone…" The man's voice trails off as the phone moves further away. It goes silent during freefall to the ground. Then the phone picks up the snarl of nearby zombies. Rick plays a new call.

"Rick? Rick? Can you hear me? Are you there?" an elderly woman says, loud enough to hear her own voice.

"I can hear her folks. You'd be surprised how many don't understand the call-in line goes straight to recording. Let's hear what granny has to say."

"My daughter. I can't find her. If she is listening, her name is Courtney. She has my grandchild, a beautiful boy, Bobby. If you see her, can you ask her to come by? I cannot reach my daughter Rick. Rick, are you there? Have you seen Courtney?" Click.

Overwhelming sounds of a large gathering. At first it sounds like a zombie horde but becomes clearer when the person speaks, that it is simply a rave. "Party, Rick! I put a post out on my socials and there's like thirty kids here. Parent's liquor cabinet is open for business. Charging five dollars a drink. I'm rich! Sandy is here, from the next grade up. She's so hot, Rick! Rrrrrick! I think I'm drunk." Screams sound in the background, subtle at first, then louder, longer. "Sorry, got to go!" Click.

"Sorry folks. I dozed off. Even those of us from the far reaches of space need to sleep sometime. As usual, I will auto play music while I get some rest. I apologize in advance for the commercials. If you are stoned and hear a fast-food commercial, do not. I repeat, do NOT head to that drive through. You will be the chalupa, my friend, not the other way around. Good night listeners."

Music and commercials play for six hours.

"Good morning, day breakers. I have an announcement to make, one that will involve some programming changes around here. But first, one more voicemail. This from a long-time listener."

"Hi Rockit, long-time listener, first time caller. I've been listening, since, you know, this whole thing started. I haven't left my house. No story, just a question. I wanted to know why. Why do you think this happened? That's all. Stay safe, my friend." Click.

"Well, Joanie. Her name is Joanie, everyone. You have asked the million-dollar question. You could gather dozens of scientists in a room, and they would likely give dozens of answers. But I'll answer as best I know how. Go back to before this started when I used to talk on air for two hours. After that

I called sponsors, typed some ads, wrote some bits, then went home. On my way, I would swing by the supermarket and get a week's worth of frozen dinners. I checked out with the same cashier every time. She was my age, pretty, and smiled a lot. Do you know what her name was?"

Silence.

"That was rhetorical. Point is, I didn't know. I saw her every week for years and did not know her name. There are people down the hall and on the floors above and below me here. We would say hi every day, when we could be bothered, but mostly we nodded. Since this began, I have had time to think. What I think is that I never got to know anyone because I did not want to be disappointed. It seemed like if ever you engaged with anyone, they would throw their politics, their religion, their Festivus grievances at you before they even got through the word hello. I get it, the world is divided in half, right? Half feel one way, half the other. But that makes every second person someone you should get along with. But where are they? I never found someone who was into the things I liked even if I bothered to strike up a conversation. Tired, folks. It made me tired."

Silence.

"So tired. But for two hours a day, fans called in and no one ever talked about that shit. They stayed on topic. Maybe we had good screeners, I don't know. But think of all the voicemails I've played for you since this all began. None threw any political views into anyone's faces. No one for once blamed the other side, not even Mr. Pop Shot on the roof. Do you see? It's as if we finally realize none of that matters in the end. A grandma is searching for her daughter and grandchild. A man wants his old life back. Well, I don't."

Suffering from hemorrhoids? Startling sound as a hand hits a button hard to silence the ad.

"Don't get me started on consumerism. What I think is we were already at each other's throats. Just now it's literally. I don't want what we had before, but I desire safety. I want people to live freely again, but I mean live! No more work, go home, sleep. Wash, rinse repeat. The reason I stayed here is that my workplace remained safe, but also because I had nowhere else to go. No one to look after. No one to look after me. I am surrounded by all of you every day but have no one in my life. And I fear the same on your end. I fear you only have me to listen to daily. No one else. Can we promise to break that cycle? If we get through this and I see you on the street, can we say hello? Can we ask how each other is doing and not get offended if the person responds with something other than '*I'm fine*?' Can we get back to being human? Because, that snarling, growling, craziness in the streets downstairs? That's been a Tuesday in the city long before this all began."

Heavy sigh followed by more silence.

"That brings me to the announcement. I am officially out of food in the station, so I must leave. I have been working behind the scenes to computerize the broadcast. This station will keep playing some best of moments, some music, and all your voicemails on an endless loop, though I do not know for how long the station will continue to broadcast. Keep the emails coming. If I ever make it back, I promise to read them all. After all, you are the only friends I have. Good luck everyone. This is Rockit Rick signing off."

A Led Zeppelin song plays as Rick exits the booth. When the song ends, someone speaks.

"Hi Rick. I'm Tessa and I'm nine years old. I'm calling because I'm afraid, and I don't know what to do. Nana got weird, so I had to lock her in the other room. What should I do, Rick? I need help. Are you there? I'm scared."

About the author

PAUL CARRO

Paul Carro is an active HWA author of the hit novel The House, Abject Fear, The Salem Legacy, and many other creepy novels. He is the author and creator of The Little Coffeeshop of Horrors Anthology. He has appeared in multiple other anthologies and is a screenwriter and producer. His screenplay Penance is set up with legendary producer Michael Phillips. He is currently developing a screenplay with horror director/writers the Winchester Brothers and is also in development on Hitchcock, Nebraska with horror flick director Rolfe Kanefsky. He was a producer on Operation Repo and currently lives in Santa Monica, CA.

About the author

JOSEPH CARRO

Joseph Carro holds an MFA from Stonecoast at the University of Southern Maine. He is the co-author of The Little Coffee Shop of Horrors Anthology and has served as an editor/proofreader for the Glyphs Productions line of comic books since 2015. He has written for itcherMag and can generally be found engaging in some kind of geeky/nerdy activity throughout the day. Oh, and he was also in a movie with Kelsey Grammer (he's going to say that every chance he gets). He currently resides in Woodford, Vermont located within the infamous Bennington Triangle although he will always be a Mainer at heart.

About the author

S. ALESSANDRO MARTINEZ

S. Alessandro Martinez is a Bram Stoker Award® -nominated author of Mexican and Spanish descent, a native Southern Californian, bat enthusiast, and suspected necromancer who writes horror and fantasy for adults and children. His work has appeared in several magazines, anthologies, and websites such as Aphotic Realm, Sanitarium, Jitter, and Indiana Horror Review. Helminth is his debut novel.

Also by Paul Carro

ABJECT FEAR

Scientists trying to cure fear must face their own when the groundbreaking experiment goes horribly wrong. In the race to cure fear there will be casualties. And blood. Lots of blood. Are you ready to face your fears?

"the horror sequences are delightfully grotesque..." —Kirkus
"Carro blends a conventional horror tale with an innovative, new concept... character backstories are incredible... intriguing and gory." --EbookFairs

THERE IS NOTHING TO FEAR
BUT PHOBIA ITSELF
ABJECT FEAR
A HORROR NOVEL
PAUL CARRO

Also by Joseph Carro

THE LITTLE COFFEESHOP OF HORRORS ANTHOLOGY

2 authors from 1 family visited 12 coffeeshops to craft 12 single sourced cups of terror!

Authors Paul and Joseph Carro the only known uncle/nephew horror writing duo visited twelve coffeeshops around the country and used the location to inspire twelve unique tales of terror. Each story is prefaced by the coffee shop we worked in and what inspired us. Volume two even adds drink recommendations. If you love naked zombies. killer hill people, and aquatic horror, you will love The Little Coffee Shop of Horrors Anthology. Volumes 1 and 2 available now!

PAUL CARRO
JOSEPH CARRO
WHERE THE SHAKING IS NOT FROM CAFFEINE
BUT FROM THE TWELVE TALES OF TERROR
THE LITTLE COFFEE SHOP OF HORRORS
ANTHOLOGY

Also by S. Alessandro Martinez

HELMINTH

Rei would do anything for those she loves.

As her best friend, Abby, struggles to cope with the sudden loss of her husband, Rei and her closest girlfriends take her to a beautiful lakeside house nestled in the forests of the Pacific Northwest, hoping that a weekend of support from long-time friends will help Abby along her road of emotional recovery.

But as the young women get settled, Rei begins to notice there's something wrong with the place. Could this peaceful, idyllic location be hiding an ancient evil below the waters of the lake? Or are the problems wholly within Abby herself, who seems to be losing her grip on reality? When unexplainable, nightmarish things occur, Rei realizes this weekend getaway may turn into their last outing.

HELMINTH
S. ALESSANDRO MARTINEZ